ONE YEAR HOME

MARIE FORCE

One Year Home
By: Marie Force

Published by HTJB, Inc.
Copyright 2019. HTJB, Inc.
Cover designer: Kristina Brinton
Interior Layout: Ashley Lopez, E-book Formatting Fairies

ISBN: 978-1950654383

www.marieforce.com

CHAPTER 1

John

Nothing has gone according to plan. From the second I was shot while capturing Al Khad, the most wanted man on earth, my life has spun out of control. I lost half my leg. I lost a month to an infection and then… I lost Ava, the love of my life, who's now married to another man and on a honeymoon somewhere in Europe. The guy's name is , and supposedly, she fell in love with him after I was deployed for more than five years. Weeks after I saw her and learned that she fell for someone else during my interminable six-year absence, it still hasn't completely sunk in that we're over for good. Thoughts of her, of , of the life I wanted so badly with her, sustained me during the long years we spent apart.

That she's gone forever is inconceivable. I've loved her from the moment I first laid eyes on her, eight years ago in a bar off base in San Diego. We ran into each other—literally—outside the restrooms, and that was that. We were together until I deployed, even when I wasn't supposed to have entanglements or relationships that would keep me from doing a job that very few service members are ever chosen to do. My unit and its mission are so top secret that I can never share with anyone the details of what we did or how we did it. And since I returned to the US, a reluctant hero after Al Khad's camp outed me in a video of the raid that led to his capture, wants the details.

I'm overrun with media requests, so many that the Navy public affairs officer assigned to me has stopped taking their calls, which means they come directly to me. How they got my number, I have no idea. I've got no choice but to hire someone to deal with it. That someone, recommended by Ava, happens to be her new sister-in-law, Julianne Tilden, who also happens to be the daughter of the New York governor. Good times. Not only do I get to deal with someone from Ava's new family, the governor's daughter is probably a pampered, privileged, pain-in-the-ass princess who has no concept whatsoever of what I'm dealing with.

I'm prepared to hate her on sight.

Her brother married my Ava. What else do I need to know about her?

If I wasn't so desperate for relief from the relentless media demands, I would want nothing to do with Ava's new sister-in-law. It would take energy I don't have to find someone else, and besides, what do I care who handles the media? As long as someone other than me does it.

I'm living in an apartment that Lieutenant Commander David Muncie, the liaison assigned to me by the Navy, arranged when I was released from inpatient treatment. I'm told being released to outpatient status is a victory to be celebrated.

Woo. Fucking.

I don't give a shit about anything now that Ava is gone. She was my reason for being, and I'm left with half a leg and a heart so broken, it might never beat normally again. What's the point? I don't know anymore, and I'm self-aware enough to realize I'm profoundly depressed. The medical professionals who deal with me on a regular basis see it, too, and have referred me to a shrink. I have his card. I just haven't bothered to make an appointment.

What can he do? Unless he can dissolve Ava's marriage and get her to come back to me where she belongs, I can't see the benefit to wasting his time or mine.

The doorbell rings, and I drag myself off the sofa to let Muncie in, moving slowly on the crutches I'm still reliant upon. I spend part of every morning on the treadmill in the fitness room downstairs, trying to get used to the prosthetic and regain my strength. I walk until my muscles tremble with exhaustion, until I'm soaked with sweat and certain I'll never get back to where I was before I lost my leg and a month of my life to infection. Every day, I tell myself it doesn't matter if I ever get back what's been lost, and still I make myself take the elevator downstairs to spend an hour torturing myself on that goddamned treadmill.

"You've got a key," I remind him.

"And you've got the ability to answer the door."

I scowl at the comment that has become predictable after weeks in this -like existence that's my new reality.

At least Muncie brought coffees, one of which he hands to me after I'm back on the sofa. He's learned the hard way not to speak to me until after I've had at least one, preferably two, cups of coffee. I'm a real joy to be around lately.

I never used to be this way. Before the deployment from hell, I had a nice life with Ava. She was all I needed to be happy, and I was all she needed. Until I disappeared without a word to her for six years, giving her no choice but to move on without me. I blame Al Khad for screwing up the loveliest thing in my life. I certainly don't blame Ava for surviving. I just wish she hadn't fallen for someone else. Her name is . I hate his fucking guts, and I've never even met him.

I had this picture in mind of what it would be like to see her again. I didn't imagine her telling me she found someone else, that she's in love and engaged and planning a life with him. Six weeks after that fateful meeting with her, I'm still reeling from having to let her go, because that's what she wanted.

Life is so goddamned unfair. I gave more than six years and half a leg to bringing a ruthless terrorist to justice, and what do I get as a thank-you? The rest of my life without the only woman I've ever loved.

"Are you going to shower before Julianne gets here?" Muncie asks from his post at the dining room table, where he's set up his laptop.

"What time is it?"

"Nine thirty."

Julianne is due at ten, and I haven't showered or shaved in days, even after sweating my ass off on the treadmill. I look nothing at all like the well-groomed naval officer I was before life kicked me in the balls. Maybe Julianne ought to see the new me, the me who doesn't give a shit about anything, even personal hygiene, so she'll know what she's getting if she decides to take me on as a client.

Because I'm still unsteady on the prosthetic, it'll take me every second of the thirty minutes I have if I'm going to shower and change. I pull myself up on the crutches and hobble into the bedroom.

Muncie follows, puts the coffee on the counter and then leaves me to shower in the handicapped-accessible stall. I'm technically handicapped now. Heartbroken and handicapped. That's me. Oh and heroic, too, if you believe the bullshit being spewed about me from coast to coast. The country is grateful. I appreciate that, but I wish they'd leave me the hell alone to wallow in my depression.

Only because it's likely that I stink, I take the damned shower. I shave days' worth of scruff and wash my hair. It's gotten long—longer than it's been since Afghanistan, when it grew past my shoulders for the first time ever. When I woke up in the hospital after I lost my leg, the hair was gone, too. I never asked who decided it needed to go. I had much bigger problems then, like figuring out how I was supposed to live without my leg.

I'm still trying to figure out how I'm supposed to go on without Ava. Standing under the warm water, I think about that first night with her, my favorite memory to wallow in when I was deployed. I could transport myself out of whatever hell I was in at the moment and be with her, my favorite place in the world to be. After I talked her into leaving the bar with me that first night, we drove around in my truck for a couple of hours, talking, laughing, listening to music and swapping life stories. She told me hers. I told her the version of mine I was allowed to share, ninety percent of it complete bullshit, such as the part about my father the general, who'd moved us from one town to another as kids.

There was no father and no "us." I was raised in the foster system and have no family. My lack of personal connections, coupled with my former physical agility, made me an ideal candidate for the elite SEAL team that deployed to hunt down

Al Khad. And we finally got the slippery bastard who'd eluded us for years before that fateful night.

But I don't want to think about him. I want to think about . And . The first thing about her I noticed was that she was young. Just barely twenty-one at the time, whereas I was twenty-nine. She was way too young for me, and I should've kept walking right on by her. That's the only regret I allow myself where she's concerned—that I sucked her into my life without giving her all the information she needed to decide for herself. I never told her, for example, that I could be deployed for years at a time, and if that happened, I wouldn't be able to contact her at all while I was gone.

I realize that makes me sound like the biggest dick who ever lived, but I wasn't to tell her. I wasn't even supposed to have her in my life. And yes, I struggled with the deception. I agonized over what would become of her if the worst should happen to our country. My only excuse is that I loved her so damned much—and loved being loved by her—that I would've done anything to have her in my life, even if that meant lying to her every day of the two years we spent blissfully together.

I told myself then that I was doing it for the right reasons. I was protecting her from having to worry about something that might never happen. But that's a bunch of crap. I was protecting myself from the possibility of losing the only person who ever truly loved me, the only person who ever belonged only to me and me to her.

I run my fingers through my hair until all the soap is out and then turn my face up to the water. I should've married her when I had the chance. What were they going to do? Drum me out of the SEAL team or out of the Navy itself? After spending hundreds of thousands of dollars to train me for the kind of mission that led to the capture of Al Khad, they wouldn't have let me go easily. However, they could've demoted me or even court-martialed me for failing to stick to the rules that were spelled out to me in the clearest possible terms when I agreed to join that particular team in the first place.

It would've gutted me to be demoted or court-martialed. Until I met Ava, the Navy and the SEAL teams had given me the first real family I'd ever had, and the thought of disappointing my commanders had been unbearable to me. That's why I didn't marry her when I knew I should have. I worried so much about her being left unprotected that I gave myself an ulcer, which was another thing she never knew about. I told her I had reflux and that was why I had to watch what I ate.

Whenever I need to escape from my new reality, I let my mind wander back to the most perfect night of my life, the night I met Ava in that nasty bar where Sanchez had chosen to celebrate his promotion. She was there with a friend who was interested in one of the Navy guys who hung out there. Never in my wildest dreams did I expect to meet the woman of my dreams in such a place. But there she was, walking out of the ladies' room as I came out of the men's room and nearly took her down.

She was so fresh and pretty and perfect. I told her when I saw her again recently that I knew I should've let her go and gone on with my life that night. The reason I didn't was because the first second I laid eyes on her, I was a goner. One second with her and it was already too late to go on as if I'd never met her.

That first night was like something out of a dream or a movie or someone else's life, because perfect things didn't happen to me. At least they never had before. But everything about Ava and me together was utter perfection, the kind of thing that comes along once in a lifetime if someone is very, very lucky. I was lucky once, and sometimes the loss of her, of her love… I wonder if I'll survive it. Losing my leg has been nothing compared to losing her.

I talked her into coming home with me that night, and we fell into bed like we'd been together for years rather than hours. She said she'd never done anything like that before, had never gone to bed with a guy she'd only just met, but we both knew right away that this was different. The first time I sank into her sweetness, I was ruined for anyone else. I haven't been with anyone since her and can't imagine ever again wanting a woman the way I still want her.

Before I was injured, I would get hard as stone just thinking about that first night and the way we came together like two meteors on a collision course with destiny. Since the injury and infection, not much is happening down south. I wonder if that's another thing that's lost forever.

The day after I met Ava, I did something I'd never done before in twelve years in the Navy and have never done since—I called in sick to work so I could spend the entire day in bed with her. She skipped her Friday classes, and we stayed in my bed for days, sending out for food so we could fuel up and go back for more. By the time we emerged on Monday morning to rejoin our lives, she had become my life and I had become hers. That's how fast it happened. I went from single to committed to her over the span of one momentous, sexually magnificent weekend.

I lose myself in the memories of what it was like to love her. I remember every nuance of her body, every reaction I could draw from her effortlessly, because I spoke Ava fluently. I knew her better than I know myself. I knew what made her sigh and what made her scream and could make her come so many times, she'd be senseless afterward. I close my eyes and vividly remember the snug fit of her pussy around my cock as it contracted with one orgasm after another. She was so incredibly responsive.

But even those erotic thoughts of the woman I love don't stir an ounce of desire in me, leaving me to wonder if I've lost my manhood along with my leg.

Muncie knocks on the door, interrupting the beautiful images in my mind with a cold, harsh dose of my new reality. "What're you doing in there? She's going to be here in ten minutes."

"Fuck off." How dare he interrupt my thoughts of Ava? The memories have retreated into a past so sweet, I wonder what point there could possibly be in trying to go on without her. It's occurred to me—on more than one occasion since she made her choice—that I could take too many of the pain meds I was given when I left the hospital and make it all go away. Who would care? Ava is gone, and my two closest friends in the world were killed in the Al Khad raid. It would be so easy to take the pills, to slip away, to finally find some peace.

I haven't done it for one very important reason. I'd never do that to Ava. I wouldn't ruin the rest of her life by taking mine and leaving her to think it was her fault. So even though losing her nearly killed me, I force myself to continue on so my death won't destroy her happy new life.

Screwed up, right? Believe me, I know.

I get out of the shower and fumble through the process of drying off and getting dressed, which I've had to relearn along with just about everything else since I lost my leg. Even with the prosthetic, my balance is precarious, and I still have a great deal of pain—real and phantom—from the loss of my leg.

By the time I'm dressed in jeans and a button-down that's come from a dry cleaner thanks to Muncie, I'm completely depleted and sweating. So much for the shower.

I hear Muncie talking to someone in the next room, which means she's here. Though it's the last freaking thing I feel like doing, I drag myself up on the crutches and make my way to the door to meet this woman Ava swears is the best at dealing with the media and the staggering amount of bullshit that has become my life lately.

I pull open the door, and the first thing I see is a pair of stunning legs. I may be heartbroken, but that doesn't mean I don't notice a great pair of legs when I see them. I let my gaze travel up the front of her until I connect with big, startled-doe eyes that scream prim and proper.

I can't believe Ava sent me Mary Fucking Poppins in black fuck-me heels and a killer red dress.

CHAPTER 2

Julianne

He's so scary looking that it's all I can do not to shrivel up in a ball or bolt for the door to get away from him. If I'd run into him on the street, I would've moved out of his way so there'd be no chance of coming into contact with him. And that's not like me at all. I talk to everyone I encounter, which drives my brothers crazy. They swear I'm going to end up dead one of these days because I'm too friendly to strangers.

I can't help it. That's just how I am. But this stranger is different, and I quickly realize he's not about to do anything to make this easier for me. He's also incredibly handsome, but I barely notice that. The scary requires my full attention.

Muncie breaks the uncomfortable silence by clearing his throat. "Captain John West, meet Julianne Tilden."

Mustering courage and determination to get through this with my professionalism intact, even if I'm quaking on the inside, I take several steps forward and extend my hand. "It's nice to meet you, Captain West. Thank you for your service."

He shakes my hand and offers a brusque nod as he lowers himself carefully onto a love seat. "Have a seat."

I take one of the straight-back chairs that face the loveseat.

Muncie produces a takeout cup of coffee, cream containers, sugar and fake sugar. "Wasn't sure if you drink coffee or how you take it."

He seems very sweet, and I offer him a warm smile, greatly relieved that he's there in case the scary captain decides to go postal on me. "Thanks. I can't function without it."

"You and the captain have that in common," Muncie says with a pointed look for John as if to say, *Get your head out of your ass and be nice.*

At least I hope that's the message he's sending, because it would be very nice if the captain would get his head out of his ass and be nice.

I stir cream and sugar substitute into my coffee. "What can I do for you, Captain West?" He's not going to make it easy for me? I can play that game, too.

"Deal with the bullshit."

"You're going to need to be more specific, I'm afraid." I take a sip of the coffee and thank God once again for whoever thought it would be a good idea to dump hot water over ground coffee beans. Did they know at the time what a service they were doing for all of humanity?

"I'm getting killed with calls from the media. Everyone wants interviews. They want me to write a book. One company asked me to model underwear for them. It's nonstop and totally insane, and I can't deal with it."

"How are they contacting you?"

"Somehow, they got my personal cell number." As he says those words, a phone on the coffee table vibrates with an incoming call. "That'll be the first of at least a hundred calls today."

"Well, that won't work. Do you mind if I take the phone and manage the calls for you?"

He hesitates, glancing at the phone with such yearning that I feel my heart soften toward him.

"I'll get you a new one and make sure she has the new number," Muncie says.

That's all the captain needs to hear. "Take it. It's all yours."

I take the phone off the coffee table. "Does it have a code?"

"Zero five twenty-five."

I write that down in the notebook that's always with me. I sleep with it under my pillow. It has all the most important information about my clients in it. My siblings make fun of my notebook, but a lot of the details contained in there are ultrasensitive, and I'd never keep them on a smartphone that can easily be hacked. We had a seminar at work about that topic last year. It scared the crap out of me and everyone I work with. Quite a few of us have switched to paper and pen since then.

Captain John West is my only client at the moment. The powers that be at the firm were so excited to land him that they bent over backward to get coverage for all my other clients so I can give the man of the moment my full attention. After ten minutes in his presence, I want to give him back.

But I won't do that for two reasons. One, everyone who is anyone in my business would literally kill to be me right now, and two, Ava asked me to take care of him, so I will. I adore Ava. She's made my brother Eric happier than he's ever been, and there's nothing I wouldn't do for her. This is a big deal to her—John is a big deal to her. She was in love with the guy for eight years, more than five of them spent wondering where he was while hoping he would return to her.

By the time he did, she was in love with Eric and they were planning a life together. I know how hard it was for her to see John again after all that time. I can't for the life of me imagine what it must've been like for him to hear she was engaged to be married.

"Why are you staring at me?" he asks gruffly, startling me.

I realize, to my horror, that I was in fact staring at him. "Sorry," I mutter.

He rubs his face. "Did I cut myself shaving again, Muncie?"

"Not this time, sir."

"I, um, I apologize. I didn't mean to stare."

"So you said." He seems to return the rudeness by taking the opportunity to blatantly stare at me.

I try not to wither under the glare of the most intense blue eyes I've ever seen, but I wilt a tiny bit, waiting to find out what fresh hell he has in store for me next. "You sure I didn't cut myself shaving, Muncie?"

The lieutenant commander laughs. "Nope. All good."

I glance at the captain and note that his scowl has softened somewhat, not into what anyone would call a smile, but perhaps the beginning of one.

"Your brother married my Ava."

And there it is, the proverbial elephant in the room. "Yes, he did."

"What's he like?"

Oh, for God's sake. I didn't expect him to ask me that and have no idea what to say.

"Is that a hard question? I take it you've known him awhile."

"All my life, in fact."

He leans forward, full of intensity and quiet rage. That's the only way I can think of to describe the vibe coming from him.

"Captain…" Muncie's word of warning goes ignored.

"He's… He's a good guy, one of the best guys I know. He'd do anything for anyone, give you the shirt off his back." I hate the cliché, but it does the job—and it's true. In a crisis, Eric would be the first person I'd call.

"What does he do for a living?"

"High-end investments."

"What the hell are high-end investments?"

"Five million dollars or more." At his look of distaste, I feel the need to say more. "He can spend a year fully investigating a potential investment, only to have the acquisition committee in his company turn it down. It's very complex work."

Judging by his expression, that doesn't help with the distaste. "Sounds like a heck of a way to make a living."

"He likes it." I take a deep breath and tell myself to get control of this meeting. "Back to the media inquiries."

"How old is he?"

"Did you ask me here to discuss my brother, Captain West, or are you interested in my professional services?" I force myself to look him dead in the eye and not to let him see that he intimidates me.

He stares back at me for a long moment before he blinks. "Both, I suppose."

"I'm only interested in the professional inquiries, if it's just the same to you. While I empathize with your situation, I love my brother, and it doesn't feel right for me to be discussing him with you."

He doesn't like that, but too bad. I'm here to do a job, not defend my brother.

"You empathize with my situation? Really?"

"Captain…" The note of warning in Muncie's tone isn't lost on either of us.

"Yes, I do empathize with your ordeal, and like the rest of America, I'm deeply grateful for the role you played in bringing a terrorist to justice at great personal and physical expense."

He begins to clap, slowly and dramatically.

Heat creeps into my face, which is infuriating. The last thing I want him to see is that he gets to me.

"Did you practice that little speech on the flight out here?"

"No." I wish I could punch him and still have a job afterward. The partners were thrilled when I told them who my potential client was. *Land him*, they said, *and we'll consider you for junior partner.* "I made it up right here."

"Nice to see that you're good on the fly."

"I'm outstanding on the fly, which is how I became one of the top young PR professionals in New York."

His cell phone rings, which is when I realize I'm gripping it tightly. With him watching me in that intense, intimidating way of his, I take the call. "Answering for Captain West."

It's a producer for *NBC Nightly News*, wanting to book an interview. "Let me take down your contact information and get back to you." The name and number go in my trusty notebook.

"And you are?" the producer asks.

"Julianne Tilden."

"Are you working for Captain West?"

"Please hold for one moment." I put my hand over the phone so I won't be overheard. "It's an NBC News producer. She wants to know if I work for you."

He holds my gaze for a long moment, during which I honestly have no idea what he's thinking. He gives nothing away. "Tell her you do."

I offer him a brief nod and return to the call. "I'll be representing Captain West for media inquiries going forward. May I give you my number so you can reach me directly?" I recite the number for my work phone and tell her again I'll be back in touch. I end the call and glance at my new client.

The first thing I do is slide my company's retainer contract across the table. "Before we go any further, I need you to sign this."

He leans forward to retrieve the document, and after studying it, he says, "Two hundred dollars an hour?"

"I assure you, I'll earn every dime of it."

"Yes, you will," Muncie mutters.

I *really* like him.

"Who's paying for this?" Captain West asks Muncie.

"We've got it covered. Sign the form."

He signs it and hands it over to me. "Now what?"

"Now we need to talk about what you're willing to do—and what you're not willing to do."

"If he had his druthers, he wouldn't do anything," Muncie says.

I never divert my gaze from the captain. "Why is that?"

"I don't want to talk about it, but the Navy has decided to make me their new poster boy for recruitment. I just want to retire and ride off into the sunset, but they're not going to let that happen."

"What's the minimum that he can do?" I ask Muncie.

"They haven't given us a minimum. They want him to take full advantage of the opportunities he's being offered, whatever that means."

I redirect my attention to the captain. "What're your physical limitations?"

If looks could kill, I'd be a goner. "I have no physical limitations."

"So you can travel?"

"Yes," he says through gritted teeth.

"Here's what I suggest… We book a New York media tour, including morning shows, nightly news, late night, and then we come back out here and do an LA leg."

As soon as I say the word *leg*, I wish I could take it back. Not that the word is incorrect, but I don't want him to think I'm fixated on what he's lost. And why would he think that exactly? *Shut up, Julianne.* I hate that inner voice that constantly critiques me. It's my mother's voice. She made a career out of critiquing my every move until the blessed day I left for college at Barnard and could breathe for the first time in my life.

He doesn't respond to my suggestion.

I clear my throat. "Would that work for you?"

"I guess."

I glance at Muncie, who shrugs as if to say, *Damned if I know what to do with him.* Great. He's been dealing with him for months, and he has no clue. What chance do I have?

I open my notebook and uncover my favorite gel pen. "Let's cover what you will and won't talk about."

"I won't talk about the raid, the mission or anything to do with Al Khad."

"That's what they're going to want to know."

"Despite the fact that Al Khad's camp released the video of the raid, the mission is still classified on our end. I'm not at liberty to discuss the particulars, and even if I was, I wouldn't."

"Can you talk about what it was like to be deployed for more than five years?"

"Yeah. It sucked."

"You have to say more than that."

"What else should I say?"

"What did you do for all that time?" The question is one that I've had since I first heard the story about him and how he deployed the day Al Khad's organization took out a US-based cruise ship with suicide bombers, killing four thousand innocent people. My sister-in-law, Ava, who was John's live-in girlfriend at the time, waited five years in San Diego for him to come back before returning home to New York to start over.

"We looked for Al Khad."

"Where did you look for him?"

He thinks about that, seeming to decide what he should say. "Our search spanned several countries that're hostile to Americans, so we had to embed and blend in with the locals to get information. That took time and patience, among other things."

"When you joined the Navy, did you know you might have to deploy for so long without any word to your loved ones at home?"

"Other than the girlfriend I wasn't supposed to have, I didn't have loved ones at home, which is why I was initially chosen for the unit. In an interview, I could only say that I didn't have loved ones at home. I can't say I had a girlfriend."

"What does it matter now?" I ask. "Cat's out of the bag."

"It matters. I don't want her dragged into this."

"Yes, that's true." I respect that he's protecting her, even now. "I agree that we're better off not arousing curiosity about her. The press would be relentless in their efforts to locate and interview her."

"Which would be inconvenient and disruptive to your brother."

Infuriated all over again, I stare him down. "It would be inconvenient, disruptive and intrusive for *Ava*. I'm sure you'll agree she's already been through enough."

Muncie makes a sound that might be laughter, but he quickly coughs to cover it up.

"I agree," John says. "Ava's been through enough, and that's entirely my fault."

My heart breaks a little for him, because even though he tries to hide it, the pain of losing her is as obvious as his blue eyes, prominent cheekbones and sexy lips.

God help me, but the man is sexy—and completely off-limits to me for so many reasons, it would take me days to list them all in my notebook.

CHAPTER 3

John

She's tougher than she looks. I like that she doesn't take my shit without giving it right back to me. Muncie likes that, too. He thinks I don't hear him laughing. As soon as I get the chance, I'll remind him of what the word *insubordination* means.

I won't go too hard on him, though, because I'd be lost without him. Not that I can ever let him know that. He's already unmanageable. How pathetic is it that the officer assigned by the Navy to tend to me has become my closest friend? Without him, I probably would've drunk myself to death after Ava told me we were done, that she was going to marry *Eric*.

Is it possible to actually hate a guy you've never met? Because I hate him for taking her away from me. Yes, I know that's irrational and unfair and ridiculous. And still… I hate him.

Apparently, I've just hired his sister to represent me with the media.

The absurdity isn't lost on me.

"So what's the plan?" I ask her.

"I'll start returning some of the calls you've received, focusing first on the New York and Los Angeles markets. There's a lot of interest, so I'll focus on the top-rated shows."

"What about timing?" Muncie asks.

"I'd expect to head to New York within two weeks."

New York. Ava lives in New York. The last time I talked to her was a couple of days before her wedding, but she promised to check in with me when she returns from her honeymoon. I'm not sure when that will be. I want to ask Julianne when they get back, but I've already asked too many questions about them.

Will Ava see me while I'm in New York, or is that too much to hope for? I have no idea what the rules of our new "friendship" are. Am I allowed to reach out to her, tell her I'll be in town and ask if she wants to get together? Or would that be out of bounds? I don't know, and the not knowing makes me edgy and cranky.

Hell, who am I kidding? Breathing makes me cranky since I lost Ava. Every day I have to remind myself that I have no choice but to go on because the alternative would ruin her. And I won't do that to her.

"Here's my concern," Julianne says. "You can't go on these shows and say nothing."

"I told you. I'm limited as to what I can talk about."

"Fair enough. The mission itself is off-limits, but you can certainly talk about the emotional elements of what you've endured."

I roll my eyes. "Seriously?"

"Yes! People are interested in what you've been through." She flips through her notebook. "You lost two friends in the raid, right?"

I grit my teeth to keep from snapping at her. "Yes."

"Can you talk about them?"

"You want me to use my dead friends to juice ratings?"

"No, I want you to tell a story that people want to hear."

"I'm not using them that way."

"Rather than thinking of it as using them, how about using your platform to bring awareness to their sacrifice?"

The thought of talking about Jonesy or Tito makes me feel sick. I'm still trying to wrap my head around losing the two men who were like brothers to me after all the years we spent training, preparing and deploying together. As close as I was to them, even they didn't know about Ava. No one knew about her. If my command had learned I had a serious girlfriend, I could've faced severe disciplinary action, so I went to enormous lengths to keep her far, far away from my military life.

I now realize the enormous disservice I did to her by keeping her isolated. After I deployed, she had no support or information. I was sick with guilt leaving her, knowing I'd be gone indefinitely and she'd have questions that no one would be able to answer.

"What're you thinking?" Julianne asks, jarring me from my thoughts.

"I'm thinking about Ava."

My confession makes her uncomfortable, but to her credit, she says, "What about her?"

"I did a terrible thing to her. I think about that every minute of every day." As soon as the words are out, I regret revealing so much to someone I've only just met, but when it comes to Ava, I never have been able to control myself.

"Why did you?"

"I loved her. She loved me." I can't tell her that Ava was the first person who ever truly loved me, that I was powerless to walk away from a feeling I'd never experienced before. "I blame myself for everything that happened. I wasn't honest with her, and it kills me to know what I put her through." What is it about this woman that has me speaking so freely?

Muncie stares at me, seeming as surprised as I am by my verbal diarrhea.

"You've both been through a lot. Do you have someone helping you?"

"He has a referral to a PTSD therapist, but he's yet to make the call," Muncie says, earning a glare from me.

"I don't have PTSD. I have a broken heart." The sympathetic look Julianne gives me makes me angry. "Are we done here?"

"We can be."

"Good." I want to get the hell away from her and her sympathy, but like everything these days, it takes a good five minutes to haul myself up, find my balance, position the crutches and get myself out of the room. I go into the adjoining bedroom, close the door and sit on the bed, exhausted from the small effort it takes to go from one room to another.

The physical therapists tell me I'll be back to fighting form in no time, whatever that means. They assure me that the daily torture hour on the treadmill will get me there sooner, which is the only reason I put myself through it. If I'm forced to continue to walk this earth, I'm determined to do it without the crutches I've come to despise.

I told Julianne I can handle the press tour, because I want to do it and get it over with. But after thirty minutes in her presence, I'm concerned about whether I'll have the stamina to keep up with her.

Julianne

"Don't be offended," Muncie says after John leaves the room. "That was him being nice."

"I'm not offended."

"Well, I'm offended for you. He's not the easiest guy to be around."

"It's okay. I understand that he's been through hell, and he's still processing everything that happened in the raid and with Ava."

"You seem like a nice person, Julianne."

"Oh. Thanks. I try to be."

"I'd hate to see him drag you down. You're not obligated to take this on if you don't want to. We'll find someone to handle him. I realize it's a difficult spot you're in with your brother married to Ava."

"It's not the best set of circumstances to begin a new professional relationship. I'll give you that. However, I feel like I can make this easier for him, and I'd like to have the opportunity to try." I don't mention that landing Captain West as a client has put me on the fast track for partnership in my firm. They don't need to know that. "And why wouldn't I do that after all he's given our country?"

"It's your funeral," Muncie says, his lips curving into a smile. "Don't say I didn't warn you."

"I appreciate your candor, Commander Muncie, but I'm quite accustomed to dealing with difficult clients."

He snorts out a laugh. "There's difficult, and then there's him."

"Why are you working with him if you dislike him so much?"

Muncie seems startled by the question. "I don't dislike him at all." He pauses. "No, wait, that's not true. Sometimes I actually dislike him, such as when he's rude to someone who's trying to help him." He gestures toward me to make his point. "That annoys me. But overall? Working for and with him has been the greatest honor of my career. What he and the others did bringing down Al Khad? It's nothing short of extraordinary."

"I couldn't agree more, and I'm looking forward to the challenge of working with him. He's got an important story to tell, and I want to help him tell it in the best way possible."

"You should know that he's only doing this because the Navy is making him go through the dog-and-pony show before they'll let him retire. Recruitment numbers have been way up since Al Khad's camp released that video, and they want to ride that wave for as long as they can."

For some reason, that angers me. "So they're basically using someone who has already sacrificed so much."

"It's not that so much as they see an opportunity."

"I still think it's somewhat unconscionable that they would force him to do something he doesn't want to do before they'll let him retire."

"This whole thing has become bigger than the Navy, bigger than him. We can't go *anywhere* without people wanting to stop him and thank him and talk to him. That's going to happen whether he does the publicity circuit or not. So the way they see it, they may as well benefit from it."

"I'll do my best to make it as painless as possible for him."

"What's the next step?"

"Tomorrow, I want to spend some time with him going over the questions he's likely to be asked and preparing his replies."

"He's gonna *love* that."

"I assume he'd rather be prepared than blindsided, but if I'm wrong about that, feel free to let me know."

"You're not wrong, but he's not going to be easily coached."

"Believe it or not, I'm not surprised to hear that."

Muncie laughs. "You've got backbone, Ms. Tilden. I'll give you that."

I put my notebook, cell phone and John's phone into my oversized purse and prepare to leave. "Call me Julianne. And I'm the youngest of four, Commander Muncie. My three older siblings are triplets. I had to develop backbone early to deal with them."

"Wow, that's cool. And I'm David or Dave."

"It's much better now than it was when we were kids and they were constantly ganging up on me." I add a smile so he knows it wasn't as bad as I make it sound. "Now they're my closest friends."

"Nice how that happens, huh?"

"Definitely. Well, I guess I'll check in tomorrow and set up a time to do some work."

"Sounds good."

"I've never been here before. Any suggestions of what I could do with the rest of my day?"

"You'll want to check out the Hotel del Coronado and the beach there, as well as Balboa Park or the famous San Diego Zoo."

I crinkle my nose. "Zoos make me sad. I can't bear to see the animals in captivity."

"So I guess Sea World is out, then, too?"

"You guess correctly."

"Mission Beach and Belmont Park are fun, and there's a great boardwalk behind your hotel with lots of restaurants and shops. Make sure you have some Mexican food while you're here, if you like that. It's the best."

"I love it. I'll check it out. Thanks for the suggestions."

"No problem. Feel free to text if you want some recommendations of where to eat."

"I'll do that."

He walks me to the door. "Thanks again for coming out and taking him on."

"No problem."

"You say that now…"

"It's all good, Dave. I'll touch base in the morning."

As I walk to the elevator, I summon an Uber to take me back to my hotel. My mind races with thoughts about the meeting with John and the work I need to do to prepare him to face the media. Like I told Dave, I've had reluctant clients before, but no one quite like him.

I'm in the Uber when my phone rings. I take the call from my sister, Amy. "Hey."

"Is this a good time?"

"Yep. I'm on the way back to my hotel."

"So you met him?"

"I did."

"What's he like?"

"That's a complicated question."

"What do you mean?"

"He had a lot of questions about Ava and Eric."

"No way."

"Yes way."

"What did you say?"

"I told him they're happy together."

"Whoa, what a spot to be in. He came right out and asked you?"

"He sort of grilled me, if I'm being honest."

"Oh my God. Eric would freak if he knew that."

"Which is why we're not going to tell him, Amy. You hear me? He's my client. I shouldn't even be talking to you about this."

"Yes, you should, and I'd never repeat it. Don't worry. So what's the plan?"

"I'm going to book him a media tour in New York and LA and try to get him through it without him killing me or the reporters."

"Is he really that menacing?"

"Ah, yeah, kinda."

"Jules! You don't have to do this! If the guy scares you, beg off."

"There's no way I'm begging off. Landing him as a client is the coup of the century, and he doesn't scare me. He's just kind of intimidating. That's all."

"Does he look as good in person as he does in pictures?"

"Um, better?"

"Wow," Amy says on a long exhale. "That's hard to believe. I hope I get to meet him while you're in New York."

"We'll see how it goes. He's not exactly what I'd call sociable."

"Still, I'd kill to meet him. When are you coming back to New York?"

"Probably toward the end of next week."

"Oh good. It's boring here with you away, Ava and Eric on their honeymoon and Rob and Camille off campaigning."

Our brother Rob is running for Congress, and Eric and Amy will be managing the campaign when Eric returns from his honeymoon. It's going to be a busy fall for our family. "Call some of your friends. It's a good chance to see them."

"I guess."

"Why do you sound so down?"

"I don't know. I've been out of sorts lately."

"Why don't you come out here and hang with me? I've got a huge hotel room, and there's an awesome pool. We could play tourist when I'm not working. Come, Amy! That would be so awesome!"

"It does sound fun."

"I'm booking you a flight."

"Wait! Let me make sure I can get the time off." She's an accountant with one of the big CPA firms in the city. "I'll let you know."

"Hurry up about it. I need you here."

"I'll call you back."

The line goes dead, but I'm filled with excitement about the possibility of her joining me in San Diego. Dealing with Captain Cranky won't seem so awful if Amy is here to entertain me between work commitments. Did I really just think of America's biggest hero as *Captain Cranky*? I laugh softly to myself, causing the Uber driver to give me an odd look in the mirror.

"Funny meme," I tell him, as if he cares.

He doesn't.

If any of my siblings were here, they'd ask me why I felt the need to tell him what I was laughing at. I don't know why! That's just how I am. I talk to people. I'm nice to people. If that makes me weird, then so be it.

Back at the hotel, I decide to go sit by the pool for a while. If Amy is coming, I'd rather do the touristy things with her than by myself. Besides, after the morning I had, I could use a little relaxation. I put on a navy-blue bikini with white piping that's one of my favorites, along with a coverup and large straw hat. I toss sunscreen, a magazine, my notebook, iPad, my personal cell phone and the work phone I'm required to have with me at all times into a tote bag, put on flip-flops and head out into the eighty-five-degree Southern California day.

In the elevator, a little girl and her mom say hello to me.

"I love your dress," I tell the girl.

"Thank you," she says. "Your hat is pretty."

"Thanks. Are you going to the beach?"

The girl shakes her head. "The zoo. I'm so excited to see the giraffes."

"Ohhh, enjoy that. Tell them I said hi."

She giggles at that, and her mom smiles at me. I wonder if she thinks I'm weird, too.

The pool is all but deserted, probably because it's really hot. I had a chat with the bartender last night while I was eating dinner, and he said it's been unusually hot this summer. I must be extra weird because it can never be too hot for me as someone who's always cold. I suffer in the frigid AC during the summer, and I suffer even more during the New York winters.

I could get used to the Southern California climate. For one thing, I absolutely adore palm trees. They say "vacation" to me, so I try to imagine what it would be like to live in a place with palm trees. Would I feel like I was on vacation every day? I wonder...

Deep Thoughts by Julianne Tilden. Maybe my siblings are right and I am a weirdo.

Alone on my lounge with no one around, I have nothing to do for the rest of the day but catch up on work emails and write up some notes about today's meeting along with potential practice questions for the captain.

I allow my thoughts to wander.

I can't stop thinking about the questions he asked me about Ava or the heartbreak in his ethereal blue eyes when he asked. And yes, I really did describe his eyes as *ethereal*. There's something otherworldly about them. I've never seen that shade on any other human being. I try to imagine Ava as a twenty-one-year-old college senior encountering those eyes in a dingy bar off base and being forever changed.

If I'd met him under different circumstances, I probably would've been similarly affected by him. But under these circumstances, I'm not allowed to have anything but professional thoughts about him, even as the "fixer" in me wants to do everything in my power to help him put his life back together.

"That's not your job, Julianne." I mimic my mother's frostiest, most patrician tone, scolding myself the same way she would if she were privy to the thoughts I'm having about my new client, who also happens to be my new sister-in-law's long-lost ex-boyfriend.

Although my mom has lost all credibility with us since she took up with the tennis pro at her club and left my dad last summer. Talk about a cliché and a hypocrite. She brought up the four of us with constant lectures about respect, honor and truthfulness, and then she stages a dramatic exit from her marriage—and her family—by bringing that guy to a family gathering?

All these months later, I still can't believe she actually did such a thing.

But I refuse to revisit that rabbit hole. It's taken me a long time to wrap my head around the whole thing. I've seen her only twice since then, once by mistake at Bloomingdale's and once on purpose when she asked if she could come by my apartment to "talk." I'm such a fool for allowing her into my home to try to "explain" herself. I lasted thirty minutes before I asked her to stop talking and leave my home.

That's thirty minutes more than any of my siblings have given her since "The Stunt," as we call it. Just thinking about that day makes me sick, so I try not to.

Is thinking about that better than thinking about how incredibly hot Ava's ex is?

I'm not sure which is worse, actually.

My ringing cell phone saves me from further thought on the matter. I take the call from Amy. "What's the verdict?"

"Good to go! I'll be there tomorrow afternoon. I bought a one-way ticket until we know how long we're staying."

"This is awesome! I'm so glad you're coming."

"Me, too, Jules. Thanks for inviting me. I really need this."

"We'll have a blast. Send me your itinerary, and I'll meet you at the airport."

"Don't worry about meeting me. I'll just come to the hotel."

"That works. I'll leave a key for you at the desk in case I'm out when you get here."

"See you soon."

"Safe travels." I no sooner end that call when my work phone rings with the tone I programmed in for my boss, Marcie. "Hey, what's up?"

"That's what I want to know. How was the meeting with Captain West?"

"It was good. He signed the retainer. I'll be meeting with him again soon to start prepping him. That's going to take some doing."

"How so?"

"He's a little… rough around the edges, you could say. It's going to take some coaching to make him ready. I'll start booking him toward the end of next week so we have a little time to get him ready."

"Should I send reinforcements? If he needs media coaching, we might want to go with an expert."

"I don't think he'd welcome that. He's barely tolerating me."

"He sounds like a real winner."

I immediately feel defensive of a man I didn't know before this morning. "He's been through a lot, Marcie. More than most people realize."

"What does that mean?"

This is where things get dicey. She has no idea that my new sister-in-law is John's ex. No one knows about Ava, and if I have my way, no one ever will. Marcie knows only that I was brought in by a referral from a friend of the captain's. She never asked me who the friend was, and I didn't volunteer the information.

Do I really need to spell this out for her? Apparently, I do. "In addition to being deployed for nearly six years, he lost his leg and his two closest friends in the raid, not to mention he's lost his anonymity since the video was released. It's a lot on top of a lot."

"I'm concerned about you being able to handle a situation of this magnitude on your own, Julianne."

"I appreciate the concern, but I've got it covered, and I'll ask for help if I need it."

"Please do. I don't need any unpleasant surprises on something this high profile." In the background, I can hear her crunching on Tums. She eats them like candy, while the rest of us speculate on how long it'll be before she suffers a heart attack or stroke. The woman is stress personified, and it's actually a relief to be on the other side of the country from her for a while. Being around her stresses me out.

My stomach aches the way it almost always does when I talk to her. "Captain West's assistant is calling me. I need to take this."

"Go ahead and keep me posted."

"Will do."

I end the call and take a series of deep breaths to decompress from talking to her. She makes me crazy. When I told her I was referred by a friend to Captain

West, her mouth fell open in shock. She tried to convince me to pass the referral to one of our more senior staffers, but I insisted on handling it myself.

Am I in way over my head with this situation? No question. Am I determined to pull off a huge success for myself and my firm? Absolutely.

Now I just have to get my cranky client to get with the program.

CHAPTER 4

John

I never had nightmares before the raid. Now I have them almost every night. I wake up in a cold sweat after reliving the horror of watching Tito and Jonesy get gunned down. I don't dream about my own injury. I dream about the two men who were by my side for years. We survived SEAL training and celebrated holidays together when we were on duty.

Losing one of them would've been horrific. Losing them both is unbearable.

My eyes burn with unshed tears that I don't dare give in to out of fear that once I start, I'll never stop the flood. Tito. Jonesy. Ava. The only three people I've ever truly loved are gone, and the pit of emptiness gnaws at me like an empty belly that won't be satisfied by all the food in the world.

I've never felt so alone, and for someone who spent most of his life alone, that's saying something.

I sit up and swing my legs toward the side of the bed. Every single time, I have to remind myself that my left leg is gone. I reach for the prosthesis and fumble my way through putting it on so I can get up and take a leak without relying on the crutches.

I lied to Julianne yesterday. I have no business going on a press junket when I'm still trying to regain my strength. The most basic things are a huge struggle for me. But I want it done. I want to do whatever I have to in order to retire and return to a life of anonymity. So I'm going along with her and the demands from my chain of command with that one goal in mind.

I've graduated from physical therapy. They've done what they can for me, and the rest, as they said, is going to take time. My doctor told me it could take a year to fully recover from the infection that nearly killed me. At least I've gotten to the point where I can bear the prosthesis and can put weight on it without excruciating pain from the stump. Due to pervasive weakness, I continue to use the crutches so I won't fall and make everything worse. Losing my leg would've been bad enough, but the infection that led to thirty days immobile in a hospital bed made everything a thousand times worse.

I pull myself up, take a minute to make sure I won't fall over and then make my way slowly and carefully to the bathroom and then to the kitchen for ice water that I drink standing by the fridge. Carrying it would require having a hand available, which I don't. Muncie got me a water bottle with a handle, but that's in the bedroom, and it would take too much effort to get it. So I drink the water before moving to the recliner in the living room. I turn on the TV, looking for something mindless to help pass the time until dawn.

This has become my routine since the nightmares started. Once I'm awake, there's no going back to sleep, so I don't bother to try anymore.

I yearn for Ava. I can't think about where she is or what she might be doing with her new husband, so I force myself to remember how she was with me the way I did during the six years of my deployment. I thought of her constantly then, and it's a tough habit to break now that I'm not allowed to think about her that way anymore.

She's married. Maybe if I keep repeating those words to myself over and over again, I'll finally get my head around the fact that she actually married someone else.

What the hell did I expect her to do anyway? Sit around and wait for me forever? She did that for five years before she couldn't do it anymore. More than almost anything else, that detail breaks my heart all over again. At the four-and-a-half-year mark, we'd nearly gotten Al Khad. We'd been *this* close, closer than we'd ever been up to that point, before he somehow got away from us again, leading to another six months of chasing our tails before we finally found and captured him.

If only we'd gotten him that first time. I would've been home before Ava's self-imposed five-year deadline, and she never would've met Eric. She'd be right here with me where she's supposed to be—that is, if she chose to forgive me for the ordeal I'd put her through.

I wish there was a pill I could take to redirect my thoughts from things that can't ever be again. I harbor no illusions that Ava is going to wake up one day and suddenly decide she married the wrong guy. He was there for her when I wasn't. I want to hate him for that, but how can I? It's the truth, even if I'd give anything to have a different outcome.

If only the doctors could've given me a timeline on how long it will take to get over the emotional wounds. Something tells me that'll take a hell of a lot longer than the physical recovery.

I find an old episode of *Frasier* and force myself to pay attention to the show, hoping the stuffy Crane brothers can help drown out the voices inside my head. I actually laugh a couple of times, which I take as a good sign that maybe there's hope for me yet. As one episode becomes two and then three, I find my thoughts wandering to Julianne Tilden.

I tell myself it's better to think about her than Ava, but is it really? She's Ava's new sister-in-law, which is a little too close for comfort, if you ask me. But Ava assured me that Julianne is excellent at what she does and a really nice person, too. What was I supposed to say? *No, don't send me your new sister-in-law?* I need the help that Julianne will provide, and since Ava herself is unable—and most likely unwilling—to do the job, her recommendation of Julianne is the next best thing.

I'm not so heartbroken that I failed to notice that my new publicist is gorgeous in a cool, patrician sort of way. She reminds me of the women who were married to the admirals. Like them, she was impeccably turned out with every blonde hair in place and makeup so artfully applied it appeared she wasn't wearing any. Not only is she beautiful, but she's also smart and efficient and committed to her work, qualities she shares with Ava. I remember Ava telling me about the clients she worked with and how much she loved helping them create a message that resonates with people.

And I'm back to Ava…

I really wish there was something I could do, perhaps a séance or a lobotomy or electric shock therapy, *anything* that would redirect my thoughts. If I believed any of those things would help, I'd do them in a hot second to get some relief from the painful memories that plague me.

I force myself to pay attention to the TV and watch a few more episodes of *Frasier*, giving thanks for the talented actors who capture my attention and keep it for a few hours. The next thing I know, sunlight is streaming into the apartment, and I realize I dozed off at some point. I'm grateful for the additional hours of sleep, even if I missed my usual gym time. I'll have to try to go later. As I sit up to stretch, I hear Muncie's key in the door.

He's annoyingly punctual in reporting for duty each morning right at nine o'clock. "Oh, hey, you're up."

"Have been for a while." I take the coffee he hands me. "Thanks."

"You didn't sleep?"

"I did. Some."

"You need to call that shrink, Captain. They might be able to give you something to help you sleep."

"Don't want it, don't need it." I quit taking the pain meds because I feared becoming addicted to them. After so many weeks in the hospital, the last thing I want or need is another doctor or pill. "The melatonin you got me helps. Let's leave it at that."

"As you wish. Julianne would like to meet with you at eleven today. Does that work for you?"

"Uh, let me check my schedule."

He gives me his trademark withering look. I get that look a lot from him, and it's almost fun to say things that'll bring it on. I have to get my laughs where I can these days.

"I'll tell her eleven is fine."

"You do that."

"Are you hungry?"

"Nope."

"You need to eat."

"I'm aware of that." We have this same conversation several times per day. My appetite is another thing that hasn't come back to life. I'm told it will eventually. In the meantime, I force myself to eat so I'll get stronger, but nothing really appeals to me.

"I can get you one of those western omelets from the diner down the street. You liked that last week."

Because it will shut him up, I agree to the omelet even if my stomach turns at the memory of trying to choke it down the last time he got it for me. I don't know why food has become such a problem for me. In my past life, I had a ravenous appetite for food and sex, neither of which is of any interest whatsoever to me now.

One of the doctors told me my appetite will be off for a while because I spent so much time subsisting on liquid nutrition that my body forgot how to eat regular food. Just like I have to retrain my muscles, eventually my desire for food will return, too, or so they say. Hasn't happened yet. I hope all my various appetites will return eventually, but for now, I don't hunger for food or sex.

Not that I can imagine ever wanting anyone but Ava, but I suppose eventually I'll have to move on and try again with someone else, even if Ava will always have my heart.

Just thinking about moving on from her makes my chest ache something fierce. The hope of a life with her kept me alive while we were apart. Without her, I feel like a sailboat that's lost its rudder and is floundering in a hostile sea.

Will I ever find my way again? I don't know, and the not knowing only adds to the hollowed-out feeling inside me.

Muncie returns a short time later with carryout containers for both of us.

We eat in silence—or he eats and I pick at mine with the usual lack of enthusiasm. He clears his throat. "The guys from the unit have reached out. They'd like to see you, if you're up for visitors."

The men I spent six years with are like brothers to me, but none of them are as close to me as Tito and Jonesy were. Seeing the rest of them and not having my two best friends there would feel like acid on a festering wound.

"Not yet."

"Might be good for you to see them." He looks over at me. "I think they need it as much as you do, sir. They need to see that you're all right."

I'm so far from all right that I could laugh at him saying that, but they were my men, and I was their commander, and he's right. Muncie can be like a dog with a bone once he gets an idea in his head, and he doesn't seem to care one bit that I outrank him when he pushes me to do things I don't want to do. Knowing that, I say, "Set it up for before we go to New York. Just the guys. No one else."

"Yes, sir."

Is it my imagination or does he sound smug? Bastard. He's lucky I need him so much.

After we eat, I go in to take a shower, shave and change into clean sweats and a long-sleeved Henley. If I have to meet with Mary Poppins again, at least I'll be clean and presentable. When I'm dressed and wearing running shoes, it strikes me that if someone didn't know my left leg was missing from the thigh down, there'd be no way to tell that I'm an amputee unless I chose to share that. Only the crutches that I keep close indicate there's anything amiss.

I sit on the bed to wait the final ten minutes before Julianne arrives, depleted from the workout required just to shower and get dressed. I recognize the vicious cycle at work here—I need food to regain my strength but have no appetite, which makes the journey back to full health that much more difficult.

I'm told I need to have patience, that things will get back to "normal" at some point, but that's not true. My version of "normal" is gone, married to some other dude and off on her honeymoon, lost to me forever.

I never knew until now how exhausting heartbreak can be, because I'd never been in love before I met my Ava. Now that I know what it feels like to lose the one you love, I hope I never fall in love again. It's not worth the agony if it doesn't work out.

Muncie knocks on the door. "Are you decent?"

"Yeah. Come in."

He opens the door, sees me sitting on the bed and takes a visual inventory, checking on me the way he does so adeptly. "Julianne is here. You ready?"

"I guess." I pull myself up and position the crutches while making a point to put weight on the prosthetic the way they told me to in PT.

Today, Julianne is wearing a pink jacket with a black skirt and the same sexy heels she had on yesterday. Her hair is up, her smile friendly and welcoming.

"Good morning," she says.

"Morning." I'm determined to try not to be a total dick to her today since she's doing the job I asked her to do, even if I don't want to deal with any of it. That's not her fault. And I don't want her telling Ava that I'm an asshole, so I need to not be one.

"I thought we'd spend some time today going over the questions you're likely to be asked and preparing your replies. Would that be okay?"

"Yes." *No*, I want to say, *it's not okay. I don't want to talk about any of it. I want to retire, buy a cabin in the mountains and be alone.*

"I'd also like to record this session so we can review it later and go over anything that needs to be tweaked. Is that all right?"

"I guess."

Undeterred by my lack of enthusiasm, she sets up her iPad on a table to record me and then returns to her seat, crossing her legs. I happen to notice again that they're nice legs, smooth and muscular, as if she played sports as a kid or is a runner or dancer.

Why the fuck am I thinking about her legs? Maybe because it's better than the other things that plague my addled brain.

"I'm going to do these in no particular order, starting with the six-year deployment. When you joined the Navy, were you told it was possible you could deploy for that long?"

"Not initially, no. That came later when I was assigned to an elite unit that trains for just this kind of mission."

"When you heard about the attack on the *Star of the High Seas*, did you know right away that you'd be deployed indefinitely?"

"Yes, I did."

"What's that like, to be living a somewhat normal life that's completely upended by something you had nothing to do with?"

"It's jarring and difficult, but it's what we trained and prepared for. You hope that your training will never be needed, but when it is, you do what you have to do, no matter what it might cost you personally. It's not about you in that moment. It's about the mission until the mission is completed."

She gives me a thoughtful look. "That's a really good answer. We should commit that one to memory."

"I don't need to memorize the truth."

"Still, that's the sort of thing we're aiming for." She consults her notes. "I know you can't give specifics about the mission itself, but can you tell us anything about where you were and what you were doing for all that time?"

"We were in the field, following the trail."

"Does that mean living in tents and eating MREs?"

"Most of the time. Sometimes we took shelter in caves. Other times we were lodged with forward-deployed troops. We ate real food when we were in camp."

"Can you talk about what you remember about the raid on the Al Khad compound?"

I'd prefer to never think about that night again, but that's not an option. The Navy is holding up my retirement papers until I complete this media tour, so the sooner I get it over with, the sooner I can get on with my life, such as it is.

"I remember being really excited that we'd finally found him. We were close a few times, most recently at the four-and-a-half-year mark, but this time we knew for sure we had him. On the way in, the hardest part was going through the steps to make sure we didn't blow it somehow. Everyone was amped and ready to get it done, so waiting for darkness made for a very long day."

Julianne barely seems to breathe as she listens to me, hanging on my every word. I can't deny that her interest in me and my story gives me a little charge. I wouldn't call it excitement, because that would be giving it too much credit. But it definitely makes me feel… something.

"I remember realizing that my two closest friends had been hit and then being hit myself. After that, everything is kind of a blur. I knew right away I was in trouble because of the amount of blood I was losing. Luckily, the team got me out of there quickly, but my friends weren't as lucky."

She consults her notes. "Lieutenant Commander Daniel Jones and Lieutenant Commander Miguel Tito were killed during the raid."

Hearing their names sends a shaft of pain through me that I feel everywhere. Life without Jonesy and Tito is almost as unimaginable to me as life without Ava. I nod in response to her question, gritting my teeth against the ache.

"Had you known them a long time?"

"We went through officer candidate school and SEAL training together. They were the closest thing to brothers I've ever had."

"I'm so sorry you lost them."

"Thank you. I am, too. They were outstanding officers, inspirational leaders and the best friends anyone could hope to have." I'm mortified when my voice catches on those last words.

"Would you like to take a break?" she asks with the sympathy that irritated me yesterday. I don't want it from her or anyone.

I shake my head. I'd rather get it over with than drag it out.

"After the raid, you lost your left leg and then suffered an infection that put you in a month-long coma. When you recovered, you learned that you'd been 'outed' by Al Khad's organization. What was that like for you?"

"It was…" The weeks that followed the coma are also a blur. I was sick and weak and grappling with the losses of my leg and my friends. My only goal then was to get strong enough to see Ava again. "It was shocking to realize everyone knew my name and my face and that people were interested in me. We operate under a necessary cloak of secrecy, which is why talking about this stuff goes against everything I believe in."

"Why are you talking about it?"

"The Navy sees this as a good opportunity to shed some light on the sacrifices our members make in the interest of national security."

"I understand that recruitment is way up since the video was released. Do you feel any sense of pride in hearing that?"

"The Navy has been really good to me. It gave me a career and a life I never could've imagined for myself growing up in the foster system. I'll be forever thankful for that, and I hope if there're other young people out there looking for a direction in life, they'll consider the Navy and the many opportunities available to them."

"I imagine it's also quite shocking to go from being a private citizen to a public figure practically overnight."

"You imagine correctly. It's very strange to be recognized in public, but people have been so nice, too. They thank me for my service and sacrifice. It's nice to feel that we're appreciated for what we did."

"Have you heard from any of the *Star of the High Seas* families?"

I glance at Muncie, who nods. "You've gotten letters from them. They're in the envelopes of mail you haven't wanted to deal with."

I gesture toward him with my thumb. "What he said."

"You're going to need to read those letters so you'll be prepared to talk about them when you're asked. I suspect that's going to be a fairly common question."

"I'll read them."

"When you deployed, did you leave anyone special behind?"

The question sparks a wildfire of rage inside me. How dare she ask me that? And just as I'm about to say as much, I get what she's doing. She's preparing me to handle that question when it's asked. I choke back the rage and force my expression to stay neutral. "No." Under no circumstances can the media ever find out about Ava. They'd go crazy tearing her life apart, and I can't let that happen.

"Just so you know, your reaction to the question was a dead giveaway that you're lying."

"I wasn't expecting it."

"Well, now you will, and if you wish to keep that aspect of your life private, you'll need to react differently."

"I'll work on it." Asking me to be unemotional about Ava is like asking me not to breathe. It actually might be less painful to quit breathing than to school my emotions where she's concerned, but I'll do it to keep her safe. There's nothing I wouldn't do to keep her as far from me and my newfound notoriety as I possibly can.

"I'm sorry to upset you, but I figure you'd rather it come from me than be blindsided in an interview."

She's right. Of course I would. I offer a brisk nod. "Are there other questions?"

"Why don't we take a little break before we continue?"

"Fine." I struggle to my feet and leave the room, closing the bedroom door behind me. I stretch out on the bed and close my eyes, exhausted from the mostly sleepless night and the toll of having to relive things I'd sooner forget. In the other room, I can hear Julianne talking to Muncie, but I don't care enough to try to figure out what they're saying.

I'm so fucking tired.

I close my eyes, just for a minute.

CHAPTER 5

Julianne

I stare at the closed door to the bedroom, feeling bad for upsetting him. "I had to ask him that."

"I know you did, and so does he."

"Does he really?"

"He knows you're only doing your job."

I wonder what he's doing in there and if he's going to come back to continue. While I wait, I scroll through email on my phone, answer a couple of inquiries from colleagues and see a longer message from Marcie that I'll deal with later. I respond to a text from Amy, who's at JFK for the flight to San Diego and excited for her trip.

See you soon!

Can't wait.

I'm glad she's excited for a getaway, and I can't wait for her to arrive. Having her here will make this difficult job a thousand times easier on me than it would be without her support. It's always been like that for me—my older siblings represent safety and security to me. While we fought the same way all siblings do growing up, I always knew that any of the three of them would kill for me and vice versa.

I glance at the closed bedroom door again. "Do you think he's coming back?"

Muncie gets up from his post at the dining room table. "Let me check." He knocks on the door, and when he gets no answer, he knocks again before poking his head in. "He's asleep, and we probably ought to leave him be. He doesn't sleep much at night."

"I feel bad about this."

"About what?"

"It's like I'm throwing salt on his wounds or something."

"I was surprised he said as much as he did just now. That's more than I've heard him say about any of it in all the months I've been working with him. Don't sell yourself short. You're good at what you do, and you're right to prepare him for what he's apt to be asked."

"That's nice to hear. Thank you for all your help." I gather my belongings and stash them in my oversized purse. "I guess we'll pick it up tomorrow. I should have an itinerary for you both by then as well." I spent hours last night returning messages to producers for all the biggest shows on TV. "Needless to say, there's a lot of interest."

"I figured there would be."

I lower my voice, lest I be overheard. "My greatest concern is that this is going to make things worse for him somehow. He seems… fragile." I no sooner use that word than I regret it. "That's not what I mean—"

"You're not wrong about that. He is fragile in many ways, but I think he understands that the damage is done as far as everyone knowing his name and face, so he may as well work it to his advantage at this point. After he retires, he'll be able to accept some of the endorsement deals that he's been offered. That'll set him up for life."

"I can't see him saying yes to any of that."

"Maybe not now, but he will. When the time is right and if the offer appeals to him. He'd be crazy not to."

That may be true, but after having known him for all of twenty-four hours, I can't picture any scenario wherein he becomes a salesman for some random product. I already know it's not his style to trade on fame that came to him the way his did.

"I'll check in with you in the morning."

"Sounds good. Did you get to do some sightseeing yesterday?"

"Not yet. My sister is coming out for a few days. We're going to do that together."

"That'll be fun."

"Definitely. I'll text you tomorrow."

"Talk to you then."

I return to my hotel, where I spend a few hours sifting through emails and answering questions from colleagues who have taken on my other clients so I can focus exclusively on Captain West. If there's an underlying layer of tension in the correspondence with my coworkers, I suppose that's to be expected when a junior account executive is tapped to represent such a high-profile client. I ignore the snark and answer their questions, even if the pit in my stomach serves as an ever-present reminder of how far out of my league I am.

Regardless, I'm determined to slay this campaign so I can tell the people in my office to suck it.

I spend an hour hammering out the itinerary for our press tour in New York. We'll start with *The Tonight Show Starring Jimmy Fallon* and then do the network morning shows, *Live with Kelly and Ryan* and *The View*. He's also booked on the big nighttime shows, including *The Late Show with Stephen Colbert, Late Night with Seth Meyers* and *The Daily Show with Trevor Noah*.

In LA, he'll appear on *Ellen, The Talk, Jimmy Kimmel Live!* and *The Late Late Show with James Corden*.

I get a little giddy when I realize how huge this is going to be and how I'm now on a first-name basis with the producers at the top shows in the business.

This is Julianne Tilden. I represent Captain John West.

Watch those doors swing wide open. Everyone wants an interview with the American hero who helped bring down the world's most wanted terrorist. And if you want to get to him, you have to go through me.

I stand up to stretch and do a little happy dance, filled with excitement for the press tour, even if my client wants nothing to do with any of it. That's his problem, not mine. I no sooner have that thought when I'm hit with the irrational fear that somehow this'll turn out to be a hot mess and everyone will blame me.

No, that won't happen. He's still wearing the uniform and representing the United States Navy. He will do so with honor and distinction, or so I hope.

With just over an hour until Amy's flight is due to land, I decide to meet her. I rush through a quick shower and change into jeans, a tank top and a sweater that I knot at my waist in case of frigid AC. I find a pair of striped wedge sandals in my suitcase, slide my feet into them, grab my hotel key and head to the lobby, where the bellman summons a cab for me.

I'm on the way to the airport when Amy texts me that she's landed ten minutes early.

On my way!

I was with Amy, Rob and his wife, Camille, last weekend before I left for San Diego, but it feels like a month has passed since then, and I can't wait to see Amy. Her presence will give me the support I need right now, and it'll be fun to have someone to sightsee with, too.

We agree to meet at baggage claim, and I'm scanning the faces coming down the escalator when there she is. I wave to her, and she smiles to let me know she sees me.

It's crowded, so I have to cool my heels for a few minutes as she makes her way to where I'm waiting for her. And then we're hugging like we haven't seen each other in a month.

"I'm so glad you're here."

"You have no idea how glad I am to be here."

She carried her bag on the plane, so we head outside to find a cab to take us back to the hotel.

"Ahhh, it's so warm, but not nasty hot like it is at home."

"I know. I love it. I could get used to this climate awfully quick."

"I'm ready for cooler weather in New York. The humidity is so gross."

"What do you feel like doing?"

"Whatever you want."

"There's a cool boardwalk behind the hotel we can check out this afternoon."

"Sounds good to me."

We arrive at the hotel a few minutes later and take the elevator up to my room.

Amy crosses the room to admire the view of downtown San Diego and the ocean in the distance. "You don't have to work anymore today?"

"Nope. I've been working mornings with…" I'm not sure what I should call him.

"John?"

"Yes. I'm never sure if I should call him John or Captain West or Captain Cranky."

She snorts with laughter. "Captain Cranky?"

Biting my lip, I nod, fearful of telling even my sister that I've thought of him that way. "He's rather miserable at times."

"The poor guy. He's been through so much. Losing six years of his life, his leg, the woman he loved and his anonymity. I really feel for him."

"I do, too. Of course I do. It's just that he's so… *bitter*. That's the only word I can think of to describe his overall disposition. I'm worried that's going to come through in every interview he does."

"If it does, it won't be your fault."

"I want this to go well for him. I want people to appreciate the ordeal he's endured and not see him as a pissed-off, bitter, heartbroken jerk."

"Is he a jerk?"

"Sometimes. But I tell myself he has good reason to be."

"Still, he shouldn't take it out on you."

"I don't think he even realizes he's doing that. He's just so… I don't know how to describe it. He's incredibly handsome and intense and sexy. I can totally see why Ava was crazy about him. But there's a dark side to him, too, and I fear that's what he'll show the rest of the world when he gets on TV. That's not really the image the Navy wants us to portray with this campaign, and if they're unsatisfied, that doesn't bode well for me."

"Hmm, I can see what you mean. How about you come right out and say to him, 'Listen, I know you've had a rough go of it, but I'm sure you don't want to air out your dirty laundry on national TV, so how about you let me help you craft a persona that'll work for what we're doing here, and when we're done, you can go back to being bitchy and moody?'"

I stare at her, agog.

"What? It's a good idea. You know it is."

"I'm just trying to picture myself saying that to a client and how it might be received."

"Who cares how it's received? He's hired you to do a job, and he needs to let you do it."

"His handler, Commander Muncie, would die laughing if I said that to him. He's had to put up with the crankiness a lot longer than I have."

"You need to just put it out there so you can do the job you were hired to do."

"Eh, enough about him. I don't have to think about him or his bitchiness until tomorrow."

"Great. Let's get a drink."

*

Overnight, John becomes the king of the one-word answer and the nonanswer.

"Tell me about your childhood."

"Why?"

"People are interested in where you came from."

"I'm from nowhere."

"So you were dropped from space and landed in a nest somewhere? Or perhaps you were spawned? That would actually make more sense." I've never in my entire life talked to a client—or anyone, for that matter—like I'm talking to him. I want to smack him, which is also new for me.

Muncie does that coughing-to-cover-a-laugh thing that's become part of my daily routine with these two.

For his part, John seems to realize he's getting to me, so he digs in, becomes moodier, if that's even possible.

"Commander Muncie." I never take my gaze off Captain Cranky. "Maybe you should let the Navy know that Captain West isn't ready to go public with his story, because he's not willing to do the work necessary to prepare for the questions he's going to be asked."

"How am I not cooperating?"

"You're not answering the questions."

"I don't understand why I have to talk about my childhood when the story is about me helping to get Al Khad."

"It's part of the overall story of your life, and for some strange reason, people are interested in your life."

"My life isn't that interesting—or it wasn't until Al Khad's minions released that video."

"Let me be the judge of what's interesting and what isn't."

"How about we put my childhood off-limits?"

"Then you'll have to talk more about the deployment, the mission, losing your leg and your plans for the future. Which is worse?"

"The childhood."

I'm instantly curious about the details of his childhood. "I know how hard this is for you—"

"Do you? Really?"

He makes a good point.

"No. I don't," I say, sighing. "But I'm trying to help you to craft a message you can take to these interviews. How about you help me do that so we can get it over with and then you can go back to being cranky and moody?"

Muncie doesn't even try to hide his laughter this time.

John sits up a little straighter, possibly about to fire back at me. Or just fire me. At this point, I'm not sure which I'd prefer.

"She's right, you know," Muncie says. "You can do this now or be blindsided by the questions they ask you in front of the camera."

"Or I could just say, 'Fuck this whole thing' and refuse to do any of it."

"Is that what you want?" My heart drops at the thought of him refusing to do the tour I've spent hours setting up for him. If I have to go back and undo all that, my name will be mud with producers who're probably already promoting his upcoming appearances.

"Hell yes, that's what I want! I want to fucking retire and be left alone."

"To do what?"

"I don't know. Nothing?"

"And you think that'll be good for you in light of everything that's happened? To sit in a room by yourself with nothing to do but think about all the ways your life has gone sideways?"

"It would be better than this."

I'm oddly wounded by that. "Would it be? Really?"

He glares at me as if to say anything would be better than dealing with me, even being completely alone with his traumatic thoughts.

Okay, then. I put my notebook in my bag.

"So that's it? You're just quitting?"

It's my turn to glare at him. "Do you know that I have never, in my entire life until now, wanted to strike another living being? And that's saying something since I grew up with three older siblings who loved to torment me."

He sticks his jaw out. "Give it your best shot."

"I wouldn't give you the satisfaction of being able to tell people that I punched an injured American hero veteran."

That earns me a genuine laugh, and it completely transforms him. I find myself staring at him, the way I would if he suddenly started speaking fluent Russian.

Then he shocks me further. "What do you say we get the hell out of here for a while?"

I'm stunned speechless. He wants to go somewhere? *With me?*

"Wow, I've finally found the secret to shutting her up, Muncie."

"Maybe she's just surprised to find that you're capable of smiling and being nice?"

Have I mentioned that I *love* David Muncie? Thank God for him.

John waves a hand in front of my face. "Earth to Julianne. Are you in there? Did you hear me?"

"I heard you. What I don't understand is why."

"Why am I offering to get out of here with you?"

I nod.

"Because I heard you want to see the sights in San Diego, and Muncie, being somewhat new to the area himself, gave you the tourist traps. I thought you might want to see the real San Diego."

"And you want to be the one to show them to me?"

"Well, yeah, I guess."

"Why? You don't even like me."

"When did I say I didn't like you?"

"Um, the first day when you could barely say hello and looked at me like I was bringing the plague to your doorstep rather than the help you requested?"

Muncie snorts and then coughs, earning another glare from his boss.

"I didn't do that."

I tip my head and raise a brow, letting him know I'm not buying his bullshit.

"Okay, maybe I did that a little, but it's not you. It's all of it. I never asked for any of this."

"So your strategy is to shoot the messenger, or in this case, the person who's trying to help you deal with a situation you didn't ask for, but find yourself in nonetheless?"

"Something like that." He holds my gaze for a long moment, during which I can barely breathe as I wait to hear what he will say. "I apologize for treating you that way. You're one hundred percent right that it's not your fault, and I did ask for your help. I've been a bitchy pain in the ass, and I'm sorry. Can we clear the slate and start over?"

Wow, I didn't see that coming. I find myself speechless for the second time in as many minutes.

Then he smiles—a real, sincere smile, and I feel like Alice falling down the rabbit hole into Wonderland. What that smile does to his already ridiculously handsome face cannot be described in mere words. *"Please?"*

I snap out of the smile-induced stupor to realize he's waiting for me to respond. After clearing my throat, I nod. "Okay." And then I remember Amy. "My sister's here. I'd like to bring her, if that's all right."

"Sure. We'll all go. Right, Muncie?"

"Yes, sir. Whatever you say, sir."

"Can the bullshit, Muncie."

"I will if you will. Sir."

John grabs his crutches and hauls himself to his feet, taking a second to get his balance. "Wait until he sees his next performance eval. The word *insubordination* will be heavily emphasized."

Despite his words, he seems amused and more relaxed than I've seen him yet, as if clearing the air with me relieved him of a burden.

"I'm going to change, and then we can go pick up your sister. Muncie will drive us."

"Um, okay, I'll let her know."

He heads for the bedroom, and I wait until the door closes behind him to turn to look at Muncie. "What just happened here?" I ask in a whisper.

"I have no idea, but I'm not asking any questions, and you shouldn't either."

"Maybe he's sick of being pissed."

"That'd be a full-fledged miracle. I give you all the credit."

"Why? I didn't do anything."

"You don't put up with his crap. That's huge."

"That's sort of mortifying, actually. I'm always respectful to my clients. But he just makes me…"

"Ragey? Infuriated? Crazy?"

I huff out a laugh. "All of the above."

"I feel your pain, believe me." Muncie glances at the closed bedroom door. "But I feel his pain, too. With everything that's happened, I give him credit for getting out of bed in the morning."

Muncie clearly respects the man he works for, even if he doesn't always like him.

I dash off a quick text to Amy. *Get up and get pretty. We've got a sightseeing date with the captain and his handler, Muncie. Don't ask. Just get ready!*

She responds right away. *Um, okay, but I have questions!*

As do I.

Curiouser and curiouser.

GET. READY.

She responds with the laughing emoji. Thank God she's here to go on this outing with me. I'd be a nervous wreck with only Muncie there to provide a buffer between me and *him*. Amy will play the role of my security blanket just by being there. It's always been like that for me where she's concerned. If Amy is there, I feel better. It's that simple.

The bedroom door opens, and John emerges wearing well-worn jeans, a white polo shirt with a Navy insignia on the chest and a pair of black Nikes that look new. "Ready?" He's combed his hair and is still wearing the same relaxed expression that astounded me before. Who is this man, and what has he done with Captain Cranky?

I could deal with the cranky. This version of him, however, is dangerous. I'm not sure why I think that. I just do.

"Am I allowed to change, too, or do you plan to drag me around San Diego in uniform?" Muncie asks.

I've never seen him in anything but the khaki uniform.

"We can run by your place."

"Gee, thanks. Do you want to bring the chair?" Muncie gestures to a folded wheelchair that I've never noticed before tucked into the corner by the door.

"No," John says quickly. "Let's go."

We head for the door, and Muncie is the last one out. He locks up while John and I head for the elevator. I walk slowly to match his pace.

"Muncie told me you're anti-zoo?" he says while we wait for the elevator.

"I can't bear to see animals in captivity, even if they're well cared for. It just hurts my heart."

"I feel the same way. What are your thoughts on seals in their natural environment?"

"Seals are so cute. I wish I could have a pet seal."

"Then we have to hit La Jolla Cove first."

"What goes on there?"

"Seals and sea lions and other fun stuff."

The elevator arrives, and the three of us step in to take it down to the lobby level. His apartment is in a building that advertises furnished residences. I wonder if he lived there before he deployed or if the place is new to him, but I don't ask. I've learned to choose my questions wisely with him.

Muncie's black Toyota Highlander SUV has a handicapped parking placard hanging from the mirror.

"Take the front," John says.

"That's okay. I'll sit in the back with my sister."

He gets into the passenger seat, and Muncie stows his crutches in the back, their routine seeming well practiced and efficient.

On the short ride to the hotel, John points out a few bars and restaurants he says he used to frequent the last time he lived here. I assume that means Ava did, too.

He gestures to a sand-colored apartment building. "That's where we lived."

He doesn't say anything else after that, and I wonder if it hurts him to see the place where he lived with Ava. I hate to think of him suffering any more than he already has.

When we arrive at my hotel, John turns to me. "Wear sneakers if you have them. The rocks can be slippery."

"Will do. I'll be quick."

"Take your time," he says. "We're in no rush."

I grab my giant purse that doubles as a work tote and jump out of the car. Inside, I take the elevator up to my floor and walk into my room to find Amy dressed in a cute dress with her dark hair in a ponytail and a sweater tied around her waist.

"They said to wear sneakers if we have them."

Her nose wrinkles with distaste. "I'm not wearing sneakers when it's seventy-eight degrees."

"We're going to see seals and sea lions."

"I'll take my chances with sandals."

While I try to figure out what to wear on this unexpected outing, she plops down on one of the two queen-size beds. "So what's the deal?"

"I don't know. We were arguing about something, and he suddenly says, 'Do you want to get out of here for a while?' At first, I was so surprised, I didn't know what to say. I could tell Muncie was, too." I change into a pair of shorts and a lightweight floral top, hoping it won't seem like I tried too hard to look good, and put my hair up in a ponytail before slathering myself in sunscreen and handing the bottle to Amy. "I'm sure it's more about me asking him questions he doesn't want to answer than some altruistic desire to make sure I properly see San Diego while I'm here."

I stop moving and stand in front of Amy. "How do I look?"

"Fine. Why?"

"Just making sure I don't look, you know, like I got dressed up or something."

"You're wearing shorts and a top."

"I know what I'm wearing, Amy!"

"Why're you freaking out?"

"I'm not."

"Ah, yeah, you are."

"I'm not!" I go into the bathroom to brush my teeth and take down the ponytail, comb my hair and redo it. And when I notice my hands are shaking, I have to admit that Amy's right. I *am* freaking out. *Why* am I freaking out?

I leave the bathroom and find Amy where I left her, still eyeing me suspiciously.

"I'm freaking out because nice John is... He's... He's not a jerk."

"Okay... And?"

"And nothing. He's just different, and I don't..." Exasperated with myself and her and especially him, I throw up my hands. "I don't know why I'm freaking out."

"Oh. My. *God.*"

"What?" I'm tossing my phone, room key, gum, sunglasses and sunscreen into a smaller bag.

"Julianne."

My siblings *never* call me that. Ever. I'm always Jules or JuJu or some other derivative of Jules, but never Julianne.

I turn to her.

"What're you doing?"

"Uh, I'm getting ready to go?"

"That's not what I'm asking, and you know it. *What are you doing?*"

"My job?"

She scowls, letting me know the nonanswer isn't going to fly. "You cannot have feelings for this man, Jules. You just can't."

The words hit me like a punch to the gut, stealing the breath from my lungs. It takes me a few seconds to recover. "I don't! Most of the time, I can't stand him."

"And the rest of the time?"

"I feel sorry for him." That's the God's honest truth. "He's been through hell."

Amy stands and comes over to me, putting her hands on my shoulders and forcing me to look at her. "You cannot go *there* with him. You *cannot.* Do you hear me?"

"I'm not going *there* with him. He's my client."

"He's Ava's ex."

I break loose from her hold. "I know who he is, Amy. I don't need you to tell me."

"You sure of that?"

"Are you *trying* to piss me off?"

"Not at all. I'm trying to keep you from doing something really, really stupid."

"And what would that be?"

"Allowing yourself to have feelings for a man who is completely and totally off-limits."

"I'd have to be dead not to sympathize with what he's been through."

"Sympathy is fine, and no one is more sympathetic than you are. But that's all it can be. Tell me you know that."

"Of course I do. Now, let's go before they think we aren't coming." Unsettled by the conversation, I grab my bag and head for the door, hoping she's following me. The unsettled feeling comes with me.

I don't have feelings for him.

He's just a client, and that's all he'll ever be.

CHAPTER 6

John

Muncie and I listen to sports talk radio while we wait for Julianne and her sister. After months of spending most of every day with him, I can tell he's got something on his mind.

"Whatever it is, just say it."

"Whatever what is?"

"That you're dying to say."

"I don't have a statement so much as a question."

Exasperated, I wave my hand to encourage Muncie to ask away.

"What's up with the field trip?"

"I just felt like getting out of that apartment for something other than doctors' appointments."

"That's all it is?"

"What else would it be?"

He hesitates, which isn't like him. He's gotten very good at speaking his mind with me, which I usually appreciate—not that I can tell the insubordinate pain in the ass that.

"You're different with her."

"Huh? Different with who?"

"Julianne. She gets to you."

"She annoys me with her endless questions."

"You know as well as I do that she's just doing her job and trying to get you ready for a media tour that you're in no way prepared for. But that's not what I'm talking about."

"How about you tell me what you're talking about, then?"

"I'm not sure, exactly. There's just something different about you since she's been here."

"What's different is that I'm being forced to do something I don't want to do."

"Nope, that's not it. I need to think about it some more. I'll get back to you."

"You do that."

"Here they come."

Julianne's sister is a bit taller than her and has dark hair, but the two women have similar gaits and builds. She's curvy like Julianne, but with one quick glance, I can see that Amy is more reserved than her more outgoing younger sister.

They get into the backseat.

"David Muncie, John West, this is my sister, Amelia Tilden. Everyone calls her Amy."

"Nice to meet you both," Amy says.

"Likewise," I reply. "Glad you could join us today."

"Me, too. I'm excited to see San Diego. And thank you very much for your service."

"You're welcome." I hear that a lot, and it never gets old that people appreciate what we did, even if it's weird that people know the role I played in it. That never would've been my choice.

After a quick stop at Muncie's apartment building so he can change out of his uniform, we head for the coast.

"What are you ladies looking forward to seeing?"

"The beach," Amy says.

"And the seals," Julianne adds.

"Yes, the seals, too," Amy says.

"And I want some good Tex-Mex," Julianne says.

I snort with laughter. "Tex-Mex is Texas. Here, it's just Mexican."

"I stand corrected. Where can we get it?"

"Roberto's. It's the best there is. We'll go there after we see the seals."

I drink in the familiar scenery of the only place that's ever felt like home to me. The view is different to me post-deployment and post-Ava. Now I don't know where I belong or if anywhere will ever feel like home to me again.

The counselor I saw when I was still in the hospital repeatedly emphasized the need to take things one step at a time—literally. My first priority has been mobility, and I'm slowly but surely getting there. With the media tour hurdle to get past, I haven't given much thought to what will come after that. Will I stay in San Diego, or will it be too painful to be here long-term without Ava? I haven't figured that out yet. While the remote cabin in the mountains appeals to me, being alone all the time doesn't.

I'm hoping the answers will come to me before I have to make decisions about the next part of my life. My Navy pension will kick in right away, so I'm not going to have to work unless I want to. While that might sound ideal, I'm concerned about having too much time on my hands to brood, so I may look for a job. Eventually.

I joined the Navy after getting into trouble as a kid. I loved the Navy from the beginning. I loved the structure I'd never had, the camaraderie, the friends, the opportunity to travel and, later, the chance to move into the officer corps. My career has exceeded all my expectations, and I loved every minute of it until the day Al Khad took down the *Star of the High Seas*, killing four thousand people and ruining the lives of so many others, including mine and Ava's.

Now I just want it to be over. I want to be free of obligations, so I can figure out what I'm going to do with the rest of my life.

I direct Muncie to head toward Ocean Beach. We'll work our way north from there.

"This is so beautiful," Amy says when we get our first glimpse of the Pacific.

"Ocean Beach is where the hippies and stoners hang out." On a quick glance, I can see it hasn't changed much in the years I was gone. It's busier and more built up, but the vibe is the same as it always was. "Makes for some good people watching."

In Mission Beach, the bustling boardwalk is mobbed on this late-summer afternoon. People are skateboarding, jogging and rollerblading, as well as eating at sidewalk restaurants and riding bikes. Muncie has no choice but to drive slowly in the congested traffic, stopping frequently to allow people to cross the street to the beach.

We make our way north, passing through Pacific Beach on the way toward La Jolla Cove, where we start to look for parking. Thanks to my handicapped placard, we're able to find a spot that's close to the main thoroughfare. As much as I hate having that goddamned placard, it does make things easier at times like this.

While the others get out, I have to wait for Muncie to get my crutches from the back. I debate going without them, but visions of toppling over in front of Julianne and her sister have me gratefully accepting the crutches from Muncie.

The others are considerate about walking slowly to match my pace. I try not to be self-conscious about how freaking slow I am. If they only knew what I used to be capable of…

"The seals tend to hang out at the Children's Pool, while the sea lions gather closer to the cliffs."

"How can you tell if they're seals or sea lions?" Julianne asks.

"Seals flop around on their bellies on land and tend to be quieter, while the sea lions have visible ears, are talkative and use their flippers to get around." I nod to a bench. "I can't really walk on sand yet, so I'll wait for you there."

I can tell they're reluctant to leave me alone. I pull a ball cap from my back pocket and put it on, drawing it down low over my face so I won't be recognized. "Go ahead. I'll be fine."

"I'll stay with you." Julianne gives Amy a nudge toward the beach. "You guys go on ahead. Take pictures for me."

An odd look passes between the sisters before Amy and Muncie head toward the beach, while Julianne and I settle on the bench. It's a gorgeous, warm afternoon, and I tip my face up toward the sun. I try not to think of the utter misery we experienced during the endless days we spent baking under a merciless sun in Afghanistan and Pakistan while we were on the hunt for Al Khad. We were either baking or freezing, or so it seemed.

"You don't have to babysit me. You should see the seals. They're adorable."

"Amy will take pictures for me."

"You like to hike?"

"I do, but I don't get to very often living in the city."

"You should hit Torrey Pines while you're here. I'd take you, but I'm not really ready to hike quite yet. Used to be one of my favorite things to do here."

"You'll get back there again. It's just going to take some time."

"So I'm told."

"Does your leg hurt?"

Normally, that question would annoy me. But I don't mind it coming from her. Why that is, I don't know. Maybe I've gotten used to her and her endless questions.

"Sorry, that's none of my business."

She's misinterpreted my silence, and that makes me feel bad. "It's fine. I don't mind you asking. It doesn't hurt like it did. My biggest issue now is the pervasive weakness from the infection I contracted after I lost my leg. I was immobile for a month, and the doctors tell me it could take more than a year to come back from that."

"Wow."

"That's why I still need the crutches while I rebuild my strength."

"I'm sorry for all you've been through and that I'm making it worse just by being here."

"You're not." I can't bear that I've made her feel that way. "It's not you. It's me."

She snorts out a laugh. "If I had a nickel for every time I've heard that..."

I turn so I can see her better. "Guys say that to *you*?"

"All the time."

"What the hell is wrong with them?"

"I think it's more about what's wrong with me. I've been told I can be a bit much, as you've probably seen."

"There's nothing wrong with you."

"That's kind of you to say, but I wasn't fishing for compliments."

"I don't give random compliments. I'm not sure if you've noticed, but charm isn't my strong suit."

She laughs, as I'd hoped she would. "I've definitely noticed."

"I'm sorry, Julianne. I've been a total dick, and… I'm sorry."

"If I'd been through what you have, I'd probably be a dick, too."

"What I've been through is in no way your fault, and it's not fair for me to take it out on you."

"It's okay. Really." She bites her bottom lip, something I've noticed she does when she's thinking.

"Whatever you want to say, just say it. Let's clear the air so we can get through this without any added drama."

"I'm all for that, but I just wonder…"

"What?"

"If you really don't want to do the tour, why don't you just say so? They can't make you do it, can they?"

"No, not really."

"Then tell them you don't want to."

I glance at her, brow raised. "Is that the sort of advice you ought to be giving me?"

"I'm not thinking about my career right now, Captain. I'm thinking about what's best for someone who's already endured a nightmare. I'd hate to be in any way responsible for compounding the trauma."

"My name is John, and it's nice of you to be concerned."

"If it's going to make everything worse, don't do it, John."

She's so sincere and truly adorable. I smile at her, and it doesn't feel forced. For the first time in a long time, it feels natural and good. "There's a reason why I haven't told them to fuck off with their media tour."

"What's that?"

I take a moment to collect my thoughts. "You asked about my childhood earlier."

She holds up a hand to stop me. "If that's off-limits, so be it. You don't owe me or anyone explanations."

"Maybe not, but I'd like to tell you if you're still willing to hear it."

"I'm still willing." She curls a leg under herself and turns so she's facing me, giving me her full attention.

"I don't know anything about my parents. I was taken in by a foster family that had to give me up a few years later when the dad got sick with cancer. After that, I bounced around a lot, and by the time I was a teenager, I was on my way to trouble. I ended up in front of a judge, who gave me a choice between jail and the military.

"That's how I ended up in the Navy. I can't imagine what would've become of me if I hadn't taken that path." I look over at her and find that she's hanging on my every word. "I'm doing the tour for all the kids like me out there who might be lost and trying to find their way. If one kid chooses the Navy over jail, then it'll have been worth it to me."

"That's amazing," she says softly. "That you're willing to put yourself through something so difficult because it might help someone else."

I shrug off praise I don't want. "I figure since I was outed, something good may as well come of it."

"It's very admirable."

"I'm not doing it for that reason."

"Which only makes it more so."

"Don't make me out to be a hero, Julianne. I'm not."

"How can you say that? The whole world thinks you're a hero."

"I've made all kinds of mistakes, just like everyone else. I'm as far from perfect as anyone can be. Look at what I did to Ava. I'd think that alone would be enough to make you hate me."

"I don't hate you, and neither does she."

"She ought to. I put her through hell."

"She doesn't. She loved you. She probably still does."

"No, she doesn't." I stare out at the endless ocean. "I ruined the best thing to ever happen to me." When the glare of the sun on the water becomes too intense, I blink and then glance over at Julianne. "I was going to ask her to marry me. The minute we got home. That was going to be the first thing I said to her. And it nearly happened. We almost had him at the four-and-a-half-year mark."

"What happened?"

"We're still not sure, but we think one of our local informants turned on us. When we raided the compound, Al Khad was long gone." I blink again when I realize I'm staring at her and drinking in the details of her pretty face. "I think all the time about what might've been different if that raid had gone as planned. I might not have lost my friends or my leg. I would've gotten home before Ava's five-year deadline, and maybe she would've forgiven me when I had a chance to explain it to her." I shrug. "I'll never know now, but I do wonder what might've been."

"I'm sorry you didn't get the chance to ask her."

"It's okay. She probably would've told me to eff off after disappearing on her for almost five years."

"I don't think she would've done that. When we first met her…"

"What?" I'm instantly on alert, greedy for whatever she can tell me about Ava.

"She was still a long way from fine where you were concerned. It took a lot of time and therapy and love. It wasn't like she moved to New York, met Eric and forgot about you. It wasn't like that at all."

"I guess I'm glad to hear that, even though you're probably way out on a limb talking to me about her."

"Kind of, but I don't want you to think she just got over you. When she heard about the raid and saw the video, she was a disaster for weeks, wondering what'd become of you."

I wince. "I was in the hospital."

"She found that out much later. She thought that maybe you'd decided not to contact her."

"I know, and I'm so sorry about that. I hate that I did that to her."

"That's the thing—it's not your fault. If we put the blame where it belongs, then it falls squarely at the feet of a terrorist who ruined the lives of thousands of people, including you and Ava."

"I should've trusted her with the truth. I regret that I didn't. I could've told her. She never would've told anyone else."

"You did what you thought was right at the time."

"And Ava paid an awful price for that."

"She's also gotten to experience true love—twice. That lucky bitch." She smiles as she says that, to let me know she's joking. "It's not really fair that she's had it twice when some of us are still looking for the first one."

I'm intrigued by the revealing statement that, coupled with what she told me earlier, has me again wondering what's wrong with the men in New York City.

A high-pitched scream from the sidewalk jolts us out of the bubble we've been in.

"You're that Navy SEAL!" An older woman has spotted me and is coming at me, iPhone in hand, ready to take a photo and make a scene.

Julianne stands, putting herself between me and the woman. "Stop."

The woman stops.

"Back off."

"I don't know who you think you are—"

"Back at you. Captain West is not available at the moment. Move along."

I sit back and watch the show, impressed by the competent, unyielding way she dispatches the woman, who storms off, sputtering with indignance. I hear her say, "What a bitch," before she rejoins her group, who stood off to the side, watching the encounter.

Julianne returns to her seat on the bench. "Anyway... Where were we?"

"You were telling me that Ava is a lucky bitch because she's had true love twice and you're still looking for the first one."

She looks down, seeming embarrassed. "Let's forget I said that."

I laugh. "You'd like that, wouldn't you?"

"You have no idea how much I wish I could take that back."

"Too late now. Your secret is out. And PS, thanks for running interference for me."

"No problem. People are ridiculous."

"Yes, they often are. I'm glad you're on my side, Julianne. I wouldn't want to cross you."

"I am on your side. I hope you know that."

"I do. I appreciate all you're doing, and I promise to be less of a dick going forward."

"That'd help, and by the way, everyone who matters calls me Jules."

Is that her way of telling me I matter? I have no idea, but I'm honored to have been let into her inner circle. "Jules." I try it on for size.

"Don't wear it out," she says, flashing a small grin.

"I'll try not to."

"John?"

"Yes, Jules?"

"I just want to say... I think the reason you're doing the media tour is amazing, and I'm positive it's going to make a difference for someone."

I'm unreasonably moved. "Thank you. I hope so."

Before I can think of anything else to say to her, I see Muncie and Amy heading back to us, talking and laughing. Is Muncie... Why is he soaking wet?

"What happened?" Jules asks when they join us.

Amy is laughing so hard, she can barely speak, while Muncie holds his T-shirt, which is wet from the chest down, away from his skin, as if that might help it dry quicker.

"Got hit by a wave."

"It was so funny." Amy has tears in her eyes from laughing. "One minute, we were watching the seals, and the next, he was soaking wet." She loses it laughing again.

"And somehow she managed to not get a drop on her, even though she was standing right next to me."

Amy is helpless with laughter.

"Glad I could provide you with entertainment." Muncie seems amused and annoyed at the same time.

Amy wipes tears from her eyes. "Oh, you did."

"I wish I could've seen that." I mean that sincerely. Muncie spends so much time poking at me that I would've truly enjoyed seeing him get doused by a wave. "No one deserves it more than you do, Commander."

He scowls at me. "I can think of someone who deserves it more than I do."

Touché. I laugh at the ferocious look on his face. Somewhere along the way, the guy has become a friend, and I like that I can spar with him this way and know that he gives as good as he gets. Sometimes people are funny about being real with officers who outrank them. I consider myself lucky that Muncie isn't one of them. I needed someone who'd keep it real with me, and he's been a godsend. Not that I can tell him that. Not yet anyway.

"Who wants to eat?" I ask them.

Jules raises her hand. "Me."

"Do we need to take you home to change first?" I ask Muncie.

"Nah, I'm fine."

"We'll sit outside so you can air-dry."

"Great."

We make our way back to the car, and I try not to notice the wet, squishy sound coming from Muncie.

Amy loses it laughing again.

Jules glances at me to share her amusement, and I feel a sense of connection to her after the conversation we had on the bench. I shared more with her in those minutes than I have with anyone, even Ava, who only recently learned the truth about my childhood. I'm not sure why I felt compelled to open up to Julianne, but now that I have, it seems we've reached an understanding of sorts. I'm glad she knows why I'm doing the tour and what I hope to accomplish. It's much better to think of her as an ally than an adversary.

I just hope I can keep my promise to change my attitude, which has sucked in recent weeks. Losing Ava almost killed me. I'm not entirely sure I'll ever recover from the blow of finding out that it was truly over between us. That blow, on top of losing my leg and my two closest friends, has turned me into someone I barely recognize. Gone is the hard-charging, hard-loving naval officer I once was. What remains is a man as fragile as a newborn, trying to find his way in a world that no longer makes sense to him.

As I watch the scenery go by on the ride to Encinitas, I vow to make an effort to be pleasant with the people who're trying to help me navigate that new world. It's not Muncie's fault that I got dealt a shitty hand, and it sure as hell isn't Julianne's fault.

Jules. She wants me to call her Jules.

I feel something inside me relax, the way muscles would after a strenuous workout. The effort it's taking to hold on to the rage is wearing me out. I put the window down and let the warm air wash over me. For the first time since I came to in the hospital after losing a month of my life to infection, I feel glad to be alive.

CHAPTER 7

Julianne

Something changed on that bench by the beach. He's like a different person—friendly, chatty, engaging, curious.

I have zero defenses against this version of him. Sitting across from him over a late lunch at Roberto's, I want to wallow in this John, listen to the cadence of his deep voice and sigh with pleasure as his eyes light up with delight when something amuses him. This was Ava's John, before his life was changed forever by a terrorist. This was the man she waited more than five years for, hoping every day that he would come back to her.

I have to admit that when I first knew her, I wondered what kind of man would have her wait so long for him, without any information about where he was the entire time. Now I get it, and I ache for her, for him, for them.

After a delicious meal, a couple of margaritas and excellent conversation about San Diego, New York and Chicago, which is Muncie's hometown, we head back to the hotel. I'm tired and sated and… confused. In the course of this enjoyable, relaxing afternoon, I've gone from dreading being around John to wanting to hear more of his stories, more of his worries, more of everything.

In the backseat of Muncie's SUV, Amy texts me.

What's wrong?

I look over at her. *Nothing. ??*

You're super quiet. Not like you.

Just thinking.

We're going to talk about this when we get back to the room.

Ok, Mom.

Amy glares at me, probably due to the Mom reference.

"Do you ladies like beer?" John asks.

"We do." I answer for both of us.

"We should hit some of the craft beer places. That's another thing San Diego is famous for."

"That'd be fun," I tell him.

Amy raises a brow in my direction.

I refuse to react. I'm not sure what she's thinking, but I'll find out soon enough.

A short time later, Muncie delivers us to the hotel door.

I lean forward into the gap between the seats. "Thank you both for a great day."

"It was fun," John says. "More fun than I've had in years, in fact."

"I enjoyed it so much," Amy adds. "Thanks for showing us your town."

"We have to make sure you see the Hotel del Coronado, too."

"Sounds good. I'll be over around nine thirty to get some work done."

"I'll be ready." This is said with a warm smile that hits me square in the chest. Dear God, the man is gorgeous when he smiles.

They see us inside the hotel before driving off. I wait for Amy to say something, but she's quiet until we're in the room.

The second the door closes behind me, she whirls around. "You have to drop him as a client. Right now."

John

On the way back to my place, we hit every red light. Each time the car stops moving, Muncie looks over at me. After the third time, I return his stare.

"What're you looking at?"

"I'm just wondering where you came from."

"Huh?" He's certainly heard my story often enough and knows I grew up in several foster homes in California before landing in San Diego after I joined the Navy. I've spent most of my career here, when I wasn't deployed.

"I've never seen friendly, fun, smiling Captain West. I've only seen surly, bitchy, bitter Captain West. This guy… He's a revelation. I wondered how you'd managed to find a woman who'd wait for you for years, but now I can kind of see why if she was with *this* guy."

The reminder of Ava is a shot to the heart after a good day—the best day I've had in a long time.

Muncie looks over at me again. "Too far?"

Yes, but I'm trying to be nicer to the people who're helping me, so I cut him some slack. "No, it's fine."

"Sorry."

"No worries." I stare out the passenger window for a long time, watching familiar landmarks go by, including the building where I spent the best years of my life with Ava. "I'm sorry I've been a dick to you. I appreciate everything you've done for me, even if I don't say it often enough."

"It's an honor to work for you, sir."

"Don't 'sir' me."

"Captain. It's an honor to work with and for you."

"No, it isn't," I say, laughing. "And my name is John. I should've told you a long time ago to call me that."

"Thank you, sir. Err, John. Thank you." At the next red light, he says, "What brought about this miraculous transformation?"

"I, um, well, while you were looking at the seals, I was talking to Jules, and she—"

"Wait. *Jules?*"

"She said that's what her friends call her."

"So now you're *friends?*"

"I don't know. I guess. Colleagues, at least. Anyway, it was a nice conversation, and it helped to… clarify some things for me."

Muncie has nothing to say to that as he takes the right-hand turn into the apartment complex that I now call home, even though nothing of mine lives there with me. What's left of my belongings is in storage with Ava, waiting for me to tell her where to send it when I'm permanently settled somewhere. I'll figure out where that's going to be after I get through this media tour that hangs over me like a dark cloud I can't get out from under. Although, with Jules guiding me through it, I stand a better chance of surviving it than I would have without her.

"Listen," Muncie says when we're parked in the spot assigned to my unit. "I know you've been through hell, and I'm glad to see you rebounding a bit. I truly am. But you have to know that becoming *friends* with Ava's new sister-in-law is… you know…"

"What?" I'm not sure where he's going with this.

"You can't fall for her, sir, er, I mean John. You can't go there."

"Whoa, I'm not going *there*. I have no interest in anything like that."

Muncie raises a brow. "None at all?"

"Not now. I've got much bigger things to be concerned about, such as being able to get around without the goddamned crutches and not making a fool of myself on national TV."

"You'll be great on TV."

"I'm glad you think so."

"People are invested in you and your story. You've been avoiding the coverage, so you have no idea how much love is coming your way."

That makes me uncomfortable. "I was just doing my job."

"You were instrumental in bringing down the most wanted man on earth, John. I know you'd rather pretend none of it happened, but you have to know your life is forever changed by that video. You may as well embrace your hero status and accept that people are going to want to thank you for what you did."

"I'm not sure how to deal with that."

"You'll figure it out. But be careful with Jules. You've had enough heartache to last one guy a lifetime. I'd hate to see you hurt again."

"Awww, Muncie. Are we discussing our feelings now?"

"Don't be an ass. You know what I'm saying."

"I do, and I appreciate your concern, but there's nothing to worry about."

The look he gives me tells me he doesn't agree, but he wisely leaves it alone and gets out to fetch the crutches. We make our way—slowly—inside and take the elevator up to my floor. "I can take it from here."

"Are you sure?"

"Positive. Thanks for going today."

"It was fun. Nice to see San Diego from the view of an insider. I'll see you in the morning."

"Sounds good." Leaning on the crutches, I reach out to shake his hand. "Thanks a lot for everything."

"A pleasure, sir."

I don't bother to remind him again that dealing with me is hardly ever a pleasure. I choose instead to end a good day on a positive note, and I pretend not to notice that he waits until I've got my apartment door open before pressing the down arrow on the elevator.

I'm thoroughly exhausted from the outing, and after using the bathroom and brushing my teeth, I remove my prosthetic, take a pain pill and change into sleeping pants and a clean T-shirt. I'd love a shower, but I'm too tired and weak to risk that when I'm here by myself. Pathetic that I can't even take a shower without worrying about falling. When I think about the things I used to be able to do...

It's better not to go there.

I reach for the phone on my bedside table that's plugged into a charger. Muncie set me up with a new one after Jules took my other one. He didn't want me to have no way to call for help if I need it. The guy thinks of everything.

I have no idea who's paying for things such as the new phone and Jules, and I find that I don't care. If the Navy is paying, I figure it's the least of what they owe me for the sacrifices I've made on behalf of my country. Not that I wouldn't do it all again, even knowing what I do now. Nabbing Al Khad and dismantling his organization was worth the hell and heartache of losing my leg, my friends and my love. If I keep telling myself that, over and over again, maybe I'll survive the losses.

I open the browser on my phone and type my name into the search bar, curious to see what's being said about me after what Muncie told me. More than one million results come up. I'm completely flabbergasted by that number. I click on the first result, a story *The New York Times* did about the raid and the subsequent release of the video that outed me and one of the Army Rangers who deployed with us. He was also gravely injured and is still in the hospital, which is why I've become the go-to guy for the media tour.

The article talks about how little is known about me, which of course is strategic on my part and the Navy's. SEALs are taught from the first day of training that discretion is key to protecting ourselves, our comrades and our missions around the world. We're instructed to never speak of what we do to anyone, even our spouses. In the unit I belonged to, there were supposed to be no spouses or significant others due to the possibility of long-term deployments.

We signed on for five years in that unit, and I was at four years and eight months when Al Khad took down the *Star of the High Seas*. Four months later and catching Al Khad wouldn't have been my job. I would've been transferred to a different unit and would've been free to propose to Ava and build a life with her.

Timing is everything, and I had two near misses. Had the attack happened four months later or had we succeeded in catching Al Khad at the four-and-a-half-year mark, I'd be with Ava now, or at least I like to think I would. She would've forgiven me for the lies I told, once she knew I'd had no choice but to lie. Instead, she's married to someone else and on her honeymoon. I can't even think about what she might be doing, or I'll go mad.

Instead, I read about myself until I fall into a restless sleep plagued by dreams of Ava and Jules.

CHAPTER 8

John

After a few hours of work with Jules in the morning, Muncie drives me to lunch with my unit. We've chosen a dive in downtown San Diego, far from the base where we'd be easily recognized. At my direction, Muncie arranged a private room and asked for discretion from the staff. Of course, that tipped them off that something big—if you'd call me *big*—was happening, and they're buzzing with curiosity about who their guest is.

When the hostess sees me, her face goes blank with shock.

"Please," I say softly to her, "don't."

Thankfully, she shakes off the shock and recovers herself. "Right this way, Captain." She leads us to a back room that you'd have to know was there to be able to find it. "I hope this is to your satisfaction."

"It is, thank you."

"It's a pleasure to welcome you to our establishment. Thank you for your service."

I offer her a small smile and a nod in acknowledgment. That's all I've got to give.

As I venture into the room where one big table has been set for twelve, Muncie confers with her about the others who'll be joining us.

"We need two more places, Muncie."

He comes into the room, his sharp-eyed gaze taking in the setup.

"We need two more places." I say it softer this time. "Please get two more."

"Yes, sir." He turns to see to my request.

I'm looking forward to seeing my guys and dreading it, too. Though I've never said as much to anyone, I feel like I let them down because Jonesy and Tito were killed in the raid. No, I didn't fire the shots that killed them, but I led them there, and their loss is on me. I've reached out to their families, let them know I'd like to see them if they'll have me, but haven't heard anything. The offer has no expiration date, and I made sure to let them know that.

We undertook an incredible journey together, spent years hunting Al Khad, and by anyone's standards, the raid that led to his capture was a smashing success. We got our guy after more than five years of looking for him. We captured the world's most wanted terrorist. But because we lost two of our own in the process, we don't see it as the same smashing success that everyone else does.

I lean my crutches against the wall, determined to stand without them to greet my guys. I only hope I don't fall or otherwise embarrass myself. I want them to see me as the same strong, determined leader I always was, even if that guy doesn't exist anymore.

One by one, they filter in: Phillips, Barker, Griff, Tonka, Dunlevy, Martinez, Soares, Turner, Blankenship, Roland. Tall, short, white, black, Hispanic, we're a hodgepodge of nationalities and backgrounds. Some of them are like me, products of the foster system. Dunlevy, a star swimmer on his high school team, had gotten into big trouble his senior year of high school when he was caught selling cocaine. Like me, he chose the Navy over prison. Today, he's a warrant officer and has a brilliant career ahead of him if he chooses to stay in the Navy—or even if he doesn't.

I return the back-pounding hug he gives me while hoping he doesn't break me. I'm not the badass motherfucker I once was, which I'm sure he can see. Dunlevy doesn't miss anything, which made him an incredible asset to me during the deployment.

When he pulls back, I'm shocked to see tears in his eyes. "It's so good to see you, Cap. You had us worried."

"Sorry to put you through that."

Dunlevy grimaces and shakes his blond head. "Been a rough few months all around. How you getting along?"

"Pretty good. I'm getting used to the peg leg and hoping to be rid of the crutches entirely before much longer. The coma is what really fucked me up."

"It's going to do these guys good to see you up and about and on the road t o recovery."

I'm glad to hear that. It's why I'm here after all. "Where's Pops?" Jimmy Popovicci, a forty-four-year-old master chief, is the oldest member of our team and my go-to guy for just about everything.

Dunlevy shakes his head, his face grim. "He's off the radar. No one's heard from him since we got back." After they were debriefed, everyone was given sixty days of leave, which has only recently ended.

I process this news with a sinking feeling. "He's got to be taking the loss of Jonesy hard." Jonesy was like a son to the salty old master chief.

"We all are. I almost couldn't come knowing he and Tito wouldn't be here." He blinks back tears that gut me. Seeing this warrior, a man who has killed with his bare hands, fighting tears guts me.

"Do I need to be concerned about Pops?"

"I honestly don't know what to say."

Neither of us has to mention that it's extremely out of character for Pops to go silent on this group of men, who're the closest thing to a family the guy has ever had.

"I'll do some recon," Dunlevy says.

"Keep me posted."

"Yeah, of course. It really is good to see you, Cap. Gotta get used to calling you that."

"I'm still getting used to hearing it." I was promoted from lieutenant commander to commander and then captain during the deployment. When I first entered the Navy as a seaman, I never dreamed of reaching the rank of O-6.

I have a few minutes to catch up with each of the guys, all of whom are emotional about seeing me after worrying I wasn't going to make it. I hate that I put them through that.

Waitresses come in bearing pitchers of beer, as well as platters of nachos and wings. The guys send up a cheer in appreciation.

I glance at Muncie, standing by the door, ready to help if needed. I give him a thumbs-up.

He smiles and nods.

"Join us, Dave. Please."

I can tell that he's reluctant when he walks over to the table to find a seat. I appreciate that he doesn't choose one of the two that he knows I want left empty, but rather he drags another chair to the table, and the waitstaff quickly provide a setup for him.

"You guys, this is Lieutenant Commander David Muncie, who's had the unlucky job of tending to me in the aftermath of... well, everything. He's one of the good guys, so be nice."

The others greet Muncie and make their way to the table. They're talking, laughing, in high spirits, which is nice to see. We saw a lot of crazy shit over there, and I worried about how they'd do at home. They seem to be doing as well as can be expected. At least it appears that way. There's no way to know what goes on inside, where they carry the wounds of what we endured together.

When everyone is seated, I stand, taking a second to make sure my legs are strong beneath me.

The others go quiet, conditioned to shut up when their leader wants their attention. "I just want to say thanks to all of you for coming out today. Means a lot to me to see your ugly faces." That gets a laugh, as I'd hoped it would. "I want you to know that I got all your messages while I was in the hospital, and they meant the world to me. Knowing you guys were pulling for me got me through the worst of it. I'm sorry that I wasn't up for seeing anyone until now."

"No worries, Cap," Blankenship says. "We're just happy to see you back on two feet and still on the right side of the grass. You gave us a helluva scare there."

"Yeah, sorry about that." I glance to my left at the two empty chairs. "I asked them to set places for Jonesy and Tito. Doesn't seem right to get together without them and Pops." I take a minute to collect myself and settle my emotions. "I'm going to get a little poetic here and quote Shakespeare. I hope you'll forgive me for this, but it sums things up rather well for me, and I hope it does the same for you." After clearing my throat, I dive into the St. Crispin's Day speech from *Henry V* that I memorized last night:

"From this day to the ending of the world, But we in it shall be remembered—We few, we happy few, we band of brothers; For he to-day that sheds his blood with me Shall be my brother."

A hushed silence falls over the usually boisterous group. "I never had brothers of my own. I have all of you, and that's a lifetime gig. As we go our separate ways, I hope you know you're stuck with me, and I… I'm exceptionally thankful to be stuck with you, my band of brothers." I raise my glass to them. "To us, to what we did. May it never be forgotten."

As I take my seat, Roland starts it with a single clap that quickly becomes a standing ovation that brings tears to my eyes. My emotions, as always these days, hover close to the surface, threatening to take me down at any second. Somehow I manage to hold it together, even as the applause goes on for quite a few minutes. It dies down only when the waitstaff come in with pizzas, burgers, more wings and refilled pitchers of beer.

Muncie was right. I needed this. Seeing the guys fills a hole inside me that I didn't know was there until I was with them again. As they dive into the food like the savages they are, I find my gaze drifting to the two empty seats, remembering the friends I'll carry with me for the rest of my life.

I can't think of them yet without the predictable blast of pain that could bring me to my knees if I were standing. The one benefit to having no family to call my own is that I've never had anyone I cared enough about to grieve their loss.

There've been times in recent months when the grief of losing my two best friends and Ava has sucked me under to a dark place I've never been before.

I've resisted the pull to the best of my ability, but it's a daily struggle to keep my head above the riptide that continues to draw me toward the darkness. Sometimes I wonder if the darkness wouldn't be a blessed relief, but fear of the unknown keeps me from giving in to that temptation. I have to believe that there're still good days ahead for me, even if my definition of "good" has been altered irrevocably.

The guys don't let me stew in my own thoughts for long. They draw me out by busting my balls about the attention I'm getting, the media tour that starts soon, the endorsements I've been offered and the nonsense that surrounds me. Being in their presence, being part of them again, goes a long way toward fixing what's broken inside me.

They give me the strength to face the next part of my journey.

CHAPTER 9

Ava

Spain is incredible. The food, the people, the beaches, the architecture… It's everything I hoped it would be and so much more. Being with Eric is the best part of an amazing experience. Having uninterrupted time together to do whatever we please is a gift after the insane few months we had leading up to our wedding.

Everything in my life would be perfect except for the vivid, heartbreaking dreams I have about John that torture me with memories I thought I'd stored firmly in the past where they belong. I had the first one on our wedding night, and I've had another every night since. I wake in a cold sweat in the arms of my new husband after dreaming about the man I used to love. Unlike most of my dreams, I remember the ones about John in excruciating detail.

During the long years of his deployment, I would occasionally dream about him, but not like this. Almost all of my post-wedding dreams include passionate encounters, some of which happened in our past life and others that are all new. I feel like I'm cheating on Eric by having dreams like that featuring another man, and I can't understand why this is happening now.

Because he's so intuitive, Eric can tell that something is bothering me, but how do I talk to him about this without giving him reason to doubt whether I'm fully committed to our marriage? I *am* fully committed. I chose him. I married him. I *love* him. It would kill me to hurt him in any way, especially after everything he's done to put my broken heart back together.

This would hurt him deeply, so I keep it to myself while wishing I could contact my therapist to get her take on it. But that's not possible when Eric and I are spending every second of every day together. I don't know how I'll survive two more weeks of this torture. The dreams are ruining the trip for me, and probably for Eric, too.

My mouth is dry and my hands sweaty after another intense dream that has left other parts of me tingling in ways that are highly inappropriate while lying naked in the arms of my new husband. I take a deep breath, trying to calm the frantic beat of my heart and the panic that grips every fiber of my being.

Eric's hand slides down my arm, letting me know he's awake.

I'd hoped to get myself together before I had to face him.

"I wish you'd tell me what's going on." His voice is as soft as the lips that slide over my cheek. "Otherwise, I'm going to think my wife is unhappy, and we can't have that."

My panic quadruples. I can't breathe or think or do anything other than blink back tears that suddenly flood my eyes. I *can't* talk to him about this. I just *can't*.

"Ava, honey… Please tell me what's wrong."

He sounds so sad, and that kills me.

"Whatever it is, we can deal with it together, but you have to tell me. Otherwise, I'm going to think you regret marrying me."

"No," I say on a sob that I can't contain no matter how hard I try.

Eric lifts himself up on one arm and turns me so I'm on my back.

I put my arm over my eyes, trying to buy some time.

"Baby, what is it?"

I'm going to have to tell him, or he'll think it's him when that's not it at all.

"It's going to upset you." I wipe away tears that slide down my cheeks despite my fierce desire to hold it together for both our sakes.

"I'm already upset knowing you are. We're supposed to be celebrating and having the time of our lives, but I can tell something is bothering you and has been for days."

I take another deep breath, trying to find fortification and the courage to tell him the truth, even though it'll hurt us both. "I've been having dreams."

"Look at me, honey."

I remove the arm that covers my eyes.

He gasps at the sight of me, which must be worse than I thought. His hand cups my cheek, and his thumb brushes away my tears. "About what?"

Closing my eyes, I take another deep breath, feeling sick and filled with despair, which I thought I'd put behind me. I should've known better. "John."

Eric goes perfectly still next to me. After a long moment, he says, "What about him?"

"*Everything* about him." My dreams are so vivid that I recall the scent and texture of his skin, a detail I choose not to disclose as it's already bad enough that he knows I'm dreaming about my ex.

Eric drops down onto his pillow, looking up at the ceiling fan. Another long pause ensues before he says, "Have you been thinking about him?"

"*No! I'm not thinking about him*. I'm thinking about *you* and *us* and our honeymoon and our life. I have no idea why this is happening." I choke on a sob that erupts from my chest.

"Come here." He gathers me into his embrace. "It's okay."

"No, it isn't. I did the right thing. I married you, and I want you."

"Wait... What? You 'did the right thing' by marrying me? Is that how you see it?"

"Of course not! That's not what I meant."

"But that's what you said."

"Please don't pick apart my words. I'm a freaking wreck over this as it is. I married the man I love, the man who loves me. That's all there is to it."

"If only that were true," he says on a long sigh.

"What does that mean?"

"We both know there's a whole lot more to it than you and me. He's part of this marriage, whether we want him to be or not."

I pull back from him, needing to see his eyes when I respond. "No, he isn't."

Eric looks over at me, his expression sad and resigned. "Isn't he? Come on, Ava. It's not like you suddenly decided you didn't want to be with him anymore. Circumstances beyond your control took him away from you, and you don't just stop loving someone under those conditions."

A feeling of desperation overtakes me. "I *don't* love him anymore. I love *you*."

He links our fingers and brings my hand to his lips, brushing a gentle kiss over my skin. "Please don't take this the wrong way—but I don't believe you."

"How can you say that? I *chose* you. I *married* you."

"Yes, you did, and I'll be thankful for both those things for the rest of my life, but just because you chose me and married me doesn't mean you don't love him anymore."

I'm stunned to hear him say that and desperately trying to process the possibility that he could be right. Do I still love John? I can't love John. "I don't want this to be happening. This is supposed to be *our* time. There's no place for him here."

"Your heart and mind are saying otherwise."

"Eric, please. You have to listen to me." I'm feeling more desperate by the second. "I don't want to be having dreams about him. I don't want to think about him or relive the hellish years I spent wondering what'd become of him. I don't want that. I want you and us and *this*." I gesture to the gorgeous hotel room in Sevilla.

"You know what I want, but we can't pretend this doesn't mean something." He glances over at me, looking as freaked out as I feel even if he sounds calm. "We should reach out to Jess," he says, referring to my therapist in New York, "and set up a time for you to talk to her."

"Now? While we're here?"

"Right now."

I'm taken aback by his serious tone and the determined set of his jaw, but what strikes me most are his eyes, which reflect pain. I did that to him, and I can't bear it. "Eric…"

"What, honey?"

"I'm so sorry."

"Please don't be. I knew we weren't completely out of the woods where he was concerned."

"You did?"

"Uh-huh. Something like that? It doesn't get resolved overnight. You haven't been yourself since you saw him in San Diego."

"What? Yes, I have."

"No, sweetheart, you haven't. There's a haunted look to you that wasn't there before you saw him, before you had to tell him it was over between the two of you. I saw it even on our wedding day."

Shaking my head, I break down into helpless sobs. "That's not true! That was the happiest day of my life!"

"I believe you, Ava. I swear I do. I'm so fucking glad you picked me. I'm thankful for that every day. But that decision came at a terrible cost to you and someone you love. I never forget that."

I'm so upset, I can't speak. I can barely breathe through the tears and sobs that keep coming. This can't be happening. I made my decision. I put the past behind me and stepped into a future bright with promise when I married Eric. How can he think I want anyone but him?

He holds me close, rubbing my back and running his fingers through my hair, until I calm somewhat. "Let's reach out to Jess and go from there, okay?"

I nod in response to his question, but inside, I'm broken, shattered once again by a situation I never had control over, even when I thought I did. I have good reason now to wonder if I ever will.

CHAPTER 10

Julianne

"What're you talking about? I'm not dropping him as a client." I toss my purse on the stiff, upholstered hotel chair and turn to face my sister. "Do you have *any* idea what it means to my career that I landed him in the first place. *Everyone* wanted him."

"Great, then let someone else have him."

"Where's this coming from?" I'm truly baffled as to why she'd suggest dropping the biggest client I've ever had—possibly the biggest client I'll ever have. "I've got every producer in the business beating down my door begging for five minutes with the man of the hour. Why would I walk away from that?"

"Because you have feelings for him."

My mouth falls open and my eyes bug. "*What?*"

Amy leans in closer to me and speaks slowly, as if she's talking to someone who has trouble understanding basic English. "You. Have. Feelings. For. *Him.*"

I lean in, too. "No. I. *Don't.*"

"Whatever. I saw the way you were looking at him over dinner, and I've only seen that look on you once before."

The reminder of the only time I thought I was in love is like a knife to the gut. "Don't," I whisper.

"I'm not saying this to hurt you, Jules. I'm saying this to keep you from getting hurt. That guy is off-limits to you in every possible way. He may as well be radioactive."

"Do you think I need you to tell me that?" Now I'm mad. How old do I have to be before my older and wiser siblings realize I can think for myself? Soon, I'll be thirty. Will that be old enough?

"I think you need some perspective."

"Actually, I don't. Today was the first time I've thought he was anything other than cranky and bitchy."

"Today you saw another side of him, and you liked what you saw."

"Yes, I did! But not for the reasons you think. Because I need him not to be cranky and bitchy on national TV. I needed a breakthrough, and today I got that. What you're seeing is relief—and that's *all* it is."

"If you say so." She gets out her nail file and goes to work on an index finger.

"I say so, and I swear to God, if you tell anyone that you think I like him as anything other than a client, I'll murder you with my own hands, you got me?"

"Don't be dramatic."

"Right, because what would be dramatic about a bomb like that going off in our family?"

"I'm glad you can see that it would be a bomb."

"Thank God you were here to tell me that. Otherwise, I never would've figured that out for myself."

"Your sarcasm isn't appreciated."

"Neither is your assumption that just because I like him as a client that I must also like him as a man." My entire system is agitated just thinking about what a shitstorm it would be if I liked him as more than a client. Amy is right about one thing—that cannot happen. Ever.

"I can see why you'd like him. He's incredibly gorgeous, wounded in more ways than one and a national hero. That's a tough combination to resist. After spending the afternoon with him, I get why Ava waited so long for him."

"Let's talk about you and Muncie."

She stops filing and looks up at me, brows knitted. "What?"

"You're not the only one who can *see* things."

"Not sure what you think you saw, but we had a few laughs when he got wet. Otherwise, nothing to see there."

"If you say so."

"I do."

"Great." I'm not used to being at odds with Amy. Not anymore. When we were kids, and especially when we were teens, we fought over everything. But when we were in our early twenties, that stopped all of a sudden, and we became best friends. Same with my brothers. Yes, we all have other friends who mean the world to us, but the four of us are tight. When our dad ran for governor of New York, we became even tighter, closing ranks around the family while on the campaign trail. And then, when my mom left my dad, my siblings were the only ones I wanted to talk to about it. With Rob running for Congress this fall, I expect to spend quite a lot of time with them, supporting his campaign. This is no time for a spat with Amy—or my brothers.

"Look, I appreciate your concern, but when I tell you there's really nothing to worry about where John is concerned, I mean it."

"I know you do."

Something about the way she says that has my hackles raised again. "But?"

She shrugs. "I know what I saw, Jules, and I saw interest. And it went both ways."

That makes me laugh. "He can barely stand me."

"Not true. He was watching you the whole time, hanging on your every word."

I shake my head, because there's no way that's true. Or possible. "If anything, I'd say we sort of reached reluctant friendship status today, but beyond that... Just no."

"Watch yourself with him. I'm not trying to piss you off or win a fight. I swear to you that's not what this is. I'm genuinely concerned."

"So noted, but no need for concern." I'm eager to get past this unusual tension between us. "Let's go get a drink."

"I'm in."

We head down to the hotel bar. I order bourbon while she gets a fruity rum concoction. While we enjoy our drinks, we talk about everything except the elephant standing squarely between us. I meant what I said to her earlier about not being interested in him that way. But I can't stop thinking about what she said about *him* being interested in *me*.

That can't happen either.

*

Everything is different the next morning. I can tell John is making an honest effort to work with me, to answer the questions, to prepare for next week. Muncie had a dentist appointment, so we're alone in John's apartment. I tell myself that's no big deal, but all I can hear are the things Amy said last night. Her voice nearly drowns out his as we go through my list of questions.

In addition to that concern, I'm startled by how awful he looks. There're deep, dark circles under eyes rimmed with red, scruff on his jaw that's unusual because he's always clean-shaven, and his hair is standing on end.

After half an hour of discussing his early years in the Navy, I decide to ask him the most important question. "Are you okay?"

He gives me a blank stare that lasts until he blinks. "Yes, I'm fine."

I tip my head and study him, feeling as if I know him a little by now, and from what I see, he's not fine. "Really?"

Diverting his gaze downward, he says, "I didn't sleep much last night."

"How come?"

He shrugs. "Sleep has been a challenge in the last few months."

"Can you take something?"

"I've tried a few things, but it doesn't really help."

I tap my lip, trying to think of the remedies I've heard people talk about. That's how I'm wired. I see a problem, I want to fix it. "Have you tried melatonin? My brother Rob swears by it."

"Yep. Sometimes it works, other times it doesn't." His lips curve into a small smile. "It's okay. I'll figure it out."

"Do you want to get some rest? We can pick this up later. I have other stuff I can do." I don't, really, but God, he looks awful.

"I could go for some food. Are you hungry?"

"I can always eat."

He laughs as he hauls himself out of the chair, balancing precariously on the crutches. "Good to know."

"Could I ask you something that's none of my business and has nothing to do with the interviews?"

"Sure."

I watch as he moves slowly toward the counter that divides his living room and kitchen to get his wallet and keys. Now that I have permission to ask the question, I'm not sure that I should.

Propped on the crutches, he studies me with the bluest eyes I've ever seen. "What do you want to know?"

"How long will you need the crutches? I'm sorry if that's something I shouldn't ask."

He gestures for me to lead the way to the door. "It's okay. You can ask."

I hold the door for him and then close it, making sure it's locked. We make our way, slowly, to the elevator as I wonder if he'll answer my question. When we're in the elevator headed down, he looks over at me. "I'm still pretty weak from the infection, although the doctors say I'll rebound eventually. It's just going to take some time."

"Are you still doing PT?"

"I graduated, but I'm supposed to be trying to get some exercise every day because that'll help, or so I'm told. All it does is wear me out."

"But doesn't that help you sleep?"

"I was in the gym from two to three a.m. and caught some sleep after that."

"Should you be, um, in the gym in the middle of the night by yourself?"

"Probably not, but I figure if I fall, someone will find me eventually." He glances at me with those intense blue eyes. "It beats trying to sleep. I, ah, I have nightmares."

I try not to overreact, but all I want to do in that moment is hug him and hold him until the haunted look in his eyes is replaced by something else—anything else. Amy's words from last night bounce around in my mind, and I want to scream at her to *shut up and leave me alone.* "About the raid?"

Nodding, he leans against the back wall of the elevator. "That and getting shot and seeing my friends killed and hunting Al Khad and trying to find Ava in places she shouldn't be. It's a jumbled mess of shit that comes at me when I'm asleep."

I feel his words—and his pain—deep inside, and I struggle to react appropriately, to retain my professional veneer.

Clearing the emotion from my throat, I step off the elevator and realize I have no idea where we're going or how we're getting there, so I stop to wait for him to lead the way.

"There's a diner a block that way." He uses his chin to indicate the direction, and we set off at the slow pace that he sets and I match, curbing my natural quick, New York pace so I won't push him to walk faster than he's able to.

It takes restraint I didn't know I had to walk slowly and to hold back the urge to pepper him with questions about his dreams. Does he have PTSD? Is it being treated? Does he have *anyone* he can talk to about it? Isn't there something that can be done to give him some relief? In my world, there's always *something* that can be done. I've never yet confronted a challenge that I didn't meet head on, giving it everything I had until it was resolved. Solving problems is my forte.

It takes fifteen minutes to walk to the diner, and by the time we arrive, there's a thin sheen of perspiration on John's face, which has gotten pale from the effort.

My heart aches for him. Under my feet, the ground seems to tip ever so slightly, throwing me off-balance. I can't let my heart ache for him. Amy is right. Allowing myself to care about him as anything more than a client would be a complete disaster on multiple levels. But I'd have to be inhuman not to feel for him as he tries to put his life back together.

The hostess at the diner, an older woman with gray hair and a kind face, lights up when she realizes who he is. "Captain West," she says breathlessly, "it's such an honor to welcome you."

John is immediately uncomfortable. "Thank you, but if you could, you know, not make a thing of it… I'd really appreciate that."

"Of course," she says in a conspiratorial whisper, as if they're in this together now. "Come this way. I'll give you a table in the back where you won't be disturbed."

"Appreciate it."

As we follow her through the restaurant, everything comes to a stop as others recognize him. John walks faster than I've ever seen him move to get to the safety of the table. And when we're seated, his pasty, sweaty appearance worries me.

He quickly drinks half the glass of ice water the hostess put on the table and seems to have trouble catching his breath.

I stay quiet and give him the time he needs to recover his equilibrium. I'm startled to realize just how compromised he is. Of course, I knew he was still recovering, but for the first time, I'm really seeing his limitations. Again, I ache for him, and I don't care that I'm not supposed to. I've seen the pictures of him from before the deployment. The change in him is dramatic and heartbreaking.

A waitress brings mugs to the table. "Coffee?"

"Yes, please," John says for both of us.

I watch the waitress, noting how she tries not to act silly in his presence. She's about to spontaneously combust from trying to contain herself.

I look up at her. "Please don't tell anyone he's here."

"Oh, no, I wouldn't do that."

Yes, you would. In fact, I'd bet money she's already texted someone.

"I'll be back to take your order in a minute."

When she's gone, I glance at John and find him watching me. "What?"

"Thanks for thinking of that."

"You know she was going to blow up her social media the second she walked away."

"No, I didn't know that, but you did."

I shrug. "It's my job to anticipate these things."

"You do it well."

I've gotten some tremendous compliments from clients over the years, but I can't say that any of them have ever meant more than those four words do coming from a client who didn't *want* my expertise as much as he needed it. My desire to protect and shield him from anything that could add to his pain seems to grow exponentially with every hour I spend in his presence. Everyone in the crowded diner would like to be me and have the chance to break bread with the man who helped to bring down Al Khad.

But I'm the one who gets to spend this time with him. I'm honored to have earned his trust and to know that he enjoys my company. Or at least he seems to.

The waitress returns, and we both order the veggie omelet with turkey bacon and English muffins.

When she walks away, I grin at him. "Copycat."

He smiles. "What? Yours sounded good."

"That comes right from the Tilden siblings, who're constantly copying each other's orders for everything from drinks to food to vacations to you name it."

My phone chimes with a text from Muncie. *Where are you guys?*

Eating at the diner.

How'd you get there?

Walked.

Whoa. How is he?

Ok.

You want me to come there?

I don't think you need to unless you want to. As I send that text, I secretly hope he doesn't come.

"Who's that?" John asks as he stirs cream into his coffee.

"Muncie, wondering where we are."

"Ah, my keeper." The smile he adds indicates the affection he has for Muncie.

"He seems like a good guy."

"He is. He's been a trouper to put up with my crap the last few months."

"I'm sure he's honored to be working with you."

"It's still weird to me that anyone would be honored to work with me."

"I'm sure it is after so many years of operating off the grid and under the radar."

"I hate it," he says softly. "That everyone knows who I am. I hate that there's video of the raid. I hate all of it."

"I know you do." I stir cream and sweetener into my coffee. "My grandmother used to tell us that we don't get to choose what happens to us in life. We only get to choose how we react to it."

"Your grandmother was a wise woman."

"Yes, she was. She died ten years ago. I still miss her."

"You were lucky to have had her. I wonder all the time if I had grandparents, aunts, uncles, cousins."

"You don't know *anything* about your family?"

He shakes his head.

"That must've been a really difficult way to grow up."

"You don't miss what you don't have, you know?"

The question is asked in a cavalier tone that belies the deeper pain of not knowing where he came from.

"Do you know," he says, "that in all the time I was with Ava, I was never able to tell her anything about my childhood or my life before her?"

Why am I elated to know something about him that she never did? I tell myself that's dangerous territory, but I'm beginning to fear that all territory with him is dangerous. "That must've been hard."

"It was. I made up a story about being the son of a retired general, told her I was from all over, when the truth of it is that I was a borderline delinquent who got in big trouble his senior year of high school and faced down a judge who gave him a break."

"What did you do?" I probably shouldn't ask, but I'm dying to know.

"I helped some of my idiot friends steal another kid's car in revenge for him stealing my friend's girlfriend."

"*Whoa.*"

"I know, so stupid. I got incredibly lucky with a judge who recognized a kid in need of some structure in his life. I say all the time that judge and the Navy saved me from myself."

Our breakfast arrives, and we dig in. As we eat, I think about the things he shared with me and how different our lives have been.

"What about you?" he asks between bites. "Any juvenile delinquency in your past?" The teasing grin that accompanies the question devastates me. Dear God, the man is handsome, and when he smiles…

It's all I can do not to sigh. "I never stole anyone's car, if that's what you're asking, but I did get busted egging houses on Halloween once. My dad made me go back and clean the eggs off every house the next day. Did you know that yolk is a bitch to clean after it dries?"

He laughs—hard—and I'm again captivated by the change in him that laughter brings. I catch a glimpse of the man he must've been before the terrorist attack changed everything for thousands, including him. That man was young, lighthearted, handsome and gorgeous.

A sinking sensation overtakes me. Amy is right. I'm attracted to him—and I was even when he was being a grumpy pain in the ass. My stomach starts to hurt. I nudge my plate toward him.

"Are you full already?"

Nodding, I sip from my coffee and try to stop the wild spinning in my mind. He's Ava's ex. Eric is so happy with her. The last thing either of them needs after everything they've been through is me developing feelings for the man who put both of them through hell, even if that wasn't intentional on his part. Amy is one thousand percent right. That can't happen. Except, it already has. I'm not sure when or how... But the feelings exist as much as I wish they didn't.

Although, to be fair to myself, how could anyone not be moved by him, his story or his valiant effort to carry on in the face of devastating loss?

All good points, Jules, but for God's sake, get your shit together!

After he finishes his breakfast, John tucks into the remains of mine and eats most of it before conceding defeat. "I can't take another bite. I think that's the most I've eaten in months."

"That'll help to build your strength."

He rubs his stomach. "And my gut."

From what I can see, he's all muscle without an extra pound on him. Once all those muscles regain their full strength, he'll be formidable again. By then, our time together will have come to an end, and that will be for the best.

"Let me get this," I say when the check lands on the table.

"No way. I've got it."

"You paid for all of us last night."

Propping his elbows on the table, he leans in, his voice low. "You know what happens when you're a Navy commander who's deployed for close to six years?"

I'm forced to lean in so I can hear him. "No, what?"

"You stockpile a *lot* of money. I got this."

I hold his gaze a beat longer than necessary. "Thank you."

He looks right back at me without blinking. "I should be thanking you for everything you're doing for me. Buying you breakfast is the least I can do."

I want him to go back to being an asshole. I could handle that guy. This guy... I'm utterly defenseless against the humble, vulnerable, wounded warrior who's slowly but surely wrapping himself around my heart.

CHAPTER 11

John

Despite the nearly sleepless night, today is turning out to be a good day. After the breakfast outing with Jules, we returned to my place and made good progress on her seemingly endless list of potential questions I might face on the media tour. As we go through the process, I'm finding it easier to talk about things I normally avoid.

I'm trying to surrender to the inevitable, to give the Navy brass what they want so I can have what I want that much sooner—retirement with full benefits. After that, I have no idea what I'll do, but I don't need to figure that out today.

By late afternoon, the sleepless night is starting to catch up to me. I'm sure she wants to get back to her sister.

"How about we hit that craft beer place tomorrow after work?" I ask her.

"Sure, that would be fun."

I don't want her to go, but I also don't want to be selfish and keep her from her sister. I'm also mindful of what Muncie said about keeping things professional with Jules in light of who her new sister-in-law is. As I have that thought, I realize it's the first time I've thought of Ava in hours, which has to be a record.

It's all thanks to Jules, who is a ray of sunshine in the bleak landscape that has become my life since I left the hospital and lost Ava. Jules is endlessly upbeat and optimistic, two qualities I used to embody before life kicked me in the balls.

Muncie left an hour ago for a meeting on base. Staring down another night alone has me feeling edgy and anxious, but I'll get through it. What choice do I have? I'm going to be spending a lot of time alone going forward. I need to get used to it.

"I checked the messages on your phone last night." Jules hands me a sheet of paper ripped from her ever-present notebook. "Lots and lots and lots of people wanting to talk to you about sponsorships, publishing opportunities, endorsements, speaking opportunities. You name it, they want you for it."

"Thank God you're dealing with that now. What will you tell them?"

"I'll return the calls and let them know Captain West will be considering future opportunities after he completes the upcoming media tour. Does that work?"

"Yeah, I guess. Just don't give them too much hope. I'm not sure what I'm doing after the Navy is finished with me." In the immediate future, I can picture myself temporarily in New York and in LA. After that is a big blank space with a huge question mark on it. Will I stay here in San Diego or disappear into a remote corner of Idaho or some other random place where no one knows me? Is there anywhere I can go where no one knows me? I have no idea.

There was a time, pre-deployment, when not knowing what happened next would've been an adventure. Those days are over. I thought I had a plan for the rest of my life after the Navy, but that plan got blown to smithereens the day Ava told me she planned to marry someone else.

Remember that. Ava is married to Jules's brother, and as I watch Jules gather her things and tuck her notebook into her humongous purse, I tell myself that I can't ever, ever, think of Jules as anything more than a colleague and a friend.

She can't be my ray of light. Someone else may be again someday, but it can't be her, no matter how pretty I think she is, no matter how reassuring her presence is to me, or how much I enjoy her company.

It. Can't. Happen.

That's the story of my life lately. It's like I'm not allowed to want anything more than to survive another day.

When she's ready to go, she turns to me. "What's on the docket for the rest of your day?"

"Uh, nothing much. Another trip to the gym and maybe a nap."

"You want to go to dinner with Amy and me later?"

. If Amy is going, too, there'd be nothing wrong with it, right? It's not like I'd be on some kind of date with Jules. It's been so long since I dated anyone that I don't even know what constitutes a date anymore. "Um, sure. That'd be good."

"We'll get an Uber and come by around six thirty? Would that work?"

That'll give me three hours to work out, take a nap and get cleaned up. "That sounds good. I'll meet you downstairs."

Her dazzling smile is right out of a toothpaste commercial. "See you then."

She leaves, taking all the energy in the room with her. I hate being alone with my own thoughts. That's the worst. My brain spins through all the bad stuff, the devastating attack on the , the years of deprivation and desperation hunting Al Khad, the loss of my two closest friends, the egregious injury that took my leg, the endless weeks in the hospital and the excruciating reunion with Ava that left me shattered. I relive it all, over and over again, like a horror movie that never ends.

In my medicine cabinet are enough pain pills to kill a horse. It wouldn't take much to kill a compromised one-hundred-and-eighty-pound man who weighed two twenty-five not that long ago. But then I think of Ava and the years she sacrificed waiting for me to come home and the happiness she's found, even if she didn't get the happy ending I pictured for her—and me. I just can't take that away from her, because it would devastate her if I took my own life.

I won't do it, but I like to think about it a little too much. I think about the sweet relief it would provide from the torture of the last few months, not to mention all the months that lie ahead in which I'll have to learn to live without the only woman I've ever loved. I can't imagine ever loving anyone the way I loved Ava.

I don't even have a photograph of her. Everything I left behind when I deployed is in storage. I have only my memories of her and us and the happiest time in my life. Those memories sustain me. is not a word I'd used to describe most of my life, but the years I spent with her were blissful. There's no better way to describe it.

All I have to do is close my eyes, and I'm right back in that life, living in the apartment we shared, rushing home to her after work so I wouldn't miss a second with her. We did everything together—grocery shopping, cooking, cleaning, laundry, hiking, bike riding. We would spend entire weekends in bed, calling for takeout to sustain us as we gorged on each other. God, I miss that. I miss doing everything and nothing with her.

I don't know what to do with myself without her, especially in this town where we lived together. This was our place, our home, and now I don't know where my home is or how I'll ever again feel at home with anyone else the way I did with her. I'd never had a true home until the one I had with her.

In addition to my ongoing heartache, my missing leg aches like a son of a bitch, probably because of the short walk I took with Jules. Ruling out the treadmill, I drag myself up and out of the chair. Even that is an ordeal. I move to the bathroom and find the pills that take away the pain, for a short time, anyway. I stopped taking them when I was still in the hospital because I was afraid of becoming addicted to them. Propped on the crutches, I take two of the pills and wash them down by sticking my mouth under the faucet. They're fucking horse pills, so it takes a couple of swallows to get them down, and they burn their way to my stomach.

I hate taking pills, especially gigantic ones that make me gag and then make me fuzzy and unfocused, but the pain is significant. How, I wonder, can a leg that's no longer there still hurt so badly? They call it phantom pain, in which my brain hasn't yet figured out that the leg isn't there anymore. I shuffle into the bedroom and sit on the bed, exhausted in every possible way. I can only hope that the meds will kick in soon and give me respite from the pain and some rest free of nightmares.

I'm not a religious man, but if there's a God up there somewhere, I hope he finds it in his heart to take some mercy on me.

I've had enough pain. I can't take any more.

Julianne

Dinner with John was a huge mistake, especially with Amy watching my every move—and his. He brought a large envelope containing letters from families.

"I don't think I could do this on my own, so I was hoping you guys might be willing to help me."

"Of course." In light of the other emotions I feel in his presence, I'm not sure I can handle taking on that additional minefield, but I'll do it for him so he doesn't have to do it alone.

We're at a steakhouse that he recalled being good from when he lived here before, and after we order, we dive into the letters.

The first one I read shreds me.

How does anyone ever get over something like that? They don't, I suppose, but somehow they find a way to live with their terrible grief.

The next one isn't much better…

Star of the High Seas.

Amy gasps. "This one is from Miles!"

John looks up from the letter he's reading. "Who's Miles?"

"He's Ava's boss in New York. He lost his fiancée and her parents on the ship and has been very active in the family group. He was supposed to have been on the trip with them, but his father had a heart scare. Miles urged them to go without him."

"God." John takes a big drink of water. He declined alcohol, saying he'd taken pain meds earlier. I want to know if he's still in pain, but I can't ask. "So many stories, many of which I'm hearing for the first time. I never got to see any of the coverage."

"It went on for months," Amy says. "Twenty-four hours a day."

"I'll never forget the heartbreak," I add. "For months afterward, everyone I know walked around with this stricken look on their faces as we all came to realize that we weren't safe anywhere. First 9/11, then this. It was almost too much for people."

Amy nods. "Yes, that's exactly how it was. It was all people talked about at work, in social settings. Over and over again, I heard the same thing: I just hope they get the bastard who did this. Since you missed all that, you can't possibly know what it means to people that you got him."

"This is perspective I really needed. Of course, I knew that people back home were pulling for us and hoping we'd get him, but hearing these stories from the families is a powerful reminder of what was lost that day." He takes another drink of water. "Could I see the one from Ava's boss?"

Amy hands it to him.

I'm sitting next to him, so I lean in to read it with him.

Star of the High Seas

Visibly moved by Miles's heartfelt words, John rubs at the stubble on his jaw. I wonder if he's thinking of the soul mate he lost to Al Khad.

I use a napkin to dab at the tears in my eyes. I know Miles, have heard his story many times before, but hearing it in his own stark words stirs all my emotions.

John continues to rub at his jaw, where a pulse of tension ticks.

I wish I had the right to reach out and touch him, to put my hand on his shoulder to offer whatever comfort I can. If Amy wasn't here, I'd do it, whether I have the right to or not. But I can't. Not with her tuned in to my complicated feelings for this man, which are becoming more so with every minute I spend in his presence. "I hope it helps to know that what you did meant so much to people," I say softly.

"It does help." His voice is gruff with emotion that he's working hard to keep in check. "Doesn't bring back my friends or my leg, but it helps to know it wasn't for nothing."

The waiter arrives with our salads, the interruption jolting us from the intense moment and thrusting us back to reality.

I glance across the table to find Amy watching me with those eyes that see far too much, and though I know it's wrong to be emotionally engaged with this man, I can't seem to help myself. In my own defense, I'd have to be a heartless monster not to feel for him, and I'm anything but heartless. I'm the opposite of heartless, which is why my siblings are constantly on me about being too open with people I barely know. They fear for my physical safety, but right now, I'm far more concerned for my emotional well-being. After reading those letters and seeing John's reaction to them, my heart feels like it's been put through a meat grinder.

I force myself to eat the Caesar salad, the petite filet mignon and the scalloped potatoes, but the food may as well be coal for all I can taste over the hammering beat of my heart, the rush of blood in my veins and the overwhelming desire for more of him that can no longer be denied.

I want him in a way I've never wanted anyone, and of course, he's the last man on earth who I should want.

CHAPTER 12

Eric

It takes a couple of days to arrange a time when Jessica can Skype with us. When we finally connect with her, it's the middle of the night in Spain. That's fine with us, since neither of us has gotten much sleep since Ava confessed her torment to me. I offered her privacy, but Ava asks me to stay. She holds on tightly to my hand as she says hello to Jessica.

Jessica's expression is full of empathy. "You look rough, sweetheart."

Ava blinks back tears. "It's been a rough few days."

That's putting it mildly. What was supposed to have been the happiest time of our lives has been the worst stretch of our relationship as we tiptoe around the grenade that threatens to blow everything between us to bits.

I suppose I was a fool to hope that once we said "I do," the issues that have been with us from the beginning would suddenly go away, leaving us to pursue our happily ever after unimpeded by the past. Yeah, right. That's not going to happen, as much as we both might've hoped otherwise.

Ava has brought the deep scars left by her relationship with John into our marriage, and just as he did before the wedding, he sits squarely in the middle of our relationship.

"Tell me what's going on. Your text mentioned dreams you've had?"

Ava nods, her misery palpable. "They're so vivid," she says softly. "And I remember every detail, which is unusual for me. I hardly ever remember my dreams."

"Oh dear. That explains why you look so ravaged when you're supposed to be having fun and celebrating."

"There hasn't been much celebrating the last few days."

Isn't that the truth? We've barely touched each other in the torturous days since she confessed to dreaming about him. She can hardly bring herself to look at me, and I'm freaking out, even as I try to stay calm for her sake. I keep telling myself she married me, but I can't forget that he's still out there—wounded and still very much in love with my wife. It doesn't help that his face and his story are everywhere I look online.

He's a national hero. How, I wonder once again, can I possibly compete with that?

"Tell me about the dreams," Jessica says.

"Uh…" Ava glances at me, visibly stricken.

"Go ahead," I tell her. "She can't help us if she doesn't know what's going on."

She's devastated to have to discuss it in front of me. It occurs to me that she looks the same way she did that dreadful day in San Diego when she had to tell John she'd fallen in love with me and we were engaged. I'd hoped to never again see that haunted, shattered version of her, but here we are.

I can't sit still for this, as much as I want to be there for her. I release her hand and stand, needing to move or do something with the energy pulsing through me. God forbid I should throw the desk chair through the sliding door the way I'd like to. Smashing something might make me feel better, but it won't do a damned thing to help her.

Ava is rattled by my abrupt withdrawal, but I can't bring myself to rejoin her. I can't comfort her through this. I just can't.

"I, um… I dream that we're back in our apartment in San Diego, living together." Every word costs her something dear while driving spikes through my heart. "Some of it is stuff that actually happened, but a lot of it is new."

"Let's talk about the new stuff."

Oh God, do we have to? I'm not sure I can hear this.

"I, ah…" Ava glances at me before looking back at Jessica on the screen of my laptop.

I wish now that I hadn't brought it, but I've got a big deal pending at work, and I need to check in every couple of days.

"Should we ask Eric to step out while we discuss this?" Jess asks.

"No," Ava says in that panicked tone that's become familiar to me in the last few days. "I want him here. I want him to know…" Her voice breaks.

This is unbearable.

"What do you want him to know, Ava?" Jess asks gently.

"How much I love him." Ava drops her head into her hands. "I love him so much. I don't want to be dreaming about anyone but him."

"Do you remember when we discussed the concept of unfinished business in regard to John and his role in your life?"

Ava nods and wipes away tears that gut me.

"We didn't dwell on it, but we talked about how things with John might feel unfinished because of how it ended between you—not because either of you didn't care about the other anymore, but due to circumstances outside your control."

"Won't that business always be unfinished in light of the way things happened?" I can't stay quiet when I feel like I'm fighting for my life in a battle I thought I'd already won.

"Possibly," Jess concedes.

Awesome.

"I… I want to move on from him," Ava says. "I thought I had, but then I started having these dreams that are so vivid and real, it's like he's right here in the room."

"Are you having sex with him in the dreams?"

My mouth goes dry, and my hands are sweaty. This is almost as excruciating as the day I had to wait for her to see him. No, this is worse. It's much worse, because I'd hoped we were past all this. I should've known better.

"Yeah," Ava says, breaking my heart and her own.

I can hear her heartbreak in the single word. I believe her when she says she doesn't want this. Who would, after everything she's already been through where he's concerned?

"Why is this happening, Jess?" Ava asks between sobs. "I thought I'd put this behind me. I don't understand."

"The brain is a strange and complicated beast," Jessica replies, sighing. "It's so hard to know the why of it, but I suspect he's on your mind, and this is a manifestation of your subconscious."

"He's *not* on my mind!"

"Really? You're not wondering how he's doing since you had to break his heart? Or how he's recovering from his injuries or dealing with life without one of his legs or curious about how he's handling the intense media interest in his story? You're not thinking about any of those things? Because I've wondered about them, and I was never in love with him."

Ava wipes away the tears that stream down her cheeks. "Of course I wonder how he's doing, but only in passing. I certainly don't dwell on it."

"Don't take this the wrong way, Ava, because I'm not saying this to make anything worse, but how is it possible that you don't dwell on the last time you saw him?"

"I don't know! I just don't. Maybe that makes me a bad person, but I can't think about that or…"

"Or what?" Jess asks in the gentle tone that is so effective.

Ava shakes her head. "Nothing."

"Ava, honey, you have to say it, or you'll never be able to really move past this."

"I can't," she says, weeping silently as if she's afraid to let me see the full extent of her torment.

I want to howl as I realize just how hard she's worked to keep it hidden from me and everyone else. If she hadn't met me, she'd be with him right now and not in Spain with me. Maybe I've been in my own form of denial, but that's the first time it's occurred to me in such stark terms. If there was no Eric, she and John would be back together.

I have to sit on the sofa because I'm fearful that my legs won't hold me if I remain standing.

"Tell me why you can't think about John, Ava."

"Because! It wouldn't be right. I married Eric. I love him, and I want a life with him. I don't want to be living in the past anymore."

"When you say it wouldn't be right to think about John, what do you mean by that?"

Ava runs shaking hands through her long, dark hair. "It would be like cheating."

"You know that's not true, right? It wouldn't count as cheating if you allow yourself to wonder how he's doing."

"It's just better if I don't think about him at all."

"Didn't you agree to stay in touch with him?"

"Yeah, but not regularly. Once in a while."

"Hmmm…"

"What?" Ava asks.

"I just think you're being unrealistic—and hear me out before you object. You loved this man for eight years. For six of them, you didn't know where he was or if he was even alive, but you remained faithful to your feelings for him. Am I right?"

"Until I met Eric and fell in love with him."

"So after you fell for Eric, you no longer had feelings for John?"

"Not exactly, but my feelings for John changed after I met Eric."

"But they never went away completely, did they?"

"No, but… that doesn't mean…" She looks over her shoulder at me, as if trying to calculate the damage her words are doing.

I keep my expression completely neutral, but inside… Inside, I'm bleeding.

"It's okay to still have feelings for John, Ava. You're not doing anything wrong by having them or acknowledging them. By denying them, you're giving them permission to flourish in your subconscious, without your consent or control."

"If those feelings are flourishing in Ava's subconscious, does that mean he's what she really wants?"

Ava spins around in her chair to stare at me, shock stamped into her expression.

"No," Jess says, "that's not what it means. Ava is awake and aware and fully in the moment when she tells you she loves you, that she chose you and married you because she wanted to. You should believe her when she says those things."

I glance down at the floor. "It's just that I can't help but wonder..."

"What?" Ava asks, sounding desperate and undone. "What do you wonder?"

"If you went through with our wedding because you wanted to or felt you had to."

Ava gasps and stares at me in horror. "Eric..."

"Guys, listen." Jess must feel like a witness to an unfolding disaster at this point. "We need to sit down when you get back and work through this. The situation you find yourself in is nearly unprecedented, at least it is as far as my practice is concerned. There's no road map that neatly lays out how you proceed from here. You're going to have to write that map yourselves, and we can do that, but it's going to take some hard work."

"O-okay," Ava says. "I-I'll let you know when we're back in New York."

"Please do, and call me if you need to talk again before then."

"We will."

"Hang in there, and be careful not to say things that can't be unsaid. This is just a speed bump. Everything will be okay. It's just going to take time and persistence and work. No one ever tells us what hard work marriage can be."

Jessica is probably hoping we won't go crazy before we get home, and I appreciate what she's trying to do. But the thing about Ava and me is that it's always been somewhat effortless between us. Take away the external factors we've had to deal with, and there's been nothing but perfection, at least I thought so.

But who knows now?

Ava ends the Skype call with Jess, and we exist in painful silence for several minutes.

I clear my throat, forcing myself to sit up a little straighter. "I think we should go home."

"Now?"

I nod.

"But we have two more weeks... It's our honeymoon."

"The honeymoon is over, wouldn't you say?"

"No! It's not over. Not unless you want it to be."

"I don't want it to be, but this... It's too much, Ava, and being here only makes it harder. It's like the beautiful scenery is mocking us because everything is such a mess."

"I shouldn't have told you about the dreams."

I look at her, incredulous. "Yes, you should have."

"No." She shakes her head, her lips pressed tightly together. "I shouldn't have. We were better off when you didn't know."

"I knew something was wrong days before you told me what it was. Don't forget that I know you better than anyone, and if you think I couldn't see that something was torturing you, then you don't know *me* very well."

"I'm sorry," she says softly, her red eyes filling once again. "I'm so, so sorry about all of this."

"Don't be sorry. We'll figure our way through it, but I can't do that here. I just can't. I want to go home."

"Okay." She looks and sounds so defeated, and I feel terrible about that. "Let's go home."

CHAPTER 13

Julianne

After another few days of intense question-and-answer practice, I feel like John is finally prepared. We're leaving for New York tomorrow morning on a military charter flight that Muncie arranged so John won't have to fly commercial. He requested permission for Amy and me to accompany them and seemed surprised to receive approval that he conveys to me by phone.

"Goes to show that the Navy will give Captain West anything he wants right now," Muncie says.

"As long as he participates in their dog and pony show."

"True."

"How's he feeling?"

Muncie called me early this morning to tell me that John was under the weather and would like to take the day off. Amy and I spent the day out at Coronado, where we toured the famous hotel and sat on the beach for a few hours as military planes came and went from the nearby base. I was concerned all day about whether he was truly ill, sick of me or heartsick after reading the emotionally charged letters. And if he's truly ill, how will that impact the trip as well as the interviews that begin the day after tomorrow?

"He seems better. He's intent on taking you and Amy to tour a craft brewery before we leave, if you're still up for that."

"Sure, that sounds good."

"Great, we'll pick you up in an hour."

"We'll be ready."

I end the call and glance at Amy, who's brushing her hair after blowing it dry.

"So he's feeling better?" she asks.

"That's what Muncie said. They'll be here in an hour to go to the craft beer place."

"I hope there's food involved. I'm starving."

"Me, too."

We get ourselves together and are waiting in front of the hotel when Muncie parks his SUV at the main doors, right on time. If there's a benefit to doing business with military members, punctuality is definitely one of them.

I'm sitting behind John, so I can't see how he looks, and I'd ask Amy for a report by text, but I can't risk that setting her off again on the many reasons why I shouldn't care how he looks. So I have to wait until we get to where we're going to look for myself.

"There're like seventy breweries in the San Diego area," John says, breaking the silence. "I'm taking you to my favorite one from when I used to live here, but if you asked a hundred people, they'd all list a different one as their favorite. I figure you ladies probably don't care too much about how the beer is made. Is that a safe assumption?"

"It is," Amy says, "though we do like drinking it."

Both men laugh.

"In that case, we'll skip the tour of the brewery and go right to their tasting room in Little Italy, where we can also get some dinner. That part of their operation was added while I was gone, so it'll be my first time there, too."

"Sounds perfect," Amy says. "We're both famished."

"The food is nothing fancy, but it's supposed to be good."

"We don't need fancy." Amy glances at me, and I can tell she's wondering why I'm so quiet.

I'm not quiet. I'm panicked. The second I saw him sitting in the passenger side of the SUV, my entire body began to hum in acute awareness of him. I wish I could make it stop, but it's not something I can control—or ignore. When he started speaking, the humming intensified to the point that I feel like someone plugged me into a nuclear reactor or something equally powerful.

Amy is right. I should drop him as a client and never go near him again. I try to imagine actually doing that. For one thing, I'd lose my job, and most of my new media contacts would shun me for abandoning the tour I set up. But my stomach really starts to ache at the thought of abandoning John, who has come to trust and rely upon me to guide him through these next couple of weeks.

I cannot desert him. I just can't.

My phone vibrates with a text from Amy. *What's wrong with u? U look like u r going to pass out.*

Everything is wrong, and there's nothing at all I can do about it.

Nothing, I reply.

I call BS.

I glare at her.

She glares right back at me, seeing me as only a sister can. Normally, I love the close bond I share with my siblings. But the bond I cherish could be jeopardized if I allow these nascent feelings I have for John to flourish. It has to stop. Right now.

I take a deep breath and hold it for nearly a minute before I release it slowly, quietly, so Amy won't hear me.

My family matters too much to me to risk their censure. I can hear Eric now. *With all the men on this planet, you had to choose him?* And he'd be one thousand percent right. Not to mention the career I've busted my ass for. Marcie would be appalled if she knew that the biggest client we've ever landed makes my body hum with desire whenever he's around—and even when he isn't. All I have to do is think about him, and my whole system goes batshit crazy.

Enough, Julianne. Stop it right now. I give myself a stern talking-to that ends when we arrive at our destination. Since I'm on John's side of the car, I hold the door for him and hand over the crutches that Muncie retrieves from the cargo area.

When he's standing, John positions himself on the crutches and then glances at me. His gaze connects with mine, and I feel the torment coming from him. It's visceral and hits me like a punch to the gut. "Are you all right?"

He offers a quick nod, but he's not all right, and I want to know why. What happened since I last saw him to knock him sideways? And dear God, he got his hair cut, which only makes him hotter, if that's possible.

The rest of us follow him, moving at his pace, which seems slower than it was the other day when we walked down the block to get breakfast. Did he have a setback because of that outing?

When we're seated at a table inside the cavernous dining space, John suggests we order flights so we can try all the different kinds of beer.

I don't want beer or food or anything other than information about what's going on with him. But I can't ask, not with Muncie and Amy there and my sister turning everything I say and do into a BFD. What if she goes home and tells our brothers that I'm crushing on my client? My stomach clenches. She'd better not, or I'll have to kill her.

"Everything all right, Jules?" John asks, gazing at me across the table with piercing blue eyes. I feel warm all over, as if the sun has just broken through clouds and decided to shine directly on me.

"Uh, yeah. All good. You?"

"Better now," he says, keeping that formidable gaze trained on me.

What does he mean by that? Dear God, my mind races and my heart beats so fast, I fear I might be having some sort of anxiety attack. I get up and manage to knock over my chair in my haste to get away.

"Sorry," I mutter to the people at the next table, who just missed being hit by my flying chair. After righting the chair, I grab my purse and tell the others I'll be right back without looking directly at any of them.

I can tell they're all looking at me like I'm crazy. I'm sure that's how I must seem. I silently beg Amy to stay at the table and not follow me. Of course, that's too much to hope for. She's right on my heels when I step outside. The cool evening air makes me realize my face is blazing with heat and embarrassment and despair. I'm almost thirty years old, and I've never felt anything even close to what I do when he looks at me with those eyes that seem to see right through me.

Amy takes hold of my arm and tries to force me to look at her. "What the hell is wrong with you?"

"I don't know. I started to feel sick."

"You're never sick. Ever. What gives, Jules?"

I shake her off. "I'm allowed to feel sick even if I'm never sick." I take greedy deep breaths of the fresh air, hoping it can cure what ails me.

"Do you honestly think you're fooling me? I know exactly what's wrong with you, and that's why I told you to walk away before it was too late."

I'm tempted to argue with her, to ask her what she's talking about, but that would be stupid. We both know exactly what she's talking about. "I can't," I say in the softest-possible whisper.

"Yes, you can. You have to."

"I really can't, Amy."

"You can get another job."

"If I walk away from this client at this moment, I'll never work in this business again. But that's not why."

She folds her arms and stares me down. "Why not, then?"

"Because of him. Because of what he's been through. He's lost everyone he ever cared about, Amy. He's put his faith in me—and that faith was hard-won. If I walk away from him, he'll be left to flounder through this on his own, and I can't let him do that. They'll swallow him whole." My throat tightens when my emotions get the better of me.

I don't do this. I don't become emotionally involved with my clients. Most of them don't deserve my emotional involvement. But this one…

I look to my older sister, who always has the answers I need. "What am I going to do?"

She puts an arm around me and walks me away from the valet parking guys, who're showing a little too much interest in us. "You're going to do your job—and only your job."

I nod. I can do that.

"You're a smart woman. You know as well as I do that this would be a disaster of epic proportions, so you have to stop it before it goes any further."

"I know. I just wish I knew how to make it stop." I grasp her arms. "*How* do I make it stop, Ames?"

"Go back to when you didn't like him. Remember how you named him Captain Cranky? Call up that version of him any time you need to be reminded of why it's not a good idea to allow him to be anything more than just another client."

"Just another client." I repeat the words, hoping they'll permeate my addled brain. "I can do that."

"You *have* to do that. You absolutely have to."

"I will. You have to believe me. I don't want to feel this way. It's the last thing in the world I want."

"Keep telling yourself that. Any time you need to, and stay the hell away from him when you aren't working. If that doesn't work, think about Eric and Ava and what they'd have to say about it."

Their names are a sobering shot of cold water in my face. I witnessed their torment firsthand, all of it caused by the same man who makes my body hum with awareness. "Yeah, okay."

"Take a minute. Get your shit together. I'll deal with the guys."

"Thanks, Amy."

She squeezes my shoulder and walks away, disappearing inside to make my excuses.

One of the valets approaches us. "Excuse me."

"Yes?"

"That guy you're with, the one on the crutches? Is he that SEAL from the video?" The young man's eyes glitter with anticipation of my reply.

This, right here, is why John needs me. "No, that's not him, but he gets mistaken for him all the time."

His face falls with disappointment. "Oh, damn. I was so sure it was him."

I shake my head, take a deep breath and try to find the grounded center that has guided me throughout my life and career. I know the difference between right and wrong. Our parents pounded those lessons into our heads when we were growing up, with lofty expectations for academic and professional success. Each of us has achieved that success, and I refuse to be the one who disappoints the others.

My feelings for John would devastate Eric, and I love my brother too much to hurt him that way. I take a few more deep breaths, trying to calm myself before I return to the table. When I'm as ready as I'll ever be, I head back inside, even as my stomach continues to churn with nerves. I hope I'll be able to eat something.

"Sorry about that." I wonder if the chipper tone I'm attempting is convincing. "I had to take a call while I was in the ladies' room. What'd I miss?"

Muncie holds up a glass full of dark beer. "Beer delivery."

I glance at the flight of six small glasses that's been left at my place before venturing a tentative look at John.

He's studying me with that intense, knowing way of his that probably made him an effective SEAL. He never misses anything.

"Which one do you like?" I ask Amy, desperate to look anywhere but at him.

"The lighter ale." She points to the glass that has the lightest-colored beer. "I can't do the heavier stuff."

"I'd be happy to take it off your hands," Muncie says.

Amy smiles and slides the three glasses on the right side of her flight across the table to him.

"Easy, sailor," John says. "You're driving."

"No worries. I'm only having a little."

The humming is so loud, it makes my ears ring. What I wouldn't give to know how to make the involuntary reactions stop. I try to ignore the humming and the tingling, but desire has my heart racing and my palms damp with sweat, which never happens. I study the menu, trying to find something that appeals to me. I was starving an hour ago. Now the thought of eating nauseates me. "What's everyone having?"

The guys want burgers, and Amy has her eye on a chicken Caesar salad.

My phone and Amy's chime with incoming texts.

She gasps. "Oh my God."

"What?" I'm almost afraid of what she's going to say.

"Rob just texted us both to say that Eric and Ava are coming home from Spain early."

"Why?"

Amy's fingers fly as she responds to Rob. "He didn't say."

All at once, we both seem to realize where we are and who we're with. Amy puts her phone on the table, facedown. "Sorry. I didn't think."

"Don't be sorry," John says. "I hope they're both all right."

"Me, too," Amy says.

"It's okay to check your phone," John says. "Now we all want to know what's going on."

The waitress returns to our table, and we order dinner. I go with the Caesar, hoping I can choke it down.

With John's blessing, Amy picks up her phone. "Rob said Eric didn't tell him why they're coming home. Just that they'll be home in the morning."

Why would they cut short the honeymoon they planned with meticulous care and looked forward to for months? I'm filled with dread when I ponder the various answers to that question.

I have no idea how I manage to get through the next hour. I'm so riddled with anxiety and despair, and my ears… The humming continues unabated, and now my skin has gotten in on the action, feeling hot and prickly. If I didn't know exactly what was causing it, I'd think I have a raging fever.

Once again, John insists on picking up the tab, and we follow him out of the restaurant.

I note heads turning as he goes by. One man starts to get up to speak to him, but I shake my head to discourage him. He gives me a foul look as he drops back into his chair. Outside, we wait for the valet to bring Muncie's SUV.

The same valet who approached me before gasps. "That *is* him. I knew it was. He lost a leg in the raid. That's why he's on crutches."

I turn toward him. "Back off and mind your own business."

"Why'd you lie to me?"

Fortunately, the car arrives before I have to explain myself.

"What was that about?" John asks when we're in the car.

This time, I'm seated behind Muncie, so I can see the left side of John's face. "He figured out who you are and was about to make a scene."

"Oh, well, thanks for running interference."

"No problem."

"So, in the morning," Muncie says, "we'll pick you up around seven, if that's okay."

The reminder of the pending trip to New York, during which I'll constantly be by John's side, turns my already upset stomach. I clear my throat and force myself to acknowledge the plan. "That works. Thanks."

"And thank you for including me," Amy says.

Muncie smiles at her in the mirror. "Our pleasure, but you have to thank the captain. The brass will give him anything he asks for right about now. Adding a friend to the flight is the least they can do for him."

"Thank you both," Amy says.

"Happy to have you." John sounds tired and stressed.

He has to be dreading this trip, the attention, all of it. His already high profile is about to get a whole lot higher, which is the last thing he wants.

I'm doing the right thing, sticking with him and doing my best to make this easier on him. I just hope I don't ruin my own life and career in the process.

CHAPTER 14

John

Jules is not herself tonight. I'm so used to bubbly, optimistic, happy Jules that seeing her obviously upset rattles me. I want to know what's wrong. I also want to know why Ava cut short her honeymoon.

It's none of my business. I'm well aware of that. But still I want to know. Is there trouble in paradise, or did one of them get sick? More than anything, I want to know that she's okay. I stepped aside when she asked me to, but that doesn't mean I don't care anymore. If only it was that simple.

When we arrive at their hotel, the sisters say good night and thank me again for dinner.

"See you bright and early," Muncie says.

"We'll be ready," Amy replies.

Jules gets out of the car, heads inside and never looks back.

Amy runs after her sister, the doors closing behind her.

"Was it something we said?" I ask Muncie as we leave the hotel parking lot.

"What do you mean?"

"Jules was off tonight, from the minute we picked them up."

"Do you know 'Jules' well enough to judge when she's off?"

"I've spent hours with her over the last two weeks. She was off tonight. Something is wrong."

"And you're aware that whatever is wrong or going on with her is not your concern, right?" After a pause, he adds, "Sir?"

I crack up. "It's far too late now to avoid an insubordination rap."

"Then I should probably go all in and tell you that you look at her like a man who hasn't had a steak in twenty years and she's a tenderloin."

The man has a way with words. I have to give him that. "Well, since I haven't had 'steak' or any kind of red meat, for that matter, in more than six years, you'll have to pardon me if I find myself attracted to a beautiful woman."

"Who happens to be the new sister-in-law of your ex."

"Oh, damn, is she? I'd forgotten that, so thanks for the reminder."

"Sarcasm aside, she's not the tenderloin you need to be focusing your gravy on."

I groan. "*Gravy?* Seriously? Way to totally ruin a metaphor."

"You know what I mean."

Yeah, I do, and he's absolutely right. But I can't help but wonder what has Jules so upset and whether it has anything to do with me. "If I forget to say it every hour of every day—thank you for everything. I mean that sincerely."

"Just doing my job, sir."

"You do it exceptionally well."

"Thank you. I'm glad you're pleased." He pulls up to the front door of my building, puts the car in Park and jumps out to grab my crutches.

When I'm standing upright and balanced on the crutches, I reach out to shake his hand. "You've also been a good friend when I've needed one. Thank you for that, too."

He shakes my hand. "It's an honor and a privilege, sir."

"See you in the morning."

I make my way inside, aware that he's waiting until I get to the elevator before taking off. He's nothing if not thoroughly committed to his mission, which happens to be me. As the elevator lifts me to the fourth floor, I think about what Muncie said. While I know I ought to leave well enough alone where Jules is concerned, I need to know what's wrong and if she's regretting taking me on a client.

What if she is? Should I let her off the hook? Christ, would that be even possible on the eve of this media nightmare she set up for me? I have no idea, but I can't go on this trip with her without knowing if something I did has upset her. Not that long ago, I found her annoyingly chipper and wanted her to go away. I've since discovered there's so much more to her than her upbeat exterior. If she's upset, I want to know why. It's that simple.

And that complicated.

Inside my apartment, I go right to the dresser to retrieve the phone that Muncie has left charging. I check the contacts, but don't find Jules's number listed. I don't think I ever put it into the contacts on my old phone.

Shit.

Wait, Ava sent me Jules's number. I asked Muncie to print out the info Ava emailed me. I tear the place apart trying to find it and locate it in a drawer in the kitchen. There's the number I need, along with the note Ava sent with it.

Full disclosure. She's Eric's sister, but she's fantastic at what she does, and she's a genuinely nice person. You'll be in good hands with her.

All those things are true. I want to text Ava and ask why she cut her honeymoon short, but I can't do that. I'm probably not supposed to know they're on their way home. And if there's trouble between the newlyweds? What then?

"Nothing. It's over with you and her, no matter what's going on with them." I have to keep telling myself that, because it's the truth. She made her decision. She picked him. She's married to him. But what if she suddenly changed her mind?

I have to sit on the bed, because that possibility has me reeling. There's no way she changed her mind.

Did she?

I type Jules's number into my contacts and set up a text message.

It's John. Are you ok?

I stare at the words for five full minutes before I press Send and then continue to stare at the screen for another five minutes, hoping she'll respond. But she doesn't. The message shows up as delivered but not read. As I get up to change into sweats and a T-shirt and finish packing for the trip, I resist the urge to check and recheck the phone.

It's so weird to even have a phone again. That was the worst part of the deployment—being completely cut off from Ava, which was necessary so as not to risk the mission in any way—and it was necessary to keep her safe. Our unit had to be ready at a moment's notice to simply disappear for as long as it took to get the job done. Now I can call her any time I want, except I can't because she's not mine anymore. She's someone else's wife and permanently off-limits to me.

Perhaps I've started to accept that fact of my life at some point, and that's why Muncie accused me of looking at Jules like she was tenderloin to a guy who hasn't eaten in years—or whatever it was he said before he ruined it with the disgusting gravy comment.

I pull my dress blues out of the closet, brush off a speck of lint and give the uniform that's defined my adult life a careful once-over to make sure everything is where it belongs. Satisfied, I load it into a garment bag that I zip closed and lay over the top of the suitcase that has everything else I'll need for this latest mission, the last one I'll make on behalf of the Navy.

In the bathroom, I take a leak—which isn't easy to do on crutches—floss and brush my teeth, wash my face and hands. Only then do I wander into the bedroom and allow myself to check the phone to see if she replied.

She did. *Nothing! All good. See you in the AM.*

I don't believe her.

Taking the phone with me, I sit on the edge of my bed to remove the prosthetic because the stump is aching like a bastard. Most of the time, I sleep with it on because I can't bear the idea of not being able to get out of here if I had to. Chalk that up to years of sleeping in caves and other unsafe locations where we had to be ready to mobilize in a matter of seconds if necessary.

I get into bed, telling myself to let it go with her. I need to follow Muncie's advice and remember who she is—and who she can never be to me.

I push all the reasons why it's a terrible idea aside and type my reply. *Aren't you the one who told me we need to be honest with each other? Why are you lying?*

I erase the part about her lying to me and then press Send.

Right away, the message shows up as read.

As I wait—and hope—for her reply, I can barely breathe. Did I go too far calling her out on her dishonesty? Will she level with me, or did I piss her off?

I startle when the phone rings. It's her.

"Hey."

"Hi."

I can barely hear her. "Why are you whispering?"

"I'm in the bathroom. Amy crashed from an overabundance of sun and cocktails."

"Ah, okay."

"I, um, I wanted to call you because... Well, I'm sorry if I was out of sorts tonight. Won't happen again. We've got a big couple of weeks ahead, and I'm ready to make this as easy for you as I can."

"How long did it take you to come up with that rehearsed bullshit?"

"It's not bullshit." She sounds wounded, and I hate that, but it doesn't stop me from pressing the point.

"Yes, it is. Tell me why you were out of sorts tonight."

"It doesn't matter. It's over and done with now, and I'm ready to get some sleep and then head for New York."

"It does matter. It, um, it matters to me if you're upset about something, especially if it's my fault."

Dead silence.

"Jules?"

"It's not your fault."

"Can you come over?"

"*What?* Now?"

"Yeah. Now."

"No, I can't come over there."

The panicked sound of her voice matches the panic brewing inside of me. I'm certainly aware of the many the reasons why this is a terrible, awful, no-good idea, but I don't care. I need to see her. "Why can't you?"

"Because it's almost midnight and…"

"Please? I want to talk to you. I'll come there."

"No!" After a fraught second, she speaks more calmly. "Please don't come here." Another long pause ensues, during which I want to ask what she's thinking—and more than anything, I want to know what's wrong. "I'll come there."

"Okay."

She ends the call.

I sit up, reach for my leg and put it back on, wincing when it makes contact with the stump. I want a pain pill, but I need to be clearheaded when she arrives. A drink. That's what I need. After pulling myself up and taking a second for my leg to throb in protest, I move to the kitchen to search the cabinets.

Muncie thought of just about everything, but there's no booze to be found here.

While I wait for her to arrive, I stand in the kitchen and try to think about when exactly it was that I stopped obsessing about Ava every second of the day and started thinking of Jules as more than just the publicist charged with shark-wrangling on my behalf.

It was the day we talked on the boardwalk. That's when things changed between us—and not just for me. She felt it, too. I'd bet the farm on that. Things between us have been different since then, and it's a difference I welcome, as it's given me some relief from the torturous thoughts that've plagued me since my life blew up in my face.

Jules is literally—and figuratively—the worst person *in the entire world* for me to feel anything for.

However, I feel *something*. I could be wrong, but I think she does, too, and I suspect that's why she was out of sorts tonight.

If I'm wrong, so be it. I've survived worse, and even knowing I could be making the next few weeks exquisitely uncomfortable for both of us doesn't stop me from answering the door fifteen minutes later. It doesn't stop me from stepping aside to let her in or drinking in every detail of her, from the hair piled on top of her head to the formfitting workout pants and zip-up sweatshirt she's wearing to the rosy glow of her cheeks to the way her chest rises and falls, as if she's out of breath or maybe…

"Jules."

"John."

"What's wrong?"

"I told you. Nothing is wrong."

"Did I do something?"

"No." She's so tense, I fear she might snap or do something awful, such as cry.

If I hadn't spent *days* in the presence of cool, competent, unflappable Jules, I wouldn't see the difference. But I do see it, and I need to know if I'm the cause. I take a step closer to her.

She takes a step back, bumping up against the wall.

"Tell me what I did to upset you."

Only because I'm watching her so closely do I notice the throbbing pulse point in her neck and the shift of her gaze from my eyes to my lips.

Oh.

"Talk to me, Jules." I set the crutches aside and lean one arm on the wall next to her, hoping I won't fall over in the next few minutes. I have a feeling that if I start to stumble, she'll catch me. In fact, I'd bet the farm I don't have on that, too.

"I can't. You're my client and Ava's ex and… I *can't*."

"Forget about me being your client or Ava's ex and tell me what has you so wound up."

"*You* have me wound up! You do. And I can't—"

I'm not sure what possesses me, but I raise my right hand to her face and kiss her. It's a somewhat platonic kiss, as kisses go, all lips and no tongue. Not yet, anyway. I have a feeling that too much too soon will send her running, and that's the last thing I want.

She kisses me back with lips so soft and so tender, I want to drown in her sweetness. Until she turns away with a whimpering sound that makes me want to roar. "Please, John. We can't." Her hands are shaking when she puts them on my chest to stop me from going back for more.

"Why not?" I feel more alive in this moment than I have since I woke up in the hospital after surviving an infection that should've killed me.

She gives me a withering look. "You know why not."

"Ava is out of my life. She got married."

"To my *brother*!"

"I know, but that doesn't mean we can't—"

"Yes, it does. It really does."

"Jules." I slide my arms around her and snuggle her into my embrace. She smells incredible, like sunshine and flowers and fresh air and life itself, and I want to breathe her in. I can't hide my natural reaction to being close to her this way or the relief I feel at realizing that I'm not actually dead down there. It's been so fucking long since I touched a woman. But it's not just any woman I want. I ache from wanting *this* woman. "Tell me you feel it, too." The attraction, the undeniable pull, the desire.

"I... I can't ..."

Empowered to know I'm not alone in this, I nuzzle her neck, making her tremble. I tighten my hold on her. "Easy. I've got you. Hold on to me."

She moves tentatively, but her arms encircle my waist, and I release the deep breath I was holding while I waited to see what she would do.

With her in my arms, I feel stronger than I have in months. I have no idea how long we stand there, clinging to each other. I want more of her. I want more of the way I feel when she's around—calm, optimistic, cared for. Safe. It's that last one that I crave more than anything after what I've been through.

"I... I should go."

I caress her back in small circles. "Don't go. Stay with me."

She shivers and holds on tighter to me.

A sense of calm comes over me that takes me by surprise. It's been so long since I've been anywhere close to calm that I almost don't recognize the feeling for what it is. My leg aches like a bitch, but I wouldn't move now if I had to.

"You should get off your leg," she says softly.

I love that she's so concerned about me. Other than Ava, I've never had anyone who truly cared about me the way Jules does, and I've missed that. "I'm okay."

"It has to be hurting."

"I'm afraid if I let go, you'll never let me hold you this way again."

"I will."

"Promise?"

She nods, but there's no pleasure in it.

I release her slowly, holding on until I'm certain I won't fall. I take hold of her hand and walk toward my bedroom, wanting to stretch out with her by my side. I don't care if we do anything more than talk and sleep. I just want her next to me.

I sit on the edge of the bed.

She sits next to me.

I raise my hand to her face, reveling in her soft skin. "You are so very lovely."

"You're rather lovely yourself."

My lips curve into a small smile as I lean in to kiss her. "Get comfortable."

She kicks off her flip-flops and stretches out on the bed.

I lie next to her and hold out my arm in invitation. We're crossing one line after the other. I know it. She knows it. We do it anyway.

With her head on my chest and her warm body snug against mine, I relax even if one part of me is anything but relaxed. I try to ignore the steady thrum of desire that beats through my body, reminding me of how long it's been since I've touched or been touched.

She rests her hand on my abdomen. "You have muscles on top of muscles."

"For all the good they do me these days."

"You'll be back to full strength soon. It's just going to take time to recover and heal."

"That's what the doctors tell me—that the only treatment left is time. It's hard to be patient when I used to be able to do everything. And now, walking a block leaves me completely drained."

"I knew we shouldn't have done that."

I squeeze her arm. "It was fine. The more I do of that kind of thing, the more I'll be able to do. I just hate…"

"What?"

"That I met you when I'm in this condition. That you don't get to see me like I was before."

"Obviously, that doesn't matter to me. Look at where I am right now. The last place on the planet where I should be."

"Is it?"

"You know it is."

His lips curve into a small smile. "And yet…"

"And yet…"

"One thing I've learned from everything that's happened is that life is short, and happiness is hard to find. If you find someone or something that makes you happy, you shouldn't take that for granted."

She moans and gently bangs her head against my chest. "You're not being fair."

"How so?"

"You're making it impossible to remember the many, many, *many* reasons why this is a terrible idea."

"Good."

"Not good."

I tug her hair free of the elastic and run my fingers through it. "So very, very good."

"John…"

"What?"

"I'm trying to understand this, but I can't. You didn't even like me. I didn't like you. How did we get here?"

"I never disliked you. I disliked the situation that caused me to need you."

"Just for the record, I actually disliked you."

I laugh—hard. "I can't say I blame you. I was an asshole. But not because of you. That was never the problem. The first time I saw you, I wondered why Ava had sent me Mary Fucking Poppins."

She sputters with laughter. "*What?*"

"You just looked so prim and proper and put together. That was my first thought." I slid my hand from her hair, down her back and up again. "But then I realized that under Mary Poppins's prim exterior was a beautiful, sexy, smart, amazing, caring, compassionate woman, and I wanted to get to know her better."

"I can't believe you thought of Mary Poppins the first time you saw me."

"Believe it, Poppy."

"Poppy?"

"That's what I'm going to call you from now on." The conversation is silly but life affirming. I'm still here. I can still feel happiness, joy, anticipation and desire. I've walked through the fires of hell and come out on the other side changed forever. But I'm still here—and so is she. I tighten my arms around her. "My Poppy."

"I'm terrified."

"*Of me?*" That possibility horrifies me.

She gives a slight nod.

"Why?"

"You really have to ask? Just being here with you this way is risking my career, my close relationship with my siblings, not to mention my friendship with my new sister-in-law, who I like very much. And I can't help but wonder…"

"What?"

"If I'm just, you know…"

"I don't know."

"Convenient."

Shock renders me speechless. "That's not it. I swear to God, the last thing I wanted when we met was to be attracted to anyone. It just happened, Jules, and it happened because of *you*, not because you were convenient. It happened because you're amazing and compassionate and fearless and so fucking good at what you do—which is a huge turn-on."

She takes a deep breath and releases it slowly.

"Tell me you believe me."

"I want to."

"You can. I swear it's true."

"What about Ava?"

"What about her?"

"There's no way you're over her."

"I don't think I'll ever get over what happened with her or how it happened. She's a big chapter in the story of my life, and part of me will always love her. But I can't have her, and I have no choice but to accept that."

"What if you could have her?"

"Uh... How do you mean?"

"Well, they cut their honeymoon short. What if that's because they realized they made a huge mistake and she comes for you? What would you do then?"

"That's not going to happen."

"But what if it does?"

"Jules... Have you ever been in love? Truly in love?"

"I thought I was. Once."

"What happened?"

"He called off our wedding three weeks before the big day."

"Oh God. I'm so sorry, sweetheart. That's awful."

"It was pretty awful. He felt terrible. He cried when he told me he just wasn't ready to be married, but he loved me more than anything."

"How long ago was that?"

"Three years."

"Do you still think about him?"

"Sometimes. Not as much as I used to."

"If he came back and begged for a second chance, what would you do?"

"I honestly don't know. I've imagined that scenario so many times since it happened, but I stopped hoping for it a while ago."

"So you know what it's like to have a relationship go sideways and how you're never really quite the same afterwards."

"Yes."

"I'm not sitting around waiting for Ava to call me. I swear to you, I'm not."

"But what if she did call you?"

"I fully expect to hear from her at some point. If for no other reason than she has my stuff in storage."

"What if she were to call you, right now, and say, 'John, I made a mistake marrying Eric. Will you give me another chance?' What would you do?"

"It's not going to happen. You were at their wedding. You told me yourself that they're happy together."

"What if it did?"

"I don't know."

She sits up and runs her fingers through her hair to straighten it. "I'm going to go."

"Why?"

"Because I feel like we're juggling with dynamite. You can't tell me that you'd turn away my brother's wife if she changed her mind about who she wants to be with. I can't tell you that I wouldn't still want my ex-fiancé if he suddenly showed up. Add to that, you're my client, I love my job and allowing this to happen could end my career."

She stands, slides her feet into her flip-flops and puts her hair back up.

"Don't I get to say anything?"

Hands on hips, she stares me down. "Sure."

"Before I met you, I was drowning. Since I met you, I feel alive again, and the only thing that's changed is *you*. You showed up and made everything better. Can you blame me for wanting more of the person who did that for me?"

Her shoulders lose some of their rigidity. "You're not being fair."

"How so?"

"I'm trying to do the right thing."

"You're trying to do the right thing for everyone except the two of us." I extend my hand to her. "Come back."

She shakes her head. "I can't. I have to go. I'll see you in the morning."

Before I can formulate a reply, she's left the bedroom. The door to my apartment closes behind her a second later.

I fall back on the pillow and exhale. I completely understand where she's coming from, but I'm disappointed nonetheless. Kissing her was amazing, and not just because I haven't kissed a woman in six years. But because of the way she responded and how I felt when it was happening. She brings a lightness to my life that was sorely lacking before she arrived, and I find myself craving that feeling now that I've experienced it.

I'm bummed until I remember that we'll be spending the next few weeks in close proximity while traveling. Perhaps during that time, I can convince her to give us both a chance to be happy.

CHAPTER 15

Julianne

I'm a hot mess in the morning, running around trying to finish packing in between drying my hair, putting on makeup to hide the dark circles under my eyes and consuming as much bad hotel coffee as I can before we leave.

Amy hasn't had much to say since the alarm woke us at six, but that's not unusual for her. My sister is most definitely not a morning person.

"Did you take the shampoo from the bathroom?" Amy asks.

"Yeah, it's in my bag."

"I can't believe you still collect hotel shampoo."

"Why not? I like trying new stuff."

"Do you still have ten thousand tiny bottles like you did when we were kids?"

"Not that many." More like five thousand, but she doesn't need to know that. I donate a lot of it to homeless shelters. The residents love what I bring back from my travels for them. As long as Amy is focused on my hotel shampoo obsession, she won't ask where I was last night.

Before I left, I sent her a text that said I couldn't sleep and was going to get a drink in the hotel bar, in case she woke up and realized I was gone. She hasn't mentioned it yet, but I'm sure she will, and that puts me even more on edge than I already am.

I can't believe I actually kissed him. Jesus. What was I thinking? I wasn't thinking, and that's the problem. I never should've gone there or said the things I did to him or kissed him. I most definitely should *not* have kissed him.

Except... It was a good kiss, a meaningful kiss. But giving in to temptation has made everything worse. Because now I know what it's like to kiss him, and all I can think about is if I'll ever get a chance to kiss him again. I inhale deeply and let it out slowly, trying to calm my nerves, my hormones and my racing mind.

I should be completely focused on the media tour that begins tonight in New York with Jimmy Fallon and kicks off in earnest tomorrow with a week of interviews on all the major morning and late-night shows. Marcie emailed overnight—does the woman ever sleep?—for an update on the tour and to reiterate once again that she wants to meet John at some point. Did she think I didn't hear her the other seventy-two times she said she wanted to meet him?

In addition to that, one of my usual clients is having an issue that will need my attention during the flight, and all I can think about are John's lips and those eyes and the ripped abs I felt under his shirt. I want to see them. Lick them.

Stop, Jules. Stop it.

I hear the shower shut off in the bathroom and throw the last of my clothes into the suitcase. I'm zipping it as Amy comes out with her hair and body wrapped in towels.

"Are you going to tell me where you really went last night?"

I keep my back to her because my expression gives me away whenever I skirt the truth. It's a problem that's plagued me all my life. "I did tell you."

"Funny, because I woke up, saw you were gone, read your text and decided to join you at the bar. Imagine my surprise when you weren't there."

Fuckety fuck, fuck, fuck. "I was there. But then I went for a walk."

"By yourself, in the dark, in a strange place when no one knew where you were? Bullshit."

She knows that's something I'd never do in New York, so it's not something I'd do here either.

"Did you go to his place?"

I fold and refold my clothes, just to have something to do that will keep my back turned to her. "For a few minutes. He was having an issue and needed my help."

"What kind of issue?"

"The kind that's between my client and me."

"So you're keeping after-midnight hours now?"

"I'm doing what my employer told me to do by taking care of whatever he needs."

"You are so full of shit, it's not even funny, and you're playing with *fire*." She comes over to me, grabs my arm and forces me to look at her. "Did you read Rob's text this morning?"

I haven't looked at my phone yet, which is also unusual for me. I'm afraid of what might be waiting for me from my client. "Not yet."

"Eric called him from Heathrow. The reason they're coming home is because Ava is having vivid, detailed dreams about *John,* and they're both so upset, they didn't want to be on their honeymoon anymore."

Shock renders me immobile. *What?* Ava is dreaming about John, and that ruined their honeymoon?

"Nothing to say?" Amy asks, her brows furrowed.

"I... I feel awful for them. But what does that have to do with me?"

Now her brows are raised in disbelief. "Are you seriously asking that? Our brother and his new wife are so upset about this guy that they're coming home from their *honeymoon* two weeks early. You were with him—by yourself—in the middle of the night, doing God knows what, after confessing to me that you have feelings for him, and you don't see the problem?"

I see the problem. I see it all too clearly. "There's nothing to worry about where I'm concerned. We talked, and that's all we did."

Her sharp gaze zeroes in on me. "I don't believe you."

"Well, that's not my problem. You'd better get dressed. They're going to be here in twenty minutes."

It's not like my sister and me to be at odds, which gives my stomach yet another reason to ache.

"Listen to me, Jules. You need to hear me when I tell you to stay the fuck away from him. Do you remember what we talked about when Mom left Dad?"

"We talked about a lot of things."

"Mostly, we talked about the way people make a disastrous mess of their own lives and then, when they're sitting amidst the wreckage, they wonder how they got there. Remember that conversation?"

"Yeah."

"That's what you're doing by indulging in this *fantasy* that he can ever be anything more to you than a client. If you continue down this path, before long, you'll be sitting in your own wreckage, wondering how you got there."

"Nothing to worry about." I affect a breezy, unconcerned tone. "He's still mourning for Ava anyway."

"He told you that?"

"Uh-huh, not that he had to. It's obvious how he still feels about her by the way he reacts any time her name is mentioned. I'm not a fool, Amy. I know the score."

"Don't forget the score, no matter how intense things get over the next few weeks. Do the job and move on to your next client. If you get caught up in him, you'll regret it."

"I hear you. Now get dressed so we're ready when they get here."

She does what I ask her to, but I'm shaken by what she said. I do remember that conversation after my mom exited her marriage and our family in dramatic fashion last summer by having her younger lover come to collect her when we were all at home for the day. It was horrific, and it didn't take long for her to regret her actions, especially when Eric refused to allow her to attend his wedding if she insisted on bringing *him* with her. Last I heard, she and the guy were "taking a break to reevaluate their relationship." Whatever. Some things can't ever be undone, and that's one of them.

I also recall feeling sorry for her because everyone was so angry with her. Not that I told anyone I felt sorry for her, but I did. My feelings toward her are complicated. I don't approve of what she did to my dad or the rest of us, but I still love her.

Amy is looking out for me the way she has my entire life, and I love her for that even if I don't want to hear the truth as I try to process everything that transpired last night. That hour I spent with him replays on constant loop as we depart our room and head downstairs to check out and wait for the guys to arrive.

I'm on pins and needles, wondering if it will be weird with John, or if he'll say or do something that'll provide further evidence for the case Amy is building against me.

The last thing in this world I want is trouble with any of my siblings. Amy is right to be concerned about the potential for massive trouble, and I like to think I'm a smart person who doesn't do stupid things that I know are going to cause a nightmare in my life or my family.

But then he arrives, and the humming begins anew, more intense than it's been so far. And when I realize he's in uniform, I nearly lose my shit over how incredibly handsome he looks. My heart feels like someone is squeezing it, and I can barely breathe as I help Muncie with our bags before joining Amy in the backseat. I make sure I'm behind John so I won't be tempted to stare at him.

During the short ride to the airport, which is located right in downtown San Diego, I check my messages, reading the one from Rob first.

This is super f'd up, u guys. They're coming home bc Ava was dreaming about John (vivid shit apparently) and they r both so upset they didn't want to be there. WTF?!?

Even though I already heard this from Amy, Rob's words further illustrate how high the stakes are in this situation—for everyone involved.

I vow to stay focused on the job at hand and not on the man at the center of the job. He is just a *client*, like all the others who came before him and the ones who will come after him. This job saved me after Andy called off our wedding. If I hadn't had my work to throw myself into, I never would've survived the crushing disappointment, the devastation or the heartbreak.

Under no circumstances known to man do I ever again want to feel like I did in the weeks that followed our breakup, and that's where I'm headed if I don't get my shit under control. I'm not a teenage girl caught in the throes of a crush on the captain of the football team. I need to stop this while I still can. The stakes are high, and self-control is the theme of this day.

When we arrive at the airport, we're driven directly onto the tarmac, where a military jet stands waiting. A man and woman, both in Navy uniforms, greet us, saluting John and Muncie before they take our bags and usher us toward the stairs.

I've flown private with other clients on swankier planes, but this beats security lines and cramped legroom on commercial flights.

"This is Petty Officer Matson," the woman says, "and I'm Chief Petty Officer Schroder. We'll be taking care of you, and may we say that it's an honor to have you on board, Captain West."

"Thank you both."

They offer coffee and orange juice.

I ask for coffee and so does John. Amy and Muncie want juice.

"Does the plane have Wi-Fi?" I ask hopefully.

"It does." Schroder gives us the password.

Thank God for small favors. I can keep busy with work during the four-hour-and-thirty-minute flight. I'd go crazy from the effort not to think about *him* if I didn't have work to focus on.

The four of us are seated around a table. Each of our seats has belts that we're asked to put on for takeoff, after which our drinks will be served.

Muncie peers out the window. "This is a very civilized way to travel."

"Sure does beat the C-141s and C-5s."

"No kidding. Those netted seats are the worst for long flights."

John laughs. "They're tough on the ass. I flew ten hours once on a 141 with a coffin on the floor between the seats. We were told not to put our feet on it or otherwise use it as a coffee table during the flight."

Muncie chuckles. "Imagine people having to be told that."

"I guess they'd had experience with people using coffins as footstools."

Though I'm face-first in my iPad, trying to concentrate on my email, I listen to what they're saying because I'm fascinated by every bit of insight I get into the life he's led and the things he's seen. His experiences are so very different from mine, so I suppose it's only natural that I find it interesting.

I can feel him looking at me, hoping I'll make eye contact, but I'm not going to do that. I'm going to do my work and keep my eyes and every other part of me away from him.

The uniform is *devastating,* or I should say he's devastating in it. People are going to fall madly in love with him on this tour. He'll be a massive star by the time it's over and will have his pick of companions. Whatever this moment of madness is between us, it's destined to fail for so many reasons, not the least of which is that his life is about to change in ways he can't begin to fathom.

It's for the best, or so I tell myself as I answer emails about one of my highest-maintenance clients, an Instagram influencer with five million followers who's driving my colleagues mad with her incessant needs. *Welcome to my world, boys,* and yes, they assigned two of my male coworkers to take care of what I usually handle on my own. I give them some pointers on how to deal with Drucilla and put them on notice that I won't appreciate it if they screw up her account. Landing her was the biggest coup of my career before Captain West came along.

As long as I'm worried about Drucilla and making sure her needs are met, I can avoid interacting with John or staring at him in that sexy-as-fuck uniform. I've never been one to go crazy over a uniform, but every hormone I have is on full alert as I fight the urge to drink in the sight of him like a thirsty fool who's never seen a hot man before.

My messenger app dings with a text from him. *Why are you ignoring me?!*

I feel like I just stepped too close to something hot. It's all I can do not to jolt as the humming in my ears drowns out the sound of the plane's engines. *I'm not.*

Yes, you are.

Sorry, just got some other clients needing me today.

I need you today. I'm freaking out about all of this.

You're going to be great. You're ready and the uniform is… God, how can I say this without sounding like a tenth-grader in heat?

What? Is something wrong with it? I'm required to wear it when I travel for the Navy.

There is NOTHING wrong with it.

He doesn't reply right away, and I stare at the screen, almost willing him to say something. After what feels like an hour has passed, I see the telltale bubbles that indicate he's writing back.

So you LIKE the uniform?

That's one way to put it…

Out of the corner of my eye, I see his face light up with a smile, and it's all I can do not to sigh. *I know this is a very difficult situation, but I want you to know…*

WHAT?! What do you want me to know? My brain goes completely haywire as I wait for him to finish that thought.

Having you around makes me feel better than I have in a very long time.

I almost wish he didn't tell me that. What can I say that would properly convey how those words make me feel? I can't go there, so I only say, *Thank you.*

No, thank you. For everything.

You might not be thanking me after a few days in NY.

Nothing that happens there is your fault. I blame the Navy for all the negative aspects of this mission.

At least it will be more deluxe than the last one. The Navy has spared no expense in putting us up at the freaking Four Seasons. I told Marcie that I could stay at my place, and she said I should do what the Navy wants me to do, so I'm staying at the hotel. It's probably just as well since there're always issues to contend with on tours of this magnitude—or so I've heard from colleagues who've done them. In addition to the primo lodging, they gave John and Muncie credit cards for any expenses they incur, and when Muncie asked what the spending limit was, they said there wasn't one. That, Muncie told me, is unprecedented in his twelve years in the Navy.

I receive another text from John. *Anything is more deluxe than that was, but you're right. That part won't suck.*

You should try to relax and enjoy the adventure. You deserve all the attention and acclaim you'll receive, and it's a great chance for you to highlight the ultimate sacrifices your friends made as well as those your fellow servicemembers make on a daily basis.

Very true. I look forward to that opportunity. Are you going to avoid me the whole time we're on the trip or just for the flight when your sister is watching you like a hawk?

I'm not avoiding you.

Whatever you say.

What happened last night... I'm almost afraid to put it into words that could be shared, not that he'd ever do that. But I've learned to be wary. *Can't happen again. I'm sorry. It's not that I don't want it to... It's just very complicated, as you know.* My finger hovers over the Send button for a long moment before I press it. Once the words are out there, they can't be unsaid, or unsent, in this case.

He doesn't reply, and I'm not sure what to make of that. For now, I decide to leave well enough alone. I told him the truth and intend to follow through. Everything Amy said to me earlier is true. My relationships with my siblings are too important to risk by juggling the dynamite-laden situation this would be with him. Especially since Eric and Ava are having problems related to him and cut short their honeymoon as a result.

The last thing they need is me making things even more complicated for them by developing feelings for Ava's ex—or acting on them.

But if I'm being totally honest with myself—and what's the point of lying to yourself?—I'd have to say that sometimes being selfless gets old. I'm constantly concerned about the feelings of other people—my clients, my boss, my siblings, my friends. When is it my turn to be concerned about my *own* feelings?

Not now, that's for sure. When I think about what Ava went through as a result of this man and how hard she fought for her happy ending with Eric, there's no way I can justify the fact that my mouth is dry, my heart is racing, my ears are ringing with that damned humming noise, and all I can think about is how he feels better when I'm around. I do that for him. I give him something he needs, and…

And I was better off before I knew that.

After getting to know him, all I want is for him to feel better about the terrible losses he's sustained. I want him to sleep through the night without the nightmares that plague him. I want him to recover his once-formidable strength and to walk with ease on the prosthetic without the crutches he hates so much. I want him to be happy, because God knows the man has earned the right to as much happiness as he can possibly find.

I want all that for him, but I don't want it at the expense of everything else I hold dear, and that would be the price of admission to his life as anything more than his media rep. That's all I can be to him, and that has to be enough for both of us.

But when I venture a glance at him across the table, I find those shockingly blue eyes watching me with an intensity that's never been directed my way by any man, even the one I almost married. I realize that even though I have a plan in place to keep things platonic between us, he's going to take some convincing.

CHAPTER 16

John

I haven't been in New York City in years, but it's just like I remember—dirty, crowded, congested and vibrant, with the kind of energy you can't find anywhere else. It's a madhouse. I take it all in through the backseat window of the car service that fetched us from Teterboro, the airport in New Jersey where we landed.

"Home sweet home," Amy says as we cross one of the many bridges that lead into Manhattan.

I'm not sure which bridge it is, but they would know. I don't care enough to ask. However, I do have other questions. "How can you stand to live here?"

"Um, well, it's home to us," Amy says. "I love it. I wouldn't want to live anywhere else."

As I watch the city whiz by, the graffiti, the litter, the chaos, I can't imagine being here all the time. "I would go mad here after a week or two."

"You'd get used to it," Amy says.

"No, I wouldn't."

"I don't know if I would either," Muncie says. "I get why people love to visit, but I don't think I could live here."

"I didn't think I could," Jules says tentatively. "At first. I was so scared to go anywhere by myself for the first six months."

"You were?" Amy seems astounded. "You never said that."

Jules shrugs. "I didn't want you guys to think I was a wimp."

"Too late. We already thought that."

I want to defend her. I want to say she's the furthest thing from a wimp. She's fearless, as far as I can tell, but I suspect my defense would be unwelcome.

Jules laughs and elbows her sister. "Shut up."

She doesn't need me or anyone to defend her. She's got this. Besides, she's probably used to her siblings picking on her, even if I'm not.

"But you do get used to it after a while," Jules adds.

"I wouldn't." There are few things in this new life that I'm sure of. That's one of them. Give me the laid-back vibe of San Diego over this zoo any day.

"I like that you can get anything you want any time you want," Jules says. "Tacos in the middle of the night? No problem. Sushi for breakfast? We've got that."

I make a note of the fact that she likes tacos in the middle of the night and sushi for breakfast.

"And the *pizza*!" Amy says.

"*To die for.*"

I feel Jules's shiver of pleasure everywhere, including my cock, which makes me want to shout out a "welcome back to the party" for the second time in as many days. I've missed him. That said, I'm well aware that this isn't the time or the place for him to make his presence known.

From the minute we arrive at the Four Seasons, I get a firsthand demonstration of what my life is going to be like going forward. Now, mind you, it certainly doesn't suck to be upgraded to the Presidential Suite with the hotel's thanks for a job very well done. I can live with that. But the staring, the gawking, the silent screaming, the autograph seekers—that's going to take some getting used to. Muncie told me the Navy brass figured I'd be left alone if they put me somewhere like the Four Seasons. They figured wrong. Everyone has something to say to me, from the bellman who greets us to the registration desk people to the woman standing next to us at the desk to the guy who brings the luggage up for us even after we tell him we can do it ourselves. They're not having that.

We take the elevator to the fifty-first floor, and the luggage guy talks to us the whole way up. I catch Jules's eyes and roll mine to let her know what I think of the star treatment. I can tell she wants to giggle, but she doesn't. She's a consummate professional, as always.

"Right this way, Captain West."

The man is wearing a uniform with brass buttons and flourishes that makes mine look shabby. Maybe I can get a job as a hotel bellman after I retire. I do like wearing a uniform.

He throws open the doors to a suite that defies description. I've never seen anything like it, certainly never stayed anywhere that could compare. I'm astounded by what have to be twelve-foot windows, the baby grand piano, luxurious furnishings and the view of the entire south half of Manhattan. As he gives us a tour of the terraces, a bedroom and deluxe bathroom with a tub that Jules says she could live in, I try not to think about recording *Fallon* later this afternoon. I'm following her advice to take things a minute at a time and try to enjoy the adventure.

"You're welcome to use it while we're here," I try not to picture her naked and covered by bubbles in my tub.

"I may take you up on that."

I glance at her in time to see the perturbed look Amy sends her way.

"I hate to say it," Amy says, "but I have to go. Back to reality tomorrow. I've got to get home and get my act together."

"Will we see you before we leave?" Muncie sounds hopeful.

"Oh, um, sure. We can make that happen."

"Let's do dinner some night soon." I make the suggestion even though I'm kind of glad Amy won't be here to keep Jules in check. I don't like her in check. I like her the way she was last night when she was clinging to me and kissing me.

"Good luck tonight and with the other interviews, John, and thank you again for what you did for all of us." Amy surprises me when she goes up on tiptoes to kiss my cheek. "I'll text you later," she says to Jules on her way out of the suite.

"I, um, I should get settled in my room." Jules grasps the handle of her suitcase. "We have to leave at four for the taping."

It's just after two now, time to take a nap or get in a workout. I'd rather have the workout, but I don't have time for that and a shower, and I don't want to go on national TV looking like shit. "Do you want to get some food?" In addition to my libido reawakening, I'm also actually hungry.

"We can order room service." Muncie grins like a loon. "It's on Uncle Sam."

"Sure." Jules gives a thumbs up.. "That sounds good."

"I'll find the menu."

Muncie leaves us alone in the huge bedroom that includes a king-size bed. I glance at it, wishing we had nothing but time and none of the complications that make the most exciting thing to happen to me in a long time also the most impossible thing.

All at once, Jules seems to realize where we are, what I'm thinking and that we're alone. "I should put my stuff in my room."

"Don't go."

She looks down, takes a deep breath and then seems to force herself to look at me. "Please don't. I just can't, John."

I hear her when she says she can't. But I *see* that she wants to.

Julianne

I'm a mess from that charged few seconds in the bedroom of his suite when I caught him staring at the king-size bed like a man who hasn't had sex in six years. Surely in all that time, there must've been someone... But recalling how heartbroken he was over losing Ava, I'm all but certain there hasn't been anyone, and that realization does nothing to bank the fire that flares inside me.

I've completely lost control of this situation and can't even begin to pretend otherwise.

Two needy, hungry words from him—*don't go*—shredded me and dissolved my self-control. I wanted to throw myself at him, wrap my arms around him and give him everything he'll ever need for the rest of his life.

I want to give him *everything*, and I don't give a flying fuck about all the reasons why that's the worst thing I could ever do. I don't care about Eric or Ava or my career or my reputation or anything other than whatever he needs. So, yeah… out of control much?

And what I need to be right now is *in control* so I can do my goddamned job. I'm taking the biggest client I'll ever have in my life to appear on *The Tonight Show Starring Jimmy Fallon*, and I need to be *on my game*.

I'm having this little conversation with myself on the short ride to Rockefeller Center, where the show tapes in the NBC building. The show sent a car for us—all the shows were asked to provide transport for my client, who is an amputee, not that I have to tell them that, but I asked for it anyway.

We're met outside and whisked into the building by one of the assistant producers, who is super professional even though I can tell she's freaking out. Can't say I blame her. He's quite something. This is a woman who deals with celebrities for a living, and she can barely hold it together in John's presence. That makes me wonder if I've underestimated just how huge this tour and his reception are going to be.

Fallon himself greets us in the reception area, and even though I've never had a client do his show before, I suspect that's unusual. John introduces him to me and to Muncie. Jimmy hugs John, his eyes brimming with emotion as he thanks him for his service, his sacrifice and for making us all safer.

I can see that John is overwhelmed by Jimmy's kind words. Hell, I'm over-whelmed by them, but he keeps his composure as he greets the rest of the staff with handshakes and a few more hugs from grateful Americans.

I glance at Muncie and can see he's as moved as I am by the reception.

The staff rolls out the red carpet for us. We're put in a room to wait and treated to a vast assortment of beverages, snacks and baked goods.

John takes it all in, seeming stunned. "This is crazy."

"Get used to it, superstar." Muncie helps himself to a Coke and grabs a bottle of water for John. "Jules? They've got iced tea."

"Sure, that sounds good." I'm full from the late lunch we had in the suite and worn out from the battle I've been waging with my emotions. I'm not accustomed to feeling this way. Even when my fiancé called off our wedding, I didn't feel quite like this, as if the world will end if I can't have what I want.

The show's various producers come in to say hello, to thank John for his service and for making their show the first stop on his tour. A woman comes in to put some powder on John so he won't be shiny under the lights.

John scowls over the fuss she's making. "This isn't makeup, right?"

She laughs. "Of course not. I'd never do that to you." When she's finished, she says we have ten minutes.

Yet another assistant comes for us. "Show time."

Muncie and I are told where we can go to watch the taping. I've asked to be allowed to stay close to John, just in case. Of what, I don't know, but I've made that request of all the places he'll appear.

Holding both crutches in one hand, John stands and gets his bearings. He turns to Muncie. "Everything look okay with the uniform?"

Muncie stands, goes to take a closer look, straightens John's tie and brushes a speck of lint from his sleeve. "You look great, sir."

"Thanks." He glances at me, grimacing. "Well, here goes nothing."

I look up at him. "It won't be nothing. Just keep breathing while you're out there. Pretend you and Jimmy are hanging out in his living room chatting like old friends. That's all this is."

He nods and graces me with one of those rare, full smiles that'll have every woman in America wanting his number. After tonight, I'll have to share him with the world, and I'm not sure how I feel about that.

"Captain West." The assistant producer signals to him. "We're ready for you."

We follow her a short distance to the soundstage. John is told where to stand until he's announced.

He hands the crutches to Muncie.

"Are you sure?" Muncie's tone is full of trepidation.

Thank God he asks, because I was going to.

John nods. "I'm sure."

My stress level just went from nuclear to thermonuclear. If he falls in front of all these people, he'll never get over it—and neither will I.

Jimmy stands before his audience hands clasped, vibrating with excitement. "I'm so very honored tonight to have as our only guest someone who needs no introduction here, or anywhere in the world, for that matter. He and his SEAL team spent more than five years hunting down the most wanted man on earth, finally capturing him in a raid that cost our guest a leg and took the lives of his two closest friends. Ladies and gentlemen, please help me welcome a true American hero. Captain. John. West."

While I hold my breath, John takes a tentative step forward and then another and another. By the third step, he seems confident that his body isn't going to betray him. I grasp Muncie's arm because I need to hold on to something so I won't pass out or vomit or do anything else that would embarrass myself and my client.

Muncie covers my hand with his, both of us barely breathing as John walks out to thunderous applause. There's simply no other word for the reception he receives. Tears fill Jimmy's eyes, John's eyes and those of many of the audience members. Hell, there're tears in my eyes and Muncie's.

John is magnificent, gracious, humble and obviously overwhelmed as the applause continues unabated for many minutes.

"He needs to sit," Muncie whispers to me.

My anxiety spikes once again, and I'm about to get the assistant producer's attention when John subtly points to the sofa, and Jimmy gestures for him to go ahead.

Once he's seated, I release the breath I've been holding, but I still cling to Muncie.

"I'm so happy you're here," Jimmy says. "Thank you for making us your first stop."

"It's a pleasure to be here. I'm a big fan of the show. And thanks to everyone for that warm welcome."

Jimmy leans in toward John. "Do you have *any* idea how thankful people are for what you've done?"

"I have a better idea after that welcome." John strikes the perfect tone as he unleashes that potent smile. *Dear God*, that smile. I can almost hear every straight woman in America sighing and all the gay men giving praise to the Lord for the gift of John West. "But I want to say first and foremost that I didn't do this alone. There were a lot of other people involved, people who sacrificed so many years of their lives for this mission. Especially Lieutenant Commander Daniel Jones and Lieutenant Commander Miguel Tito."

Per our request, their photos are displayed on the monitor when he mentions their names. He was adamant that they be given top billing on this tour, and I was happy to make sure his request was honored.

Another round of applause follows.

"They were your friends?" Jimmy asks.

"My closest friends. We were like brothers."

"I'm so sorry for your loss."

"Thank you. It's been a tough blow for everyone on our team."

"What can you tell us about the effort to find *him*? I refuse to say his name."

"I don't blame you. If I never hear his name again, that'd be fine with me. All I can say about the mission, which is still classified, is that it was a team effort involving all branches of the armed forces, the intelligence community and support from our allies. None of us do what we do for this kind of attention." He gestures to include the audience and soundstage.

"In fact, it goes against everything I've been taught to talk about my job in any kind of public forum."

"It must've been shocking to realize you'd been outed by the other side."

"It was. I woke up from a month-long coma to find out I was a household name in the US and around the world. Needless to say, that's going to take some getting used to."

"People are so incredibly thankful."

"I know, and we appreciate that. Believe me. I've heard from family members of those who were lost on the *Star of the High Seas*. Their letters have touched me so deeply. To know that we were able to give them some closure… That means everything to me and everyone else who was involved."

The audience applauds enthusiastically.

"We have a surprise for you." Jimmy is giddy with excitement.

I glance at Muncie. "What's this?"

"I figured you'd know."

"Nope."

From the other side of the stage, I watch as Miles Ferguson walks out. "Captain West, meet Miles Ferguson, who lost his fiancée, Emerson Phillips, and her parents on the *Star of the High Seas*."

I'm frantic. "Is he going to be able to stand?"

"Let me go help him." Smooth as silk, Muncie appears behind John on the sofa and hands him the crutches.

From where I'm standing, I see the grateful look John gives his faithful colleague. He hauls himself up to shake Miles's hand.

"Thank you." Miles speaks after the crowd settles once again. "On behalf of all the *Star of the High Seas* families, thank you so much."

Tears stream down my face. Knowing both men and how terribly they've suffered, seeing them together is incredible. I thought I knew what to expect on this tour, but watching this first appearance, I realize I had no idea.

CHAPTER 17

Ava

After endless hours of travel, we arrive at Eric's Tribeca apartment, which became ours when I moved in before the wedding. That feels like a lifetime ago, when it's been only a month. While I boil water for tea, more to have something to do than because I want the tea, Eric disappears into the bedroom, taking both our suitcases with him.

I'm stirring honey into the tea when he emerges, pulling the suitcase of his that he just took into the bedroom.

My heartbeat slows to a crawl, and anxiety touches every part of me. I want to ask him what he's doing, but I can't form the words.

"I'm going to stay with Rob for a while."

No! The single word is ripped from my soul, but I can't get it past the enormous lump in my throat. I shake my head.

"It's not forever, and I'm not leaving you, Ava. I just need space and some time to think, and I can't do that here."

I want to beg him to stay. We can't work this out if we aren't together. Tears roll down my face, but I still can't speak over the panic and despair that hold me hostage.

He comes to me, wipes the tears from my face and puts his arms around me. "I'm so sorry about this, Ava. I love you, and I'm not giving up on us. I swear to you I'm not." He holds me for a long time before he kisses my forehead and lets go. "I'll be in touch."

He's gone before I can think of any way to stop him.

I'm on my knees where he left me, sobbing and calling for him, but he can't hear me because he's gone. He said he isn't leaving me, but he's not here. And he went to stay with Rob, who's married to my sister, so she'll be descending in no time, I'm sure.

I can't do this. I just can't. I thought I'd put all this shit behind me, and here I am, once again crumpled up in a ball on the floor, reeling from heartbreak. How many times can one heart break before it can't be put back together again?

I'm not sure if minutes, hours or days pass while I'm on the floor sobbing. I hear my phone ring, and I ignore it.

It rings again, and I shut it off. The only person I want to hear from is not the one calling me. I don't want anyone else. I finally pick myself up off the floor, stagger over to lock the door and go into the bedroom, where I fall into bed without removing the clothes I've had on for what feels like a week. The trip home was endless and awkward and largely silent.

I don't care about anything or anyone. I just want to be left alone. I want my own mind to leave me alone and stop making everything worse. I want to go back to the day before the *Star of the High Seas* was blown up, back to when my life made sense in a way it rarely has since then.

I pray for sleep to take me, but I slept a lot on the plane, and my body has no idea what time it is. After tossing and turning, I get up for a glass of water and take some Advil for the massive headache brought on by all the crying.

I hate feeling this way, shattered, heartbroken, despondent, afraid. I worked so hard to put my pieces back together, only to end up right back where I started, as if all the hard work never happened. I think about reaching out to Jess, but it's late in New York, and she has kids.

After refilling my water glass, I go back to bed and flip on the TV out of desperation, anything to take my mind off the new disaster imploding inside my life. I want Eric to come home and tell me everything will be okay, the way he has from the beginning. He made me feel safe and secure and happy again, until I ruined it by obsessing, albeit subconsciously, about my ex.

I wish I better understood how the mind works. Then I might be able to explain how it's possible for thoughts I've never actually had to ruin my brand-new marriage.

With the remote in hand, I keep flipping mindlessly, barely paying attention to what I'm seeing until I land on the one face I can't forget.

John is on *Fallon* tonight.

I sit up in bed and adjust the volume so I can hear the commercial about tonight's show. He's talking about the men he served with and the many people involved in bringing the terrorist to justice. He's humble, gracious, gorgeous in his uniform and on the cusp of becoming a massive star, although that reality probably hasn't registered with him yet. It will after this. I hope Jules is prepared for what's going to happen.

Fallon, who interacts with celebrities on a daily basis, is obviously starstruck by John, and rightfully so. The commercial is no more than thirty seconds, but it's enough to rattle me even more than I already am.

After spending nearly six years wondering what'd become of this man, seeing him on TV, alive and well and smiling as he banters with Jimmy Fallon, makes me feel seared by what could've been, what should've been and what is.

He's no longer my concern. I told him we were over the day I saw him in San Diego. I told him I was in love with Eric, engaged to marry him and planning to go forward with the wedding, despite his reappearance. I saw his devastation, tasted the salt of his tears and carried his heartbreak with me back home to New York, where I apparently did a piss-poor job of trying to carry on as if the ground beneath me hadn't suddenly disappeared, leaving me free-falling through space.

I still love him.

Of course I still love him. He never did anything to make me stop loving him. Did he keep things from me, things I had a right to know? Yes, he did, but only because he had to, not because he wanted to.

I still love him, and I still love Eric. He's the one who got down on one knee and asked me to be his, which John never did. Eric is the one who stood before our family and friends and promised to love me forever. John never did that. I made the best possible decision I could in an unbearable situation, and I have no regrets.

I did the right thing marrying Eric, even if I still have feelings for John. I'll always have feelings for him, my first love. But Eric is the one I want a life with, and somehow, I have to convince him of that. I can't let this happen. I can't let our marriage fall apart before it ever has a chance to get started. I'd never get over that, and Eric wouldn't either.

I get out of bed and run for the shower, tearing off my clothes as I go. Standing under the hot water, I wash off the trip, the turmoil, the tears and emerge prepared to do battle for my marriage. I don't want to spend a single night without him.

At the curb, I grab a cab and give my sister's address. "Please hurry. It's an emergency."

The cab driver floors it, and we arrive at Rob and Camille's place ten minutes later. I give the driver a twenty for a nine-dollar fare. "Thank you."

I run up the stairs to the vestibule and push the number for their apartment. Camille answers.

"It's me. Let me in."

The buzzer sounds, and I go inside, running up the stairs to their apartment, where my sister greets me outside the door.

"You shouldn't have come here, Ava," she whispers.

"I need to see him."

"He said not tonight."

"But—"

"Ava." Her eyes convey her torment. "He said no."

This can't be happening. He won't even see me? This is worse than I thought. He really has left me, despite what he said. Nodding to my sister, I turn and go back down the stairs, ignoring Camille, who calls out to me. I end up back outside and begin to walk toward the home that's not really mine. It's his.

If we break up, I'll have to move. Again. I'll have to start over. Again.

I don't know if I can do either of those things again.

For some reason, I think about a girl I knew in middle school who took her own life because she thought the boy she liked had made fun of her. We later found out he'd been talking about someone else entirely. I haven't thought about her in years, but for some reason, she's on my mind tonight. Maybe because I finally understand how she must've felt to know that the guy she wanted most didn't want her. I've never been in that position before.

I know... Cry me a river, right? I've been in love only twice, and both times, they wanted me the same way I wanted them.

But Eric doesn't want me anymore. I ruined us, and for the first time, I get why that thirteen-year-old girl couldn't handle the pain. Why it was too much for her to bear. It's not like your love for him goes away when he stops loving you. What're you supposed to do with all those feelings that you no longer need? Do they dry up like breast milk does once the baby stops needing it? Or are they with you forever, tormenting you with what you had and what you lost?

I walk for a long time, well past home and up toward the chaos of Times Square, where I blend into the madness of lights and people and traffic. In front of the Marriott Marquis, I look up, and my gaze snags on the giant picture of John in a promo for *The Tonight Show*. I stand there and stare at him for the longest time, drinking in the details of the face I never forgot and wondering where he is tonight. Is he close by?

And why do I care? That's over, too. I made sure of it.

Standing in the midst of thousands of people, staring up at the handsome face of the first man I ever loved, I've never felt more alone.

CHAPTER 18

John

This will go down as one of the best nights of my life, and I certainly didn't expect to think that when we left the hotel earlier. The reception I received from Jimmy Fallon, the *Tonight Show* staff and the audience has bolstered my confidence as the tour I've dreaded kicks off. Maybe it won't be total hell.

Jimmy and his management team have taken us up to the Rainbow Room for dinner and drinks after the taping. I'm sitting next to Jules, but we're surrounded by people, so I can't ask her how she thinks it went or what I should do differently next time. Hopefully, she'll be up for a debrief when we get back to the hotel to make sure I'm ready for the *Today* show in the morning.

Miles and his girlfriend, Skylar, join us. I learn that he is Ava's boss, and she was Ava's roommate when she first moved to New York. Sky doesn't have much to say to me, so I assume Ava gave her an earful about all the many ways I failed her. I deserve any disdain that Ava's friends direct my way. I was grossly unfair to her, even if I had no choice in the matter.

I like Miles, though. He seems like a good guy, and Jules obviously knows them both quite well. She whispers to me that he had dark hair before the ship was attacked. His hair is now almost completely gray, even though he can't be more than forty-five, if that. In some strange way, it helps to meet other people whose lives were changed forever on that fateful day. It makes me feel less alone with my own pain.

People keep coming over to our table, wanting to talk to me. One of the assistant producers is great about thanking them for their interest but asking them to give me privacy and space.

If she wasn't handling it, Jules would. I have no doubt about that. With her by my side and the others acting as a buffer, I relax somewhat as the adrenaline from the taping starts to wane, leaving me tired but not so tired that I want to leave. Under the table, I nudge Jules. "You okay?"

"Yep."

"You're quiet."

"Just taking it all in. I don't get to have dinner and drinks with Jimmy Fallon every day."

"I figured this was all in a day's work for a high-powered publicist like you."

"Ha! I wish. I've never done anything like this, which I probably shouldn't tell you. You might fire me and get someone more experienced."

"Never. You're just what I need, Poppy."

She gives me a small, personal smile that just does it for me.

"You think it went okay? With Fallon?"

"You were amazing. The promos for tonight's show must've gone live, because my phone is on fire with producers wanting to add their shows to your tour."

"Is that what's bothering you? Is it too much?"

"No, of course not. It's fine. I'm not adding to the tour, though. You're doing enough as it is."

"Whatever you say. You're the boss." I stretch my arm out behind her, and she startles when my sleeve brushes against her neck. "Sorry."

"I, um, I should go back to the hotel and deal with these inquiries."

Is it that, or does she want to get away from me? I suspect it's the latter. "Not yet. We'll go soon."

She receives a text that makes her go rigid.

I know I shouldn't read her private texts, but I do it anyway and see the note from Rob that says Eric is staying at their place.

Jules types a quick reply. *For how long?*

Not sure.

This is not good.

Not good at all.

Eric *left* Ava? No way. They just got married. What the hell could've come between them that fast? I want to ask Jules, but I'm not supposed to know what's happening, so I don't ask. I tell myself it's none of my business. Ava made her choice, and regardless of what happens between the two of them, there's no going back for the two of us.

I lean in closer to Jules. "I need to talk to you tonight."

She looks at me. "About what?"

"I'll tell you when we get back to the hotel. Just save me a few minutes, if you would." I'm a manipulative bastard, because I know she'll do it. I'm her client, after all. But it's not business on my mind. I just want to spend more time with her. I want to talk to her and get to know her better and hear about her life and figure out what matters most to her.

I've got a few weeks with her before we go our separate ways and return to our regular lives, even if nothing about my life is "regular" anymore. Regardless, I don't want this opportunity with her to get away from me. I want to make the most of the time we'll have together here and in LA to convince her to give me a chance.

She doesn't want that, and I understand why, but if there's one thing I've learned from the last six years of my life, it's this: I don't care what anyone else thinks. I know that's easy for me to say because I don't have parents, siblings or anyone who would care about who I get involved with. She does, and that makes things complicated for her.

While I respect that, it's not complicated for me. I gave up six years of my life, my leg, my two best friends and the woman I loved in service to my country. I don't owe anyone anything. This next phase of my life is going to be about me and what I want.

I want her.

I want to get to know her better. I want more of the kisses we shared, and I want to feel the way I do whenever she's around—off-balance but in a good way, uncertain, excited to hear what she has to say, hopeful.

That last one is big for me. I haven't had any reason to feel hopeful since I lost Ava, and now I do. And it's all because of her.

If she thinks I'm going to let that feeling slip through my fingers, she's about to find out otherwise.

Julianne

It's nearly ten o'clock when we return to the Four Seasons. Muncie's room is first, and he says he'll see us in the morning.

Propped on his crutches, John turns to face Muncie. "Did you find out about the gym?"

Muncie nods. "They said no problem on five to six a.m., but after that, they have to open it to everyone. Your room key will get you in."

"Great, thanks for arranging that."

"No problem. Try to get some sleep."

"Will do."

I tell myself to head straight to my room and pretend he didn't ask to talk to me after we got back. We've covered all the business that needs to be addressed for tomorrow. He knows we have to be back at Rockefeller Center for the *Today* show at seven thirty. He's on in the eight o'clock half hour. After that, he's on *Kelly and Ryan*. It'll be a busy morning, but we'll have the rest of the day free. I'm planning to use that time to go home, do some laundry and pick up more clothes.

What could he want to talk about?

If I pretend not to know the answer to that question, I can act like it doesn't matter that he wants to spend more time with me. Alone with me. I swallow hard as we walk to the end of the long hallway where my room is the last door on the left, right next to his.

"Can you come in for a minute?" he asks.

"I, um, I probably shouldn't. I've got some things to confirm for tomorrow anyway."

"Liar." The statement is softened by the curve of his lips and the light in his eyes.

"I'm not lying!"

"Yes, you are. You've had everything confirmed for a week now, and there's nothing left to do but show up at the appointed times."

What can I say to that? It's absolutely true.

"Come in for a minute." He withdraws the keycard from his pocket, opens the door and holds it for me, all while managing crutches.

I'm frozen in place, indecision racking me. I know what I *should* do. And I know what I *want* to do. I take a step forward and then another until I'm inside the room.

The door closes behind me with a loud click that echoes through the vast space.

John goes to the bar that the hotel has outfitted with anything and everything he could possibly want. I love that they're giving him top-level VIP treatment. He certainly deserves it. "Drink?"

I figure I can have one more glass of white wine before I venture into the realm of tipsy. I most definitely need to maintain control of my senses right now. "White wine?"

"Coming right up. Make yourself comfortable."

I kick off my heels and curl up on the sofa with my legs under me.

He walks over without the crutches, bringing a glass of wine for me and a bottle of beer for himself and, after turning on the gas fireplace, sits next to me. He's removed his tie and coat and released the top few buttons of his shirt.

"A fire in August?" I ask him, brow raised.

"I love fires. Bonfires, beach fires, fireplaces. I've never lived in a house with a fireplace, but I've always wanted one."

"You should get one in the next place you live."

"It's at the top of my list."

"Will you stay in San Diego?"

"Probably. It's the only place that's ever felt like home to me, even if it's different now."

Without Ava, he means.

"How do you really think it went with Fallon?"

I glance at him. "You have to ask?"

He shrugs. "It seemed to go well, but it's hard to tell when you're the one being interviewed. It was like a blur."

"You honestly don't get it, do you?"

His brows come together in an adorable look of confusion. "Get what?"

"You were *magnificent*. They *loved* you, and everyone who sees it tonight will love you, too. You're going to be a very big star after this."

"I'm still not sure how I feel about that."

"You probably ought to figure out how to feel about it, because it's happening. My phone—and yours—have been ringing nonstop all night long with people who want you for something. I haven't taken any of the calls or listened to the voicemails because our focus needs to be on the tour, but afterward? You're going to have your pick of anything you want to do."

"I haven't heard phones ringing all night."

"I had them on silent."

"If that's how it's going to be, you can't quit me after the media tour. I'm going to need you far beyond that. I have no clue how to deal with any of this."

My heart kicks into overdrive at the thought of more time alone with him. My brain tells my heart to stand down, but the heart apparently has a mind of its own and it's looking hard in his direction. "Let's get through the next couple of weeks and figure out a plan then."

"You aren't going to leave me here to watch the show by myself, are you?"

I glance at my watch. It's not on for an hour yet. "I'll watch it with you, but then I have to go to bed and so do you if you're planning to work out at five. We need you well-rested for TV."

"God forbid I should have bags under my eyes."

"Exactly."

"I just want to say… Thanks for all the prep work you did with me. At the time, I didn't really see why we had to do that, but I get it now. When I was out there tonight, at least I felt ready to not make a complete fool of myself."

"There's no way you would've made a fool of yourself."

"I might've without all the time you spent getting me ready."

"I'm glad you felt like it was worth the bother."

"It was definitely worth it."

At some point, he turned so he's facing me, giving me his full attention, which is more than my fragile willpower can handle.

He reaches for my hand and links our fingers.

My mouth goes dry, and the humming gets so loud, I almost can't hear anything else over the roar inside my own head.

"Could I say something else?"

"John…"

"Poppy…"

It's all I can do not to whimper. Other than the mess with my ex-fiancé, I haven't often had reason to feel that life isn't fair. With this man sitting inches from me, gazing at me with the most beautiful blue eyes I've ever seen as he holds my hand, I'm acutely aware of how unfair life can be. If it weren't for Ava and Eric, I'd leap into whatever this is with him with everything I am. To hell with my job and the career I've worked so hard to have.

He grins. "You know what I was thinking earlier?"

"What's that?"

"You got to ask me all kinds of probing questions, but I haven't gotten to do the same with you."

I should remove my hand from his grasp and get the hell out of there. Right now. But I'm riveted by the way he looks at me and the small, subtle movement of his thumb over my hand. My heart beats so fast, I fear I might pass out or have a heart attack or vomit or something equally embarrassing.

"Wh-what do you want to know?"

"Everything."

I take a deep breath and let it out slowly. That does nothing to slow the galloping beat of my heart. I guzzle the wine, which only makes me feel more lightheaded.

"What're you most ashamed of?"

Other than holding hands with Ava's ex, the man who broke her heart and is now endangering her marriage to my brother? I look down at our joined hands, trying to think of something worse than this.

"When I was in middle school and high school, I was bullied." I never talk about this.

He frowns. "By who?"

"One of the mean girls who decided I was too pretty, too popular, too successful in school and sports, and I needed to be taken down a few notches. She was relentless."

"There was nothing anyone could do?" He seems dismayed for me, which makes me like him even more than I already do.

"My parents would've been all over it, but I didn't tell them about it."

"Why not?"

"I was afraid that would make it worse."

With his free hand, he tucks a strand of hair behind my ear, the light touch of his fingertip setting off a powerful wave of desire that I feel everywhere. I'm never going to survive this. He's going to incinerate me and leave the life I had before him in ashes, and even knowing that, I can't force myself to move, to leave, to run. Whatever it takes to get away from this powerful trap he's set for me.

"What happened?"

"Our junior year, she was raped and murdered by another kid we went to school with."

"What? Oh my God. That's awful, even if she was awful to you. No one deserves that."

"It was horrifying. I hated her, but I was so deeply affected by what happened to her."

"Of course you were. Even after what she'd put you through, she was still just a kid."

"Yes." I'm relieved that he understands when so many people in my life, who'd known what Tori did to me, didn't get my pervasive grief over what'd happened to her. "I've always felt guilty over hating her, and I've tried to make up for it by giving volunteer time to women's crisis centers. I also organize an annual fundraiser in her name in our hometown. I feel like the least I can do is make sure people never forget her name."

"You're amazing," he whispers. "That you do that for someone who made your life hell says so much about who you are."

I shake my head. "It's not like that."

"Yes, it is. Putting aside what she did to you to make sure she's remembered—it's truly amazing. Not everyone has the ability to forgive the people who've hurt them the way she hurt you."

"It helped me to get over what happened to her by doing something meaningful."

"It's incredibly impressive."

"We've raised more than a million dollars for women's shelters and resource programs, all in her name."

"I'm in awe. Truly. And I bet that most of the people who've been involved in the effort with you have no idea how she treated you."

I shrug. "What does it matter now?"

"It matters. *You* matter. You're as beautiful on the inside as you are on the outside."

Before I have a second to catch up, he's leaning in and his lips are touching mine. Over the humming, which gets louder by the second, I can hear my brain cells frying and taking with them every reason why I shouldn't let this happen. The brain cells are overruled by desire so sharp, so intense, that it outweighs everything else, even my common sense.

My hand curls around his neck, my empty wineglass falls to the floor, and my lips open to his tongue.

A groan seems to come from the deepest part of him as his arms encircle me, possibly to make sure I can't escape.

I'm not going anywhere.

His lips are hungry, ravenous, devouring.

I've had boyfriends since I was fourteen. I've been kissed—many times. I've had sex with six men. I have never experienced anything even close to what it's like to kiss this man. One taste of him, and I'm addicted.

"Poppy," he whispers when we come up for air. "You taste like heaven."

That nickname does it for me. Everything about him does it for me.

He goes back for more, and I give it to him. I'd give him anything he asked for. My resistance crumbles like a house of cards, and not even the thought of what Eric would have to say about me kissing the face off Ava's long-lost ex can stop me from tipping my head to get a better angle. I lose all track of time and place as the kiss goes on and on. I'm under him, the hard ridge of his cock is pressed to my core, he squeezes my ass through my dress, and all I want is to remove the barriers standing between us and the need that's stronger than anything I've ever felt.

His lips skim my ear. "Tell me to stop and I will."

"Don't stop."

He raises his head to look me in the eye. "Jules."

"John." I'm defiant, determined. In that moment, I don't give a single fuck about consequences or condemnation or anyone other than him and me and what I now realize has been inevitable almost from the day we met.

"I don't want you to hate me tomorrow."

"I won't."

"Do you promise?"

"I promise." I might hate myself, but I won't hate him.

"We need a bed for this."

He sits back, and as I stand to offer a hand to help him up, I keep waiting for my common sense to resurface, to call this off while I still can. But I don't call it off. Rather, I take his hand and walk at his pace to the bedroom, where we turn to each other and take another good long look, as if we're both deciding something that can't be undone once it happens.

"You can say no at any time." He releases my hair from its updo and then brushes it aside to kiss my neck.

"I'm not saying no."

"Tell me the truth."

"About?"

"Was it the uniform that did it?"

I didn't expect to laugh right then. "It certainly didn't hurt anything."

"Good to know."

I slip my arms around his waist, wanting to touch him everywhere now that I've given myself permission to have him. "You said you wanted the truth…"

"Mmm." He's unzipping my dress while continuing to nuzzle my neck.

It's all I can do to remain standing. "It wasn't just the uniform. I was so proud watching you do the interview earlier. I thought my heart would burst with pride for who you are and what you've endured. That you can still be so incredible after what you've been through… This is as much about admiration as it is about attraction."

"You give me way too much credit. I might look good on the outside, but inside is still a bit of a mess."

I cup the face that's become so dear to me, even as I tried to resist him. "You're doing great."

"I'm much better since Mary Poppins showed up to whip me into shape. I feel hopeful again, and that's entirely thanks to you."

"Now you're giving me too much credit."

He shakes his head and uses his fingertips to push my dress down over my shoulders.

It falls into a pool at my feet, leaving me in only a black bra and matching thong.

"So fucking sexy, my prim and proper Poppy. Do you have any idea what your legs look like in heels? It ought to be against the law for you to walk around in heels in front of a guy who hasn't had sex in six years."

Once again, he makes me laugh, which I love because I can't be nervous when I'm laughing. I attack the buttons on his shirt, powered by the craving to touch him the way he's touching me.

"Easy on the buttons, babe. I only have one other uniform shirt with me."

I grasp the hem of his dress shirt and undershirt and lift them both over his head, gasping at the muscular landscape of his chest and abdomen. I expected him to be well put together, but this... This is a masterpiece. "*Damn.*"

"Used to be better. It will be again. Someday."

I hate that he sounds self-conscious about his body when he has absolutely no reason to be. "You're beautiful."

"I will be."

I lean forward to kiss between well-honed pectorals. "You're perfection right now."

He releases the clasp on my bra, pushes it down my arms and then pulls me in so my chest is tight against his. We stand there for the longest time, sharing the same air, absorbing the magnitude of this moment.

One of his hands slides down to my ass as his hard cock presses against my belly.

I'm on fire for him, and when I look up at him, I see the same fire coming tenfold from him.

We kiss again, his lips and tongue ruining me for anyone who isn't him. Only when I feel his muscles start to tremble from the effort to remain standing do I gently encourage him to sit on the edge of the bed. I kneel between his legs, untie and remove his shoes and go to work on his belt buckle as well as the various hooks and fasteners on his pants.

"Is it the Navy's goal to make it difficult to get your pants off?"

Laughter does miraculous things to his face. "It wouldn't surprise me." He takes over, quickly freeing himself before lifting his hips to help me get his pants and boxers off. I make a point of completely ignoring the prosthetic, because I don't want him to worry about that. Not now. When his long, thick cock springs free, I lick my lips in anticipation. I wrap my hand around the base and ease him into my mouth.

His sharp inhale encourages me to bring him the ultimate pleasure.

"Poppy… Not sure I can handle that."

I ignore him and double down, taking him as deep as I can, until the thick head breaches my throat.

His fingers tangle in my hair. "*Fuck.*"

I love that after all the pain and suffering he's endured, I'm the one bringing him this pleasure. I pull out all the stops with my tongue, lips and hand.

"Jules. Stop."

I don't stop. Rather, I suck hard and feel his entire body go tense in the second before he comes hard, flooding my mouth and throat with his essence. I take it all, everything he has to give, crossing a line that can never be uncrossed.

CHAPTER 19

John

I nearly go blind from the pleasure. Sweet, beautiful, oh so competent Jules nearly stops my heart with her enthusiasm. I fall back on the bed, sucking in deep breaths while she continues to clean me up. My cock leaves her mouth with a fitting "pop."

"Poppy."

She kisses my abdomen, outlining each muscle with her tongue as she works her way up, giving each nipple her attention. Before she makes it to my lips, I'm already hard again.

"Yes?"

I put my arms around her, running my hands over her back and down to cup her sexy ass. I have no idea why she changed her mind about letting this happen, but I'm not about to ask. "Shit."

"What?"

"I don't have condoms."

"Do we need them?"

"Um, well, you tell me."

"You haven't done this in years, and I'm on long-term birth control. I had a physical a month ago, and I'm healthy."

"Okay, then." I'm raring to go again after years without. For weeks after Ava left me for good, I wondered if I'd ever want to do this with anyone else. But with Julianne warm and sexy in my arms, Ava feels like another lifetime ago. A beautiful lifetime, but I don't want to think about the past right now, and that, in and of itself, is a priceless gift that Jules has given me.

"You have no idea how much you've done for me." I frame her face between my hands. I kiss her softly, not wanting to scare her away with the ferocity of the desire I feel for her, and not just because I haven't done this in so long.

It's *her*. She's the only reason I feel ready for something like this. Because it's her. I'm not sure if my missing leg will make me clumsy, but if it does, she won't care. I know this for certain. I feel safe with her, comfortable and protected from the madness circling all around me these days. She's my buffer, my shelter from the storm, and I want to show her what she's come to mean to me.

I don't have the same strength I used to, so I have to use my words to get what I need, when in the past, I would've taken matters into my own hands and arranged her where I wanted her. "Let's move to the pillows. I want you comfortable."

She gets up, offers me a hand and pulls me up. That she does this instinctively, without fuss, moves me profoundly. She knows what I need and makes sure I get it, not just in here but everywhere else, too. A man who's gone without softness and kindness for so long could very easily become addicted to her brand of care and concern.

I pull back the covers, my gaze fixed on her ass as she gets in first. By the time I slide in next to her, I'm desperate to be inside her. But first I need to see to preliminaries, when the starved caveman inside me would skip them to get to the main event. *She* is the main event, and if I make this great for her, maybe she'll come back for more.

We make out like teenagers, only this is better because we're naked in the most comfortable bed on the planet.

As we kiss, she runs her fingers through my hair while I fill my hand with a plump breast, running my thumb back and forth over the tip that tightens under my touch. She squirms, trying to get closer, which is fine with me. I want her as close as I can get her. I gorge on her sweetness, the sexy caresses of her tongue against mine, the softness of her lips and the fragrance of her hair and skin.

Moving from her lips to her elegant neck and down to the tender tips of her breasts, I give her tenderness while battling the inner beast that wants to *take, take, take* of what she so willingly offers. Soon enough, I tell the beast. First I'll give, and then I'll take. I wish I could trust my arms to hold me up, but I don't, so I stay on my side as I move down, drawing one nipple and then the other into my mouth while letting my hand wander down her body.

She parts her legs to let me in, encouraging me with the subtle shift of her hips and the tightening of her fingers in my hair.

I push the scrap of fabric between her legs out of the way to press one finger and then a second into the tight, wet heat between her legs, loving the way she gasps from the impact. Using my thumb, I caress her clit while sucking hard on her nipple.

She explodes in my hand, crying out from the pleasure, her responsiveness making me crazy for more of her. "John," she says, panting. *"Please."*

It's been a long, long time since I did this, but I know what she wants, and she doesn't have to ask me twice.

"Get on top." I want this to be perfect for her, and I just don't trust my own body to not let me down. I now have another reason to work hard in the gym so I can get back the strength to be everything she needs in bed and out.

I shift to my back, and when she straddles me, I realized she's removed the thong, leaving nothing between us.

Her hands are flat on my chest, her gaze fixed on mine, the emotion arcing between us potent. I only hope she feels it as much as I do.

"I should apologize in advance if this is quick." I offer a wry grin. "I'll make it up to you the next time."

"I'm not worried about it, and you shouldn't either." She moves to take me in, coming down slowly, her head falling back and her mouth opening on a silent scream that sends a surge of heat to my cock. God, she's beautiful and sexy and responsive and… When her internal muscles tighten around me, I have to bite my lip to keep from losing control too soon.

My hands fall to her hips, holding on for dear life as she sets a demanding pace, almost as if she's trying to break me.

Her gaze collides with mine. I see challenge, fearlessness, sexiness and desire in hers. I see joy and pleasure and the zest for life that's so much a part of who she is. I've latched on to those qualities in her, and they've become my life raft in stormy seas. I slide my hands over her back to her shoulders, bringing her down to me. I need to kiss her, to feel her breasts against my chest.

I surprise myself and her when I turn us and break the kiss. "Hot damn. Wasn't sure I could do that."

Her smile lights up her face. "You can do anything."

I push into her, giving her all I've got in one deep thrust. "You make me believe that."

She spreads her legs farther apart and lifts her hips as her hands move over my back and down to grasp my ass.

Only because she took the edge off before am I able to keep up with her. I'm determined to make her come again before I give in to the burning need that has me sprinting toward a spectacular finish.

"Touch yourself," I tell her gruffly, wishing I could do it, but I'm not able to multitask yet.

She reaches down to where we're joined as I bend my head to roll her nipple between my teeth. The combination has the desired effect, and when she clamps down on my cock, I'm done. I come so hard, I see stars. The pleasure is bone-deep, heating the blood that flows through my veins and making my heart swell with emotions I thought I might never experience again.

"Poppy." I turn us again so I won't crush her with my tired body.

"Yes?" She's sprawled on top of me, her hair tickling my chest as aftershocks ripple through us both.

"That was awesome."

"Mmm, sure was."

"Are you okay?"

"Uh-huh. You?"

"Better than I've been in a long time." Now that I'm allowed to touch her, I can't stop. My hands move over her soft skin, memorizing every dip and valley, every handful of sexy ass and muscular thigh.

She shivers when goose bumps break out on the surface of her skin.

I go hard inside her.

She laughs, and the sound of her joy is the sweetest music I've ever heard. Then she lifts her head and stretches to see the bedside clock. "It's almost time for the show."

"Don't care." I squeeze her ass cheeks and thrust into her like the randy bull I am. The floodgates have opened, literally, and now that my libido has returned, I want to fuck until I can't move, until she's too sore to take me, until I sate the desire that burns through me so hot it threatens to consume me.

"Yes, you do. Let me go, and I'll grab the clicker."

"I'll only let you go if you return to exactly where you are right now."

"I will." She smiles as she kisses me.

I let her go and push myself up on my elbows so I can watch her move around the room. Her breasts are bigger than I expected them to be, and they bounce when she moves. Sexy as fuck.

The clicker is behind the TV. She points it at the TV and turns it to the local NBC channel. I forget that she lives here and knows all things New York. I experience a pang of concern. What will we do when I'm back in San Diego and she's returned to her life in New York?

Stop. Don't get ahead of yourself. You've got weeks yet to make yourself necessary to her. Right then and there, that becomes the primary goal of this media tour—to make myself necessary to her.

"You promised to come back."

Smiling widely, she returns to her post on top of me.

"Um, that's not exactly where you were."

She shifts her hips and takes me to the hilt. "Better?"

Gasping, I say, "So much better." Being inside her is like touching heaven.

"I can't see the TV," she says.

Holding her hips, I thrust in deeper. "You don't need to. You were there. You saw it live."

"I want to see it," she says, laughing.

I turn us so we're on our sides, facing each other, my cock still embedded deep inside her. I'm not sure where I'm getting the strength for these sexual gymnastics and wonder if I'll pay for it with soreness tomorrow. If so, who cares? It'll be so worth it. "Better?"

She nods, but stares at me and not the TV, her hand on my face as she kisses me.

The show comes on with music and announcements. I hear my name, but I keep my gaze fixed on her, fucking her slowly but deeply, my hand on her ass to keep her right where I want her. I shouldn't be able to do this, but for once, my body cooperates, and I don't ask any questions. It feels so good. I just want it to continue for as long as possible.

We listen to Jimmy's entertaining monologue as we kiss and touch and move together in an erotic dance. After commercials, Jimmy introduces me. My heart gives a lurch when I recall the fear I had of falling after I made the spontaneous decision to leave the crutches with Muncie.

"I was so proud of you for walking out there," she whispers against my lips.

"I was scared shitless that I'd fall and make an ass of myself."

"No one ever would've known you were anything but cool and so sexy in that uniform. Every woman in America would like to be me right now."

I laugh. "Shut up."

"Shut me up."

I thrust my tongue into her mouth and fuck her harder, moving to the sound of my own voice coming from the TV. I couldn't care less about the interview or anything other than the pleasure I'm finding in her arms. I've been deprived of pleasure for so long that I am greedy for it, rougher with her than I should be, but I can't help it.

"Jules." I break the kiss to suck in a deep breath. "This is so good, you… You're so good, so good." I bury my face in her neck and breathe her in, wanting to drown in the scent of her.

Her fingertips dig into my back, letting me know she's close.

This time, I want to own her orgasm. I reach down to caress her clit, teasing her and then backing off several times, until she's all but clawing at my back, begging me to give her relief. I tease her some more before finally letting her have what she wants.

She screams when she comes, and I can only hope Muncie is far enough away from us that he can't hear her.

I power into her, over and over again, riding the waves of incredible pleasure until I can't hold back anymore. I tighten my arms around her and come hard, right as Jimmy brings Miles out to surprise me.

We're quiet for a long while as we listen to the interview and come down from the high we found together.

"Did you like meeting Miles?" Her hand makes small, soothing circles on my back. It's been so long since anyone touched me this way. I want this night to last forever.

"Yeah, he seems like a really great guy."

"His story is so sad. He was crazy about Emerson."

"That came through in his letter. Did he meet Sky through Ava?"

"Yes. She fixed them up, actually. She became very close with Miles while working with the family group."

"Sky doesn't like me very much."

"It's not that…" She bites her lip as if she's hesitant to fill in the blanks for me.

"What is it, then?"

"Sky and Ava lived together during the time that Ava was trying very hard to get back on track. It wasn't like she left San Diego and her life there behind and never looked back. There were a lot of potholes for her on the road to happily ever after with Eric."

I run my hand from her shoulder to her hand and then back up again. Her skin is so soft and so smooth. It's like silk. "Have they hit another one because of me?"

After a long hesitation, she says, "Could I ask a favor?"

"Anything you want."

"Can we please not talk about them? I can't talk about them and do this, too." She gestures between the two of us. "I have to keep it separate, or I'm apt to lose what's left of my mind."

"Fair enough. I'm sorry if I made you uncomfortable."

"You make me very uncomfortable." Her lips curve into a small smile. "I've never done anything remotely like this. I have no idea how to handle the potential repercussions."

"My sweet Poppy. Always such a good girl."

"Sad but true. I don't know how to be any other way."

"I know it may be selfish of me to say this, but for once, I want to see you take care of yourself rather than everyone else. I want you to put *you* first."

"It's sweet of you to want that for me, but it's very difficult for me to put myself first when people I care about will be hurt by my actions."

And that, right there, is the crux of our dilemma.

CHAPTER 20

Eric

I can't escape the guy, no matter how hard I try. I don't want to talk about the disaster my marriage has become, so Rob gets us both fresh beers and we settle in to watch TV. Who's on *The Tonight Show* but the man of the hour, the one face in the entire world that I can't bear to look at right now.

He gets a hero's welcome that he certainly deserves, but it makes me feel sicker than I already do.

Rob reaches for the clicker on the coffee table and nearly knocks his beer over in his haste to change the channel.

"Leave it."

Maybe it makes me a masochist, but I can't help being curious about him, even if I wish he'd go away and never come back.

Rob eyes me warily. "Are you sure?"

I nod. I'm not sure of anything anymore, but what harm can it do to watch him on TV? The crowd cheers for a full five minutes.

Fallon has tears in his eyes.

John, who is incredibly impressive in uniform, has no idea how to cope with the welcome from the grateful audience members.

I watch with a sinking feeling inside. "I never stood a chance."

"That's not true."

"Yes, it is. Look at him. Every woman in American is going to want him after this. How can I compete with that, with what she had with him?"

"You don't have to compete with him."

"Don't I? My wife was having X-rated dreams about him while we were on our fucking *honeymoon*." I spin the wedding ring I'm still getting accustomed to wearing on my finger, wondering if it'll be gone before I get used to it being there. "Clearly, I'm not getting the job done if she's having sex dreams about him."

It goes against everything I believe in to have walked away from her earlier. I'm a guy who sticks around and does the work, but in this case… I just had to get out of there before I said or did something that would ruin us forever.

"It's hardly fair to blame her for dreams, man. She can't help that any more than you can help what you dream about."

"I dream about her—and only her."

"I still say she can't be held accountable for things outside her control."

"So you'd be fine if Camille suddenly started fucking her ex in her dreams?"

"I wouldn't like it, but I wouldn't blame her for it."

"Sure, you wouldn't. Talk to me when it actually happens, and let me know how you feel about it then."

"You're going to push her away by being angry with her about something that didn't actually happen."

"She's already gone."

"She is not! She was here an hour ago wanting to see you, and you turned her away."

"I don't want to see her." At some point during the interminable trip home, I started getting angry, and now the anger is all that's left.

"Eric, you're making a huge mistake."

"The huge mistake happened on July third." Our wedding day was the best day of my life, but even that day, I knew something was wrong. I chose to ignore it because I was getting what I most wanted. Since then, I've learned that ignoring obvious problems can make everything worse.

Rob stares at me, his face blank with shock. "You don't mean that."

"Yeah, I do. The only reason she went through with it was because of Brittany."

He shakes his head in total disbelief. "*What?* What the fuck does that bitch have to do with any of this?"

"If she hadn't done what she did to me, Ava would've called off the wedding after she saw him." I gesture to the TV, where the man of the moment holds court on Fallon.

"You've lost your fucking mind. That is *not* true."

"Yes, it is." It feels good, actually, to finally say out loud what I've suspected for some time now. "She would never do to me what Brittany did. She knew it was a big deal for me to take a chance on her, just like it was a big deal for her to take a chance on me. She would've cut off her right arm before she put me through what Brit did."

When my fiancée ghosted me, exited our life together without a word to me, I thought it would be the worst thing to ever happen to me. I was wrong.

"She even said as much in Spain. She said she did the right thing by marrying me."

"She meant that she did the right thing for herself."

"I'm not so sure about that. I suspect she really means that she did the right thing by not putting me through another hideous breakup when her first love returned from a six-year deployment and wanted her back." I stare at him on the TV, my jaw so tense, it feels like it could snap from the intense pressure building inside me. "From the second she returned to me after seeing him, she was a completely different person."

"How so?"

"She was haunted. She didn't sleep or eat. She didn't give a shit about the wedding. She went through the motions, and I let her because I was so afraid of losing her that I didn't sound the alarm. I asked her about it. We talked to Jess about it. We aired it out, and she pushed forward with the wedding and all our plans, but she wasn't herself. She did it because it was what I and everyone else expected her to do, not because it was what she wanted."

"I refuse to believe that. I was there that day. I saw how happy she was and the way she looked at you. She wasn't faking it."

"No, she wasn't. She genuinely loves me. I have no doubt about that. But she loves him more."

"Eric, this is insanity. She married you. Who would do that if they didn't want to be with someone for the rest of their life?"

"Ava would." The more I talk about it, the more certain I am that I'm right. "She did the right thing, but at what cost? I love her. I really, really do. But I don't want to spend the rest of my life with someone who wants someone else. I can't do that."

"You shouldn't have to, and if I know her at all—and I think I do—she just needs some time to get herself sorted. The timing of all this, of him coming back right before your wedding and wanting to see her… That would've fucked up anybody. You just have to give her some time to get her head on straight. You guys are happy together. I've seen that with my own eyes."

"You saw that before he came back."

"I saw it *after*, too. I saw it on July third."

I want to believe him, but I'm done with blowing smoke up my own ass. I have to face the truth that's staring me in the face on TV and at home. I can't pretend this isn't happening, as much as I might want to.

Camille comes out of their bedroom, phone in hand. "I can't get in touch with her. Her phone is going right to voicemail."

"She must've shut it off," Rob says.

"I want to go over there and check on her."

"You're not going over there now. It's almost midnight."

"I'll get an Uber."

They live at one end of Tribeca, and we live at the other. The close proximity to my brother's place was the reason I bought my loft. That, like everything else, has been permanently tainted by the events of the last few years. If my marriage ends, I'll sell the fucking place where *two* disasters unfolded.

"If you insist on going," Rob says, "I'll go with you."

"I'd feel better knowing she's okay." Camille gives me a look that conveys a world of disappointment and concern. She was pissed that I wouldn't see Ava when she came by earlier. I'd apologize, but I'm not sorry. For once, I'm taking care of myself in this situation, rather than putting her first the way I have from the day I met her at Rob and Camille's wedding.

It was all so sweet—brothers marrying sisters. *The New York Times* even featured us, the governor's sons, in their Vows column.

I wonder if they'll also cover the divorce.

CHAPTER 21

Julianne

I wake alone in John's big bed, the scent of his cologne clinging to the pillow we shared during the most spectacular night of my life.

In the bright light of day, I have zero regrets. I'm not sure what exactly has happened to me in the last few weeks, but whatever it is, I'm down with it. I've met an amazing man who makes me feel things I didn't know were possible, which has me thinking about Andy and how I almost married someone who made me feel nothing compared to what happens when John simply walks into a room.

I loved Andy. I truly did. But this, with John… This is different in ways I'm still processing after the best sex of my life. It wasn't just the sex, though. It was the *connection* that made it different, more intimate than anything has ever been. For me anyway. I know he's had that before, but I haven't.

And now that I've had a taste, I'm completely hooked.

Where is he, anyway?

I start to get up to see if he's in the other room when I hear the door slam shut and a commotion coming from the living room.

Two voices.

John and Muncie.

Shit!

I fly out of bed, grab my dress, panties and bra from the floor and go into the bathroom, shutting the door and locking it. I get dressed as fast as I can with hands that don't want to cooperate, all the while trying to come up with a story that Muncie will believe.

John let me use his tub.

Right. That'll work, after he heard me mention it yesterday.

Except it's six in the morning…

Shit, shit, *shit*!

"Don't go in there," I hear John say.

My ear is pressed to the door.

"We need a towel. You're bleeding like a stuck pig."

What? He's hurt? What happened?

"Use this."

Is Muncie seeing his uniform strewn around the room? Oh God, my shoes are out there and the wineglass is probably still on the floor where it fell when we were making out on the sofa. Crap!

I lean my forehead against the cool wood door, trying to decide what to do. I want to know what happened to John, but I don't want Muncie to see me in last night's clothes, put two and two together to get that I'm fucked in more ways than one.

My concern for John overrides any potential fear of humiliation. I open the door and walk out of the bathroom and then the bedroom, as if I have every good reason to be emerging from John's bedroom in last night's clothes. And when I see the bloody T-shirt pressed to the back of John's head, I nearly pass out when I realize he's seriously injured.

"What happened?"

Muncie looks at me. He does the math in two seconds but quickly returns his attention to John. "He fell in the gym."

John sends me an apology in the look he directs my way. "It's nothing."

"Do we need a doctor?"

Muncie says yes at the same time John says no.

"It's laid open. He probably needs stiches."

"I don't have time for stitches. I'm on the *Today* show in two hours."

My stomach clutches with stress over the idea of having to contact the *Today* show to tell them he's not coming. They won't be happy. "Let me call down to the front desk. Maybe they can get us someone."

"Worth a shot," Muncie says.

I make the call. When I tell the front desk that the injured person is Captain West, she snaps to attention and says she'll send someone up immediately. I thank her and convey the information to the guys.

"Do they have medical personnel on staff?" Muncie asks.

"Probably for things just like this." My gaze is fixed on John's pale face. I can tell by the way his mouth is set that he's in pain that he doesn't want us to know about. He's had more than enough of medical issues and people fussing over him.

I go into the bathroom and wet one of the superdeluxe washcloths and grab one of the towels, bringing them back to the main room, where John is seated at the dining room table. "Let me see it." I steel myself for whatever I might see.

He removes the ruined T-shirt to reveal a two-inch cut on the back of John's head. Muncie is right. That's going to need stitches. I gently press the washcloth to the cut, cleaning it up even as it continues to bleed quite profusely.

John looks up at me. "Sorry about this."

"Don't be. It was an accident. Shit happens."

"I'll be fine for today. I won't let you down."

I want to hug him and kiss him and hold him. I want to tell him he could never let me down, but I can't do any of those things in front of Muncie, who is watching us like someone who's fallen into the scoop of the century. I know him well enough to be certain he'd never breathe a word of it to anyone, but I hate that he knows. We haven't had even one day to ourselves to enjoy our change in status, and now someone knows.

I tend to John until the doorbell rings.

Muncie runs to let in the doctor, who comes in carrying an old-fashioned medical bag. I estimate that he's in his late sixties, with white hair and bushy white eyebrows. He introduces himself as Dr. Carey.

The doctor quickly assesses the situation. "That's a lot of blood. What happened?"

"I was, um, jogging on the treadmill and tripped, fell backward."

Hearing that, I swallow hard, realizing he could've been hurt even worse. And why was he *jogging* when he can barely walk without the crutches?

The doctor steps behind him. "Let me take a look."

I move aside to let him in, gathering up the bloody towels and T-shirt and rolling them into a ball. While the doctor puts John through a series of neurological tests, I stand with Muncie, who seems as tense as I feel. "Why was he jogging?" I keep my voice down, not wanting John to overhear us.

"I have no idea what the hell he was thinking."

"I have commitments this morning," John tells the doctor. "Can you patch me up?"

"Yep, but you're going to need a couple of staples, and I want you to get a CT scan just to make sure you don't have a bleeder inside."

John's gaze darts to me. "Can we fit that in?"

"We'll make it happen." I'll figure something out. That's my job.

"I'll make some calls," Dr. Carey says. "See if I can't get you in somewhere so we can keep it under the radar."

I'm immediately relieved. "That'd be excellent."

"Saw you on *The Tonight Show* last night." Dr. Carey cleans the wound and applies butterfly bandages. "Security says there're people camped outside, hoping to catch a glimpse of you."

I look at Muncie.

"How do they know he's here?" Muncie asks.

My stomach aches with stress. "Hard to keep secrets in the age of social media."

"I'll set something up so you can get in to be seen without any fuss," Dr. Carey says.

"Thanks, Doc."

When he finishes tending to John, I consult with him about our schedule for the day, give him my phone number so he can let me know where we have to be and when. "We really appreciate your help."

"Least I can do for him. My neighbor's son and his family were on the cruise ship."

"I'm so sorry for their losses."

"Worst thing I ever lived through. What the captain did... What they all did, means so much to so many. We'll take care of him."

"Thank you."

"I'll call you shortly."

After he leaves, I return to John's side, eager to help in any way that I can.

"What was he saying?"

"His neighbor lost family in the attack on the ship."

"Oh. Wow."

"What do you need?"

"A shower. I'm covered in blood."

"Do you need help?"

"Nah, I'm good."

"You might be lightheaded," Muncie says. "You lost a lot of blood."

"I said I'm fine. I'll be ready when it's time to go."

"You want something to eat?" I ask.

He shakes his head as he hauls himself up, leaning heavily on the table. "Just some coffee."

I hold my breath as I watch him get his bearings and walk toward the bedroom. I don't exhale until the door closes behind him with a loud slam.

I want to chase after him, to be there for him, to help if he needs it, but he made it clear he doesn't want my help or Muncie's.

Muncie glances at the closed bedroom door. "He called me from the gym. He couldn't get himself up. I think he's embarrassed more than anything."

"He has no reason to be."

"Try telling him that. I'm going to run and grab a shower. I'll be back ten minutes before we have to be downstairs." His gaze drops to the floor, where my heels from yesterday are sprawled on the carpet next to the wineglass.

I feel my face flush with embarrassment. "I'll see you then."

After he leaves, I debate whether I should stay or go. I want to be sure John is okay in the shower, but I don't want to invade his privacy.

To hell with it, I decide, opening the bedroom door and walking over to the closed bathroom door. I don't hear the shower running yet, so I knock. "You need anything before I leave?"

"No, I'm fine. Thanks."

I want him to need me. I want him to invite me in and ask me to shower with him. I don't want to leave him, especially knowing he has to be upset about what happened. But I refuse to force myself on him. "Okay, I'll be back with coffee before it's time to go."

He doesn't reply.

I force myself to retreat, to grab my shoes and purse and go back to my own room, even when everything in me wants to stay with him.

John

So fucking stupid. That's what I am. I had no business jogging on the treadmill, but my night with Jules had me feeling powerful and strong again, which I now know was an illusion. I'm not strong. I'm weak and addled, and the body I'd built into a finely honed machine continues to let me down.

My head is killing me, and I'm dizzy from the blood loss. Not a good state of being for an amputee adjusting to a prosthetic and already dealing with balance issues.

Because I absolutely cannot fall again, I hold on to the rail in the shower while washing up and shaving with one hand. Somehow I manage not to slice my face open, which is small comfort. I've lost enough blood for one day. The water in the basin is tinged with red, and I wince when the shower hits the wounded spot. Thank God it's on the back of my head so I don't have to go on TV with bandages on my face.

I stand under the hot water for a long time, letting it soothe the aches and pains from the night of pleasure and the fall that brought me, literally, back to earth, reminding me I'm still a long way from fine.

I hate the way Jules looked at me with compassion and sympathy. I don't want those things from her or anyone. I'm sick of people's compassion. I just want to go back to normal, whatever that is these days.

Hearing there're people camped outside my hotel, hoping for the chance to see me, sort of freaks me out. Losing my anonymity on top of everything else is yet another thing I have to adjust to in this new life.

My thoughts wander to last night, the best night I've had in years. Jules... Poppy, she's amazing, and thinking about her has me hard and aching for more of her. I feel a little stab of guilt about what we did last night. Regardless of everything that's happened, I still feel loyal to Ava, and sleeping with someone else was a big deal for me.

Not that I regret it, because I don't. How could I when Jules is so great? I care about her. I honestly do. Is it the same thing I felt for Ava? No, it's not, but that doesn't mean it couldn't be at some point. I shouldn't get ahead of myself where she's concerned. This situation is far more complicated for her than it will ever be for me. I half expect her to balk in the bright light of day when she's stone-cold sober and realizes how big of a step we took last night.

I get out of the shower and lean against the vanity as I towel off, alarmed by how weak I feel. Ugh, this is the last freaking thing I needed right now. It's the last thing any of us needed with a tight schedule packed full of obligations. I had a concussion once in high school when I was playing football and collided head on with a defender. This doesn't feel quite as bad as that did, which is a relief.

I go into the bedroom, gather my uniform pants off the floor where they landed last night, and get a clean shirt out of the closet. I need to ask Muncie if we can send yesterday's out to be cleaned. He'll know how to make that happen. I bend to pick up the shirt off the floor, and the room tilts like a carnival ride. Stumbling, I land on the bed, where I take a few minutes to breathe through the dizziness.

Fuck!

I'm so pissed with myself. This is a self-inflicted setback, and it's going to complicate an already complicated day.

I struggle my way into clothes, lying back on the bed to zip my pants and fasten my belt. I'm sweating and nauseated by the time I get socks and shoes on. Maybe this does feel as bad as the concussion I had in high school.

The main door to the suite opens and then clicks closed. Either Muncie or Jules has returned.

A soft knock sounds on the bedroom door. "John?"

Jules. "Come in."

She opens the door and gives me a quick visual inspection that I instantly resent.

"I'm fine. No need to worry."

She walks over to hand me a coffee.

"Thank you."

"Are you pissed with me?"

I immediately feel like shit for giving her reason to ask that. "I'm pissed with myself."

She sits next to me on the bed. "How come?"

"I shouldn't have attempted jogging. Clearly, I'm not ready for it."

"Why did you? Attempt it, that is?"

"I want to be strong again. Like I used to be. I want you to see me that way, not like this."

"John." She puts her hand on my face and gives a gentle tug, asking me to look at her.

"What?"

"You want to know what I see when I look at you?"

"Not really." When pushed into a corner, I revert to being the bitchy asshole I was when she first met me. Having her around has softened my rough edges, but that's left me defenseless where she's concerned.

"I'm going to tell you anyway." With her hand flat against my cheek, she caresses my face with the subtle stroke of her thumb. "I see the strongest person I've ever met. I see a man who gave up everything in service to his country. I see a man who helped to get justice for thousands of people and everyone who loved them. When I look at you, I see a fierce warrior, a strong, sexy hero. And that is *all* I see."

I'm overwhelmed by her kind words. "I like how I look to you."

"I like how you look to me, too," she says with a suggestive brow waggle that makes me smile.

I lean my forehead against hers, wallowing in the support she offers so willingly.

"This is just a setback. I'm sure there'll be others, but you'll get back to where you were in time. I know you will. Please don't accelerate anything on my account. If you thought for one second that last night was anything less than perfect for me, you're not giving yourself enough credit."

I curl my hand around her wrist. "It was perfect for me, too."

"I wish we didn't have anywhere to be."

"You have no idea how much I wish that."

"I think I have a small idea." She offers a reassuring smile. "The sooner we get through it, the sooner we can come back here and relax. I'd love to take a soak in that magnificent tub of yours."

"My tub is your tub."

"Could I ask one thing of you?"

"Whatever you want."

"If you need anything today, even if you need someone to lean on when you don't feel strong enough on your own, lean on me. I'm right here for whatever you need whenever you need it."

"Yeah." My voice is gruff as my emotions hover painfully close to the surface. At some point in recent days, she's become my touchstone and my rock. There's no one else I'd rather lean on than her. "I can do that."

CHAPTER 22

Ava

I wake up feeling hungover, even though I haven't had alcohol in days. The events of yesterday flood my mind, reminding me that Eric is gone, perhaps for good, and I'm alone. Again.

Well, not entirely alone. My sister is asleep next to me, in the spot where my husband should be. She bombed her way into my space last night, refusing to take no for an answer when she insisted on staying with me.

Rob, who came with her, apologized for her pushiness.

"It's fine," I told him, because what else could I say? I wanted to ask him how Eric is, but I already know he's as shitty as I am.

So here we are, day two after Armageddon, camped out with our siblings who're married to each other. What was once such a fun coincidence now feels like another thing that needs to be mourned in the aftermath of disaster.

I have no idea what I'm supposed to do with myself today. There's nothing scheduled because I'm supposed to be on my honeymoon for the next two weeks. I could let Miles and my immediate supervisor, Trevor, know I'm back early and up for working if they need me. But if I tell them that, they'll want to know why we came home early, and I'm not at all prepared to answer those questions.

So I don't reach out.

There's only one person I want, and he doesn't want me. Not anymore. His refusal to see me last night shocked me, although it probably shouldn't have. He's been steadfast in his love for me, even on the emotional roller coaster I've had us on since we met. He's never once wavered. Realizing that he'd hit his limit was like being slapped in the face by reality. How much nonsense can any guy tolerate from the woman he loves before he says enough?

Apparently, sexy dreams about my ex were Eric's limit, which is hardly fair in light of the fact I can't exactly control what I dream about. But stacked on top of everything else I've subjected him to where John is concerned, it's no wonder he's had it with me and my never-ending drama.

Hell, I've had it with me and my never-ending drama. I'm sick to death of it all. I'm sick to death of John and the nightmare of his deployment. So I can hardly blame Eric for feeling the way he does.

"Oh, you're awake."

I glance at my sister. "Yep."

"How're you feeling?"

"Never better."

"Ava."

"What do you want me to say? I feel like shit. I'm supposed to be on my honeymoon, and I'm in bed with my sister. Not how I expected this day to go."

"What can I do for you?"

"Arrange a lobotomy for me?"

"Other than that."

"I have no idea."

"I'm sorry you're going through this."

"So am I." I glance at her. "Thank you for coming over last night, but I'm sure you and Rob had plans today. You don't need to babysit me. I'll be okay."

"I'm sure whatever plans Rob had for today are canceled, since his brother needs him."

"He can't cancel plans during a campaign for Congress."

"He'd do it for Eric. You know how tight the four of them are. Amy and Jules are back in town, too. They'll probably come over."

"Don't you have to work today?"

"I called out sick."

"You don't need to do that, Camille. Seriously. It's not necessary."

"I want to help you guys, and so does Rob."

"There's nothing you or anyone can do. Eric won't even talk to me."

"That was last night. I'm sure he's changed his mind by now."

"I'm not so sure."

She twists her mouth the way she does when she's thinking about whether or not she should say something.

"Whatever it is, just say it."

"It's big," she says softly.

"Bigger than my new husband leaving me?"

"Yeah." She bites her lip and looks up at the ceiling while I try not to scream at her to just fucking say it. "Eric thinks you married him only because of what Brittany did to him."

I hear what she says, and it registers, but the notion is so shocking, so incendiary, that I can't fully process it. "How do you know that?" I somehow manage to ask her in a voice that's barely a whisper.

"I heard him say it to Rob last night. Rob tried to tell him that was ridiculous, but Eric is convinced if he hadn't had that happen to him before he met you that you would've called off the wedding after you saw John in San Diego."

I have no idea what to do with this information. *How* can he possibly think that? I never, for one second, considered calling off our wedding.

"I wasn't sure if I should say anything. I don't want to make it worse."

"How can it get any worse? He left me, won't talk to me and thinks I married him only because I felt I had no choice." Where do we even go from here? I have no idea, and I need professional assistance. I can't unravel this mess on my own. I reach for my phone and text Jessica.

I need you. Badly.

She writes back a minute later. *What time works for you?*

ASAP.

Come at noon. I'll be there.

It's ten now. Two hours. I can handle two hours. *See you then.*

"I'm seeing Jessica at noon," I tell Camille.

"Oh, good. That's really good."

I'm not sure even the formidable force of nature known as Jessica can help me fix this situation that feels so broken.

I get up to shower, and when I emerge from my bedroom, Camille has made coffee and breakfast. I hope the eggs she used are still good. I can't recall when I bought them.

The coffee burns my tongue and throat. I barely feel it. I hate this. I hate being back in the place I fought so hard to get free of when I left San Diego to start a whole new life in New York. I hate feeling the same way I did when I learned John was alive but hurt and then heard nothing from him for weeks. I hate feeling the way I did after I saw him for the first time in nearly six years and had to tell him we were through, that I had someone else and was going to marry him. I hate feeling the way I did when he cried and begged me not to go.

I hate that after all the work I put into my relationship with Eric and the plans we made for our future, I'm once again standing in the ashes and wondering how I got here. With zero interest in food, I push the eggs around on my plate and manage to eat a half piece of toast smothered in grape jelly.

I appreciate that Camille remembers I loved toast with jelly when we were kids and slathered the jelly on the toast for me, hoping I'd eat something.

"I know you're upset and worried, but you don't need to be."

"Can't help it. Rob and I care about you guys. It hurts us to see you hurting."

At some point, my annoyingly perfect little sister grew into a woman I'm proud to call a friend. "It means a lot to me that you came last night and that you stayed. But I have to figure this out on my own."

"I get it." She sips from her coffee mug. "I just hope you know you can talk to me about it. I'd never repeat anything you say about Eric to Rob. I promise. If you need me, I'm here."

"I'll let you know, okay?"

She nods. "If I don't hear from you, I'll worry."

"I'll check in later."

Before she leaves, she does the dishes and wipes down the kitchen. Then she comes over to hug me. "Hang in there."

"Trying."

When she leaves, the sound of the door closing echoes through the vast space. I loved this place the first time I ever saw it, with its high ceilings and industrial touches. Now it feels like somewhere I shouldn't be. This is his place, not mine, and he shouldn't have had to leave it. Later, when I check in with Camille, I'll ask her to tell him he can come back. I'll get a hotel or an Airbnb apartment or something to hold me over until I figure out what's next.

I haven't even finished unpacking the boxes from moving in, and I'm already thinking about moving out. Didn't see that coming.

I'm half out of my mind by the time an Uber delivers me to Jessica's office on Third Avenue. Usually, the smells coming from the street-level deli make my mouth water. Today, they only add to the nausea.

Once upon a time, Jessica Trudeau put me back together. I'm hoping she can work her magic once again. She buzzes me in, and I take the stairs to the third floor, where she's waiting for me. Her curly blonde hair is up in a clip, but her trademark animal-print cat-eye glasses bring me immediate comfort.

I break down at the sight of her.

She hugs me for a long time while I cry it out.

"Sorry," I mutter many minutes later.

She hands me the tissues she always has at the ready. "No need to apologize. That's what I'm here for." After sitting in the chair across from me, she leans in, puts her hand on top of mine. "What's going on?"

"Eric left me."

Her mouth falls open in shock that she does nothing to hide.

Normally, I love that she keeps it real. Today, her reaction only ratchets up my anxiety. If she's shocked, this must be really bad.

"*What?*"

"As soon as we got back from the trip, he packed a bag and went to Rob and Camille's. When I went over there last night, hoping to talk to him, he wouldn't see me."

"That doesn't sound like the Eric I know."

"I guess I finally pushed him too far."

"By having dreams you have no control over?"

I shrug, feeling helpless and defeated. "Camille told me she overheard him telling Rob that the only reason I married him is because of what his ex, Brittany, did to him."

Jessica shakes her head as if she doesn't understand. "How so?"

"Well, you remember how she left him in the worst possible way, right? Apparently, he thinks that because he went through that before he met me, I never would've ended it with him even if that's what I wanted. But that isn't what I want." I start to cry again. "I want *him*. I married him."

Jessica sits back in her chair, clearly trying to process this. I know how she feels. It's a lot for me, and it's my life we're talking about. For a long time, she says nothing, which isn't like her. I'm about to ask what she's thinking when she leans forward.

"Is it possible?"

"Is what possible?"

"That you went through with the wedding because you couldn't bear to hurt Eric the way Brittany did?"

"No, it's not possible! I never once thought of calling off the wedding."

"Maybe not consciously, but after you saw John, it never occurred to you that you could get back everything you'd lost with him now that he was back and telling you that nothing had changed for him?"

"No." I refuse to so much as entertain these possibilities. "That's not what happened."

"No one would blame you, Ava," she says gently. "You loved John with your whole heart and soul. At no time did either of you consciously decide to end your relationship. Neither of you ever wanted it to end. It's only natural that once you saw him again, you might rethink the plans you made in his absence."

"That's not what happened. I'm married to Eric. I love him."

"I know you do, Ava, but—"

"No buts. I want Eric, and I've tried to tell him that. How am I supposed to save our marriage if he won't even talk to me?"

Jessica takes another long pause to think. "Eric has been a trouper through all this, wouldn't you agree? He's rolled with things that other men would've found to be too much. He went with you to San Diego so you could see your long-lost love. He supported you every step of the way through an unimaginable situation. His devotion to you never wavered."

"I agree with all that. So what's your point?"

"Would it be okay if I spoke to him alone?"

"Of course. I'd do anything necessary to resolve this. I want him to know…"

"What do you want him to know?"

"That I love him." Tears spill down my cheeks. I mop them up with the new tissue she hands me. "That I want him and the life we have planned."

"You're going to have to sell that to him, Ava."

"I thought I already had."

"He's not convinced." She seems to choose her words carefully. "I think you'd agree that your relationship with Eric came somewhat easily to you once you gave yourself permission to be with him. He was agreeable, understanding and supportive of the situation you were in with John's whereabouts being unknown. Right?"

"He was very good to me through it all. I'd never say otherwise."

"Would you agree that he was good to you at his own expense at times?"

"How do you mean?"

"Roll with me here… Imagine you're Eric in this situation. You've been through the dreadful ordeal with Brittany and come out on the other side a changed man. You're jaded and bitter about what she did and not at all interested in other women. Until you meet an amazing woman at your brother's wedding, and suddenly, everything is better. You're looking forward rather than dwelling on the past, and life is good again. There's only one small problem—she's still pining for a guy who's been gone for years, who may or may not be alive. We know he's most likely off on a valiant mission on behalf of the country, hunting down a terrorist. I mean, you can't even hate the guy.

"So, that guy is gone. Eric is here, with her, and he's falling hard for her and she seems to be falling just as hard. He proposes, she accepts, they begin to plan a wedding, and everyone is happy. And then, all hell breaks loose when the special forces guys get the terrorist. That changes everything. Suddenly, she's on pins and needles wondering what became of the man she loves—present tense, not past—and when there's no word on him, she's obviously in agony over what became of him. Still, Eric stands by her, offering support and love and compassion. Then the terrorists release a video that shows her guy was right in the middle of it, he was wounded, perhaps killed, but no one knows for sure, and she's going mad waiting to find out what happened to him.

"Still, Eric stands by her, holds her when she cries, uses his connections to get the info she needs and finds out that her guy is alive, badly wounded, but alive. And when she hears nothing from the guy and begins to think he's probably forgotten about her, Eric helps her over that hurdle and remains steadfast in his devotion to her, even when it turns out the guy hasn't forgotten her and would very much like to see her."

I listen to Jess's recitation of events with a growing sense of dread. Look at what I put him through. No wonder he's done. Anyone else would've been gone a long time ago. But not Eric. He stayed, and how do I thank him for that? By having vivid dreams about John while we're on our honeymoon.

"Do you understand where I'm going with this?"

"Yeah, I do, and I don't blame him for calling it quits. He was a fool to stay with me as long as he did."

"That's not my point, Ava. My point is that Eric did most of the heavy lifting in your relationship, and now it's your turn. If you mean it when you say you had no doubts about marrying him and never once considered calling off your wedding, you're going to have to *sell* that to him. *You're* going to have to do the heavy lifting."

"I'm willing to do whatever it takes to make it work with him, but I can't do anything if he won't talk to me."

"I'll take care of that."

CHAPTER 23

Eric

I get a text from Jessica that says we need to talk and that it's urgent. I don't want to talk to her or anyone. I'm holed up in Rob and Camille's guest room, trying to get some work done. I'm supposed to be on my honeymoon, so I wasn't expected at the office today, but I fired up my laptop because I need to keep busy while I try not to lose my mind. I've also got shit to do for Rob's campaign, which I'm supposed to start managing as of the Tuesday after Labor Day.

But my focus is nonexistent.

I'm such a fool. That's the bottom line. I didn't learn anything from what happened with Brittany, not that I would ever compare Ava to her. What I didn't learn was to set limits for how much of myself I'm willing to give to someone else. Once again, I went all in, and once again, I got burned. I should've bailed on Ava when she first told me about John. That would've been the smart thing to do after hearing she had unfinished business w ith him.

Sure, he'd been gone more than five years at that point, but as far as she knew, he was still alive. I should've known he'd return in a blaze of glory that would make him the most celebrated man on earth, and that he'd want Ava back. Of course he would. Anyone would want her.

So I blame myself for the mess we find ourselves in. I never should've gotten so caught up in the magic of falling in love with Ava that I became blind to the massive obstacles standing between us and our happy ending.

Namely, one Captain John West. Why not say his name? He's the third person in our marriage, after all, so he deserves to be called out and given top billing right along with Ava and me.

The phone rings with a call from Jessica. I take it only because I figure she's not going to give up until she talks to me. What does it matter? It won't change anything as far as I'm concerned.

"Hi, Jess."

"Oh, Eric, I'm glad I reached you. I was wondering if you might have time to come in later today."

"By myself?"

"Yes." That's the only scenario I'd consider right now. "Is that allowed?" She's Ava's therapist, first and foremost.

"It's all set." In other words, Ava gave Jess permission to talk to me. Whatever. "When could you come?"

She's a crisis counselor and doesn't take a lot of regular appointments so she can be available when her clients need her. I guess Ava and I are the crisis du jour.

"An hour?"

"That works. Do you have the address?"

"Yes."

"See you then." She ends the call before I can change my mind.

I instantly regret agreeing to see her, because that means I have to shower and get dressed and leave the sanctuary I've found in my brother's guest room. By the time I go through the motions of showering, I'm exhausted. But I told Jess I'd be there, so I text Rob to let him know I'm leaving for a bit and head out into a warm, sunny late afternoon in New York City.

Some people flee the city in the summer, but that's my favorite time of year here. I love to take long walks and eat outside and have drinks on rooftop decks.

Sure, it gets hot and smelly, but the pluses outweigh the minuses for me. Today, everything looks different to me after yet another relationship has blown up in my face. I couldn't care less about summer or roof decks or cocktails. I don't give a shit about work or Rob's campaign or anything else. What does any of it matter?

I grab a cab and direct the driver to Third Avenue. I use my phone to look up the actual address and give it to him. Then I sit back and watch the city go by without seeing much of anything. My brain keeps wandering back to that morning in Spain when Ava told me about her dreams.

I know she can't help what she dreams about, but hearing that she was dreaming about *him*, that she was dreaming about having *sex* with him… That broke something in me, and I'm not sure it can be put back together. I'm not sure I want to put it back together.

We pull up to the street-level deli, and I hand the driver a twenty. The smells coming from the deli remind me that I haven't eaten anything all day. Maybe I'll stop there after I see Jess. She buzzes me in and waits for me outside her office.

"Thanks for coming."

My normal response would be to say "no problem" or "happy to" or some other such thing that would be a lie. It was a problem to come, and I'm not at all happy to be there.

"I saw Ava earlier."

I figured as much, so I have nothing to say to that.

"She's upset that you won't talk to her."

"I'm upset that she's dreaming about her ex. At least we're both upset."

"I have to be honest with you. I expected this to happen after San Diego."

I'm confused. "Expected what to happen?"

"For you to say enough. I expected you to call off the wedding."

"That's funny, because I expected her to."

"Did you, really?"

"Yes, I really did. She was a zombie after she saw him. The first week, she barely had anything to say to me, and then she seemed to rally leading up to the wedding. But the whole time, I was waiting for her to say, 'I can't do this.' I wouldn't have been surprised."

"I think she'd be surprised to hear you say that."

"Really?" I'm well aware of the bitter edge to my voice, but how am I supposed to feel? "My friends told me not to marry her."

"Did they?"

I nod, recalling the boys' night out that Rob organized for me before the wedding. "My brother got a bunch of our friends together. I didn't want a traditional bachelor party or a weekend in Vegas or anything like that. In hindsight, that was probably because I was afraid to leave Ava for even a few days at that time."

"Because you were afraid she'd change her mind?"

"Among other things. She was fragile. You saw her after San Diego. You know what I mean."

"Yes, I do. So what happened with your friends?"

It pains me to think about this and how stupid I was not to listen to them. "I hadn't seen them in a while, and none of them had met Ava. I confided to them that Ava had been with John before the deployment, that no one knew that and how important it was to keep it quiet. When they heard the whole story, my friend Rory said, 'Dude, you're seriously going to marry this girl?' He could see disaster looming, but I refused to go there. The others weren't quite as blunt as Rory was, but they didn't disagree with him."

"What did Rob say about it?"

"Not much. He was in a weird spot, being married to Ava's sister. It wasn't like he could encourage me to call off the wedding to his sister-in-law without causing trouble in his own marriage. But with hindsight, it was clear that he had reservations, too. Everyone who knew the situation probably did."

"I didn't."

I'm taken aback by the forceful way she says the two little words.

"If I'd thought Ava was making a mistake by marrying you, I would've said so. I'm not sure if you've noticed, but I don't beat around the bush with my clients. If I see them about to do something that's going to make whatever brought them to me in the first place worse, I jump in front of that. I saw no need to do that in this case. Before your wedding, Ava never gave any indication that she was having second thoughts about marrying you. She never once said, 'Jessica, what should I do?' She spoke only of how amazing you were, how supportive and understanding. She said she wasn't sure how she would've gotten through the trauma of John's reentry into her life without you. Earlier today, she sat right where you are now and told me that all she wants is to be married to you."

I listen to what she's saying, and the words register with me, but I still feel... I don't know... removed from it all, as if I'm watching this happen to someone else. One of the things Ava and I have both liked about Jessica is her no-nonsense approach. It's helped us through more than one crisis, and it matters to me that she saw nothing to be concerned about before the wedding, despite having a front-row seat to the entire drama.

"What I know for sure," Jessica continues, "is that you can't save your marriage if you don't talk to your wife."

"I'm not sure I want to save my marriage." There. I said it. It's out there and can't ever be taken back, not that I want to take it back. It's the truth.

"I have to confess... I'm truly stunned to hear you say that. Do you honestly think Ava wants any of this to be happening?"

"I'm quite sure she doesn't want it. Who would? But something just kind of snapped for me in Spain, and now... I don't know. I just don't know."

"Here's what I know. A few weeks ago, you married the woman you told me you love more than life. You married her knowing full well about her past and how traumatic it was for her. You married her knowing that while she'd made considerable strides in putting that traumatic past behind her, she was certainly not finished with the process. You knew exactly who and what you were getting. So how is it fair for you to now decide that maybe that wasn't what you wanted after all?"

The question infuriates me. "You want to talk about what's *fair*? Is it fair to me that there will *always* be another man in my marriage, in my wife's heart, in our lives? Is that *fair* to me?"

"Eric, you knew this before you married her. You knew he was part of the package."

"I didn't know he was going to be in our bed with us! I had no idea that was going to happen!"

"Neither did she."

"Look, I get that you're on Ava's side here—"

She holds up a hand to stop me. "*Whoa.* I'm not on anyone's side. I want both of you to get what you want, and right up until yesterday, that was each other, or at least I thought that's what you wanted."

"It was."

"And now?"

"I don't know." Filled with despair, I look down at the floor. I can't believe I'm back in this fucked-up place again. "I just don't know if I can do this."

I can feel the disappointment coming from her even though she doesn't say anything for a full minute.

"I told my friends about you."

Raising my head, I meet her gaze. "What?"

"No names or specifics, of course. I just mentioned that I had this couple come through my practice and that the woman was dealing with some heavy stuff, and her partner was nothing short of amazing in the way he supported and cared for her through it all. I told them I was inspired by you both, but by you in particular."

"Now I *really* feel like an asshole."

"You're not an asshole, Eric. You're the furthest thing from that. But if you check out of this marriage, I think you're going to wake up one day and realize you've made the biggest mistake of your life. Ava *loves* you. She truly loves you. She wants to be married to you and have the life you two planned to spend together."

"I need some time."

"Okay."

"Just okay?"

"What else should I say? You need time? Take the time, but don't take too long. I'd hate to see you have regrets down the road."

I get up to leave.

"Eric? When you're ready, let me know. I'd like to have you in together."

Nodding, I walk through the door and down the stairs to the street level. The smell of the deli invades my senses and turns my stomach. The thought of food revolts me. I head home on foot, keeping my head down as I cross over midtown on my way back to Tribeca. I see nothing but the dirty sidewalk as I cover miles while rethinking the things Jessica said as well as what I said to her.

I should call my wife, but I have no desire to talk to her, which is the first time I can say that since I met her more than a year ago. The weekend her sister married my brother was the best time I'd had since the disaster with Brittany, and that was largely due to Ava. We were matched up as the best man and maid of honor, and I liked her from the first minute we met. I think about her getting drunk at the reception and how I "saved her life" with my miracle pizza cure. We spent the night together in her room after the wedding, but nothing happened. Not that night, anyway.

I fall in love fast. That's my modus operandi. It's happened three times now. The first one burned out when we went to separate colleges more than five hundred miles apart. The second one became an epic disaster when Brittany exited my life without so much as a word to me. The third one…

I don't know how or if that one will end. I just don't know.

CHAPTER 24

Julianne

After the appearance on *Kelly and Ryan*, we spend an hour at a clinic where John receives three staples in the head wound that he says "hurt like a motherfucker."

The thought of staples to the head makes me queasy, so I encourage him to keep the details to himself before we have a second patient on our hands. I suck with medical stuff. I can't believe I didn't faint earlier when I saw the blood pouring out of his head.

Muncie surprises the hell out of us when he tells us in the car on the way back to the hotel that Amy is taking him sightseeing this afternoon.

"I've never been to New York City before, and she offered." He shrugs, looking adorable and flustered. "Do you guys want to come?"

"I don't," I tell him. "I've got work to catch up on, and I'm going to run home to do some laundry."

"I'm going to take some Advil and hope my head stops pounding."

"Maybe I should stick around," Muncie says. "In case you need anything."

"Nope, you're off duty," John says. "That's an order."

"Are you *sure*?"

"Positive. I'm going to chill for the rest of the day."

"I'll be back after a while and can check in."

"Go have fun." I'd love to see something transpire between him and Amy, that sneaky devil. She never mentioned anything about this to me. I text her.

I hear you're taking Muncie out on a date??

It's not a date. He's never been here before. I thought he might like to see a few things.

Is that all it is?!?

Yep. How are you? Saw J on Fallon. He slayed it.

He really did, and on Today and Kelly & Ryan, too.

Everyone is talking about him at work. People are obsessed with him.

My phone rings nonstop. I need three days to wade through all the messages, texts and emails I've gotten in the last twenty-four hours.

You've got your hands full, that's for sure.

If only she knew... *What's up with Eric?*

Rob said he wouldn't talk to Ava last night when she went over there. It's bad... I guess they both saw Jessica today. Separately, though. Waiting to hear how that went.

That news makes my stomach hurt. *Keep me posted?*

I will.

Have fun with Muncie. I include heart emojis and get back the middle finger, which makes me laugh.

"Holy shit," John says when we pull up to the hotel, which is surrounded by people and press. Hundreds, maybe thousands of people. The NYPD is there, working to establish a perimeter, but the situation is a long way from under control.

"We need security." There's no way I'm chancing John's safety by subjecting him to crazy crowds.

Muncie looks as freaked out as I feel. "I'll see what the Navy can provide."

"We need people who know this city and how things work here. I'll ask my office to arrange for something."

I fire off a text to Marcie telling her we need security for John. *The hotel is surrounded with people. Need help 911.*

She responds quickly. *I'm on it. Will get someone there asap.*

Hurry.

"How are we going to get him in?" I ask Muncie, my nerves stretched to the limit at the thought of people coming at him and possibly knocking him over.

The driver speaks up. "We can take him around the block to the service entrance. I've got a buddy that works here. I know where it is."

Muncie puts down his window, just enough to call over one of the bellmen who's helping the cops try to control the chaos. "We're going around to the service entrance. Have someone let us in."

"Will do."

The driver hits the gas and gets us out of there, rounding the corner with squealing tires. "We got lucky that the intersection was clear. You hardly ever see that around here."

John is tense as he stares out the window. The poor guy is probably shocked by that crowd. I know I am. I can only imagine how he must feel.

"We've got top-notch security people my boss, Marcie, is contacting." I wish I could touch him, but I won't do that with Muncie in the car. It's bad enough he knows what happened last night. Oh Christ. He won't tell Amy, will he? *Oh my God…* I'm almost thirty years old and right back in junior high. How is this my life?

You know exactly how…

I want to tell my own brain to shut the hell up. How am I going to get a minute with Muncie before he leaves? I won't, so I text him. He's sitting next to me, so there's no chance of John, who is across from us, seeing the text.

Um, this is hella awkward, but please… Don't tell Amy. Anything. Please? I'm breathless waiting for his reply.

I would never. None of my business.

Thank you.

I'm worried about him.

I'll keep an eye on him.

"Are you two talking about me?" John asks.

"Nope," Muncie and I say together, which basically confirms that we were, in fact, talking about him.

"I'm fine. I swear."

"We believe you." I send him a warm smile. I'm dying to wrap my arms around him, to let him know that everything is okay, that *he* is okay, that he did great today, that I'm proud of him, that I'll do whatever it takes to protect him. If we can just get him inside...

The service door opens, and the same bellman Muncie talked to out front, a man named Brad, is there to greet us. We go through the routine of getting the crutches, handing them to John and walking slowly behind him as he makes his way inside. He's moving slower than he did yesterday, which leads me to wonder if his head was the only part of him injured in the fall.

Muncie sees it, too, and sends me a concerned look.

"Welcome back, Captain West. I apologize for the situation out front."

"Not your fault."

"We'll get it handled, sir. And if I might add, you were great on *Fallon* last night."

"Thank you. Glad you thought so."

"*Everyone* thought so. The entire staff has been talking about it today." He leads us to the service elevator and escorts us to the top floor, where he checks to make sure no one is lying in wait to pounce, before he signals for us to exit the elevator. "All clear."

Leaning on his crutches, John offers his hand. "Thank you, Brad."

"A pleasure, sir. Thank you for your service."

My heart swells with pride every time someone thanks him. Everyone should thank him. The whole damned world owes him a debt of gratitude for capturing that scum-sucking piece of shit Al Khad. We stop at Muncie's door.

"Home by midnight and use protection," John says.

I snort with laughter and then cough to try to cover it up, knowing Muncie won't appreciate it.

Muncie's face turns bright red. "Fuck off. Sir."

John loses it laughing, and the sight of him in hysterics is so overwhelming, so amazing, that neither Muncie nor I can look away. We've never seen him laugh like that, and it's quite a revelation to both of us. Slowly but surely, we're starting to meet the man he was before his life was changed forever, and God help me, I like that man. I like him so much.

When he recovers himself, John says, "Seriously. Have a good time. Enjoy the break. You've earned it."

"Thank you. I'll see you both in the morning. Call me if you need anything."

"I won't need anything."

Muncie goes into his room. The door clicking shut behind him echoes through the hallway like a gunshot.

John flinches and then seems to catch himself.

I'm not sure if I should ask if he's okay, so I don't. I sense he wouldn't want me to.

"If I could hold your hand, I'd grab it and lead you straight into my room."

His words, spoken in a gruff tone, are the hottest thing anyone has ever said to me.

"Would you let me?"

"Yes." My voice is barely a whisper. I'd follow him anywhere. As that realization settles in on me, I experience a moment of clarity in the chaos of everything that's happened in the last few days. My life is changing, possibly forever. I'm allowing that to happen by allowing *this*, with him, to happen, and my eyes are wide open to the potential price I'll pay for taking what I want. He draws the keycard from his pocket, swipes it over the door and gestures for me to go in ahead of him.

I honestly planned to go home to my place this afternoon. I planned to do laundry and catch up on work and actually read the hundreds of emails and texts I've received. I was going to listen to my voicemails and start a list of offers for John to consider once the initial tour is complete. But instead, I drop my purse and reach for him at the same second his crutches fall to the marble floor with a loud crash.

The kiss is incendiary. His hands are inside my suit coat, pulling at my blouse and on my bare skin before I can catch up to what's happening.

His head. He's injured. We shouldn't. I turn to break the kiss. "John, your head."

He presses his hard cock against me.

"Not that one!" I sputter, laughing.

"I'm fine. Shut up and kiss me."

"You have a concussion. You're supposed to take it easy."

"Poppy," he whispers, his lips soft against my neck and his cock hard against my belly. "It's a *mild* concussion. *Please?*"

I shiver and cave like a house of cards caught in a stiff breeze. "Only if you let me do all the work."

"Whatever you want."

Once again, we tear at each other's clothes like lunatics. I've never had sex like this. It's always been slow and sweet and civilized. This is none of those things. It's wild and untamed, the craving desire I feel for him turning me into a version of myself I've never met before. He's equally uncivilized, and the sound of fabric tearing only makes me crazier than I already am.

We fall on the bed in a tangle of limbs, and I almost forget about the concussion that's not holding him back in any way.

"John," I gasp between the most passionate kisses of my life, "your head."

"Is fine. Kiss me." With his hand on the back of my head, he pulls me into another kiss that's all tongues and teeth and flat-out insanity.

I keep thinking that this can't be real, that this sort of thing doesn't happen to actual people. It's something you see in movies or read about in books. It can't be happening to me. But it's real, and it's happening, and it's *divine.* His hands are everywhere, his mouth ravenous. We come together like two comets on a collision course as he pumps into me deep, fast and rough.

I come hard, crying out from the shocking pleasure that zips through me, and I'm on the way back up before I begin to recover from the first one.

His teeth clamp down on my nipple as his fingers dig into the flesh of my ass. We're both sweating as he hammers into me, his big cock stretching me to my absolute limit, but I'm right there with him, lost in this moment that's changing me forever. Even as I'm swept away in a riptide that takes me far away from everything I've ever known, I have the presence of mind to know there'll be no recovering from this man. If this doesn't work out, I'll never get over it. I'll never get over him.

"Poppy," he whispers, straining against me and holding me so tightly I can barely breathe, "come with me."

Nothing has ever felt so good or so right or so perfect.

As we come down from the highest of highs, I hear my work phone ring with the tone I assigned to Marcie. "I have to get that."

He holds me tighter, his muscles trembling. "Don't go yet."

"It's my boss."

"Tell her you were tending to your client."

That makes me laugh. Marcie will be furious if I don't take her call, but I can't bring myself to care when I'm lying in John's arms, still breathing hard from the best sex I've ever had.

"I'm sorry I was rough with you," he says after a long silence.

"In case you couldn't tell, I loved it. But you were supposed to let me do all the work."

"You can do the work next time." His eyes are closed, and his face is free of the tension that's so much a part of him.

I caress his cheek, wanting to bring him every bit of comfort and peace that I possibly can. "Does your head hurt?"

"Like a bastard."

"Let me up. I'll get you some ice and pain pills."

"You don't have to."

"I want to."

He opens his eyes, looking at me with eyes the bluest blue I've ever seen, as well as the vulnerability he tries so hard to keep hidden. "I don't want to seem weak to you."

I can't help but laugh at that. "In light of recent events, you have absolutely no need to worry about that."

"It was good for you?"

"You can't seriously be asking me that."

"I'm seriously asking you."

"It was… life changing." I kiss his lips, both cheeks and his forehead. "*You* are life changing."

"And that's a good thing?"

"I think it might be." I'm in so deep with him, deeper than I've ever been. I should be terrified, but I'm oddly calm. At almost thirty years old, I've been around long enough to know that something like this is rare and special, and I intend to treat it as such. "Let me up."

He releases me, and after a quick trip to the bathroom, I go into the other room to get ice from the freezer and the pain pills they gave him at the clinic. I bring them back with a glass of water. He's right where I left him, facedown in bed, his muscular back on full display, along with the red scratches I left on his back. Those scratches fill me with satisfaction even as my body continues to quake with aftershocks. I want to lick him, bite him, scratch him. I've never had those thoughts about any man.

But this isn't just any man. I'm a little bit afraid of how powerful my feelings for him have become. It's like being on a freight train with failing brakes that's headed down a big hill. Even knowing I'm heading for an epic crash can't stop me from jumping on that train and hoping for the best.

"Ready for some ice?"

He grunts in response and takes the pills I hand him, washing them down with a gulp of water.

After stashing the glass on the bedside table, I put the makeshift ice pack on the back of his head and hold it in place while using my free hand to caress his back.

"Feels good."

Long moments pass in silence as I hold the ice in place and continue to massage his back. He's completely relaxed when my phone rings again.

"Ugh, if I ignore that again, I won't have a job."

He reaches up to take over with the ice pack. "Go ahead."

I run for my purse, which was dropped inside the door. I take the call right before it goes to voicemail. "Marcie. Hey."

"What the hell, Julianne? Why didn't you answer when I called before?"

"Did you call? It didn't ring." I wince at the lie. I'm the world's worst liar. I absolutely suck at it, which is why I try to never do it. "What's up?"

"I wanted you to know that security is on the way. They'll be working the main entrance of the hotel to help provide additional coverage there as well as the top floor where Captain West is staying."

I realize with a sinking feeling that the presence of security could put a damper on our extracurricular activities. "Okay."

"I gave them your number in case they have any questions. If they call, answer the phone, Julianne."

I wince at her tone. "I will."

"Also, you need to do something about the inquiries you're getting regarding the captain. Everyone who is anyone is reaching out, and when they can't get you, they're calling here."

"I'll take care of it."

"Are you sure you don't need additional support from the office?"

I've never been more certain about anything. "Positive."

"One more thing… Victor Carlin wants him on his show."

"No." I hate Carlin and his whole shock-jock persona. There's no way I'm subjecting John to that guy.

"I'm not asking, Julianne. I owe him a favor. I told him I'd make it happen."

"You shouldn't have told him that without consulting with us first."

The dead air that follows has my stomach twisting with nerves. I've never spoken to her that way before, and there's no question that she doesn't appreciate it.

"Make it happen."

The line goes dead. No freaking way is he going on that show. I don't care what Marcie promised him.

"Everything okay?" John asks when I return to the bedroom after having a conversation with my boss while completely naked.

"Victor Carlin wants you on his show."

"That'd be *awesome*. I loved to listen to him before the deployment. I got satellite radio just so I could get his show. I'd love to meet him."

I cringe and wrinkle my nose. "I knew there had to be something about you that I didn't like."

He laughs. "You didn't like *me* when we first met."

"That was *so* three weeks ago."

His smile makes my heart happy because I know he hasn't had much to smile about in a long time. "Your boss wants me to do Carlin. I want to do Carlin. Sounds like you're overruled, Poppy."

And when he calls me that… I die. I'm dead.

"I'll set it up, but don't blame me for whatever happens."

"I never would. I'd be rocking and drooling in a corner without you to run interference for me." He reaches for me and draws me back into bed with him, the ice bag abandoned to the floor.

When he nuzzles my neck, I'm reduced to the consistency of Silly Putty. He could ask me for anything, and I'd give it to him. "You're so sexy, Poppy. Your skin is like silk, and you smell so good. I want to stay in this bed with you for the rest of my life."

Every defense I might've had crumbles to dust. His words and the gentle, reverent movement of his hands ruin me. *Yes, I want to say. Let's stay in this bed for the rest of our lives. Let's never leave this suite. Let's be this way forever.*

If the last time was wild and untamed, this time is tender and sweet. It's even more devastating, though, because of the way he looks at me as we make love. As he gazes deep into my eyes, I can't get enough. I want him deeper. I want him so far inside me, he can't ever leave. I want him in ways I never imagined possible, and when I think about how I might've married Andy and missed this, I feel ridiculously relieved.

Thank God I didn't marry Andy or anyone else before I met John.

The relief is so overwhelming, it brings tears to my eyes.

"Am I hurting you?" he asks.

I shake my head.

"What's wrong?"

"Absolutely nothing."

He doesn't understand, and with him moving inside me, I lack the brain cells to form a coherent sentence. I'll tell him later, after. What's happening right now requires my full, undivided attention even as my work phone rings again.

My personal cell chimes with texts. I. Don't. Care. I, who am normally chained to my phones, my iPad, my email, my social media, couldn't care less about any of it.

The lovemaking may be tender and sweet, but the finish is explosive. We cling to each other like lifeboats in a stormy sea, which is my last conscious thought before I sink into deep sleep.

CHAPTER 25

John

I know I'm no longer in Afghanistan. I know Ava is gone and I'm in New York, in bed with Julianne. I know those things, even in sleep, but I'm flashing back to before the deployment, to the day the ship was bombed, when I woke up with Ava and thought about how I had only four months to go before I'd be free to resume the life I put on hold when I agreed to the five-year assignment to one of the military's most elite teams.

It was an honor to be asked, the thrill of a lifetime to train with those incredible men, to stand ready to deploy at a moment's notice, should the need arise. But after meeting Ava almost two years earlier, I wanted other things. I wanted a wife and a family and a real home. I wanted a life that couldn't be ripped from me without warning.

I was four months away from having it all.

I was watching *SportsCenter* on ESPN when the broadcasters interrupted their show with the news about the attack on the *Star of the High Seas*. I switched immediately to CNN and watched the coverage in stunned silence for two minutes before the phone rang.

I knew in my gut it was the call I hoped to never receive. I took the call and heard the one word that confirmed my life as I knew it was over.

"Go."

Without replying, I put down the phone.

"Who was that?" Ava's face is pale and stricken from watching the horror unfold on TV.

They were estimating at least four thousand people were on the ship, all of them likely dead.

I should've told her. I should've told her at the beginning and given her the choice. And now it was too late. I put my hands on her shoulders, drank in the details of her sweet face and tried to commit her to memory in the seconds we had left. "I'm sorry, Ava."

"For what?" She sounded frantic, as if she was tuning in to the fact that whatever was happening, it was big.

"For having to leave you." I kissed her, hugged her, told her I loved her, and then I grabbed my go bag from the front hall closet. Then I was gone, leaving her and everything else I owned behind. I wept all the way to the base, knowing it'd be a very long time before I'd see her again. I wasn't sure, in those first minutes, how I'd survive without her or how I'd stand not knowing if she was okay in my absence. I had that fifteen-minute ride to mourn the loss of life as we knew it and to prepare for the mission ahead.

I hated myself for doing that to her. I hated myself almost as much as I loved her. I hated that I was too weak to leave her when I knew I should have. I hated that she'd be left alone with no support, no information, no nothing. I took a big gamble, and I lost. The one I loved most would be hurt terribly when she figured out I wasn't coming back. That was unbearable to me.

For a second, only a second, I thought about declining the mission. My career would be over, but I'd get to keep Ava. In the end, I couldn't do it. As much as I loved her, I couldn't let down the men who were like brothers to me.

I arrived at the base, and the mission took precedence. The rest of my dream was on fast-forward—the long, uncomfortable flight, years on the trail of Al Khad, nights in caves, blazing-hot days, freezing-cold nights, crap food, loneliness, fear, fury, agony, grief and never-ending love for Ava. The near miss at the four-and-a-half-year mark, the raid on the compound, the deaths of Tito and Jonesy before we were even inside the building, being shot in the leg, the certainty that I was bleeding to death, pleading with the medics not to take my leg, waking from the coma, my leg gone, my body ravaged, finding Ava, seeing her, hearing she had someone else and was planning to marry him.

It's a dream-slash-nightmare that plays on repeat, over and over and over again like some sort of unfunny version of *Groundhog Day*. I've had it before, and like then, I struggle to break free, to wake up, to escape the images that haunt me. This time, though, there's a light that hasn't been there before. It's far off in the distance, beckoning me to walk toward it. If I can only get there, I might have a chance. But my leg hurts, my body is tired, my head is pounding, and the light is still so far away.

I wake up sobbing, sweating, shaking.

Jules is there, soothing me, wiping away my tears, talking to me in that calm, competent tone I latch on to like a lifeline. She draws me into her arms, and even though I don't want her comfort, I can't bring myself to reject it. She is softness and safety and sweetness. She is the light waiting for me on the other side of the nightmare.

I hold on to her, taking her strength and making it my own.

If you ask me later, I won't be able to tell you how long we stay that way. It's a long time before I'm calm enough to apologize to her.

"Don't."

I start to pull back from her. "I shouldn't..."

"Shhh. Stop. Everything is fine." She holds on tighter, so tight I can't escape, not that I want to.

With no choice but to stay put, I sag into her embrace, close my eyes. My face is pressed against her breasts, but this isn't about sex.

It's about something so much bigger.

Julianne

I'm undone by whatever happened with John. I was asleep when he began thrashing next to me, and when I saw that he was crying...

God, my heart. It just exploded with compassion for him, realizing he was having some sort of flashback. I want to know more. Does that happen a lot? Does he need treatment?

He's sleeping peacefully now, hours later, but I'm wide awake, wired, worried about him and a tiny bit concerned for myself as I fall deeper into this thing with him, knowing full well there'll be no way out once I hit bottom.

I don't care. Not now, anyway. I will when it's over, but for now… I'm like fierce, fearless Jules, who has no fucks to give for anything that isn't him and whatever he needs when he needs it.

I get out of bed and put on the T-shirt he wore under his uniform earlier. It smells like him, and I love how he smells. I've never been the girlfriend who wanted to wear her guy's clothes, but maybe I am now. In the entryway to the suite, I find my purse and grab the bag I carry with me at all times and take it into the bathroom, where I floss, brush my teeth and put in my retainer. And yes, I still wear my retainer because the orthodontist told me I have to if I don't want crooked teeth again.

With my oral hygiene seen to, I settle on the sofa with a bottle of water, my personal phone, my work phone, John's phone and my iPad. I go through the hundreds of texts, emails and voicemail messages we've received in the last few days.

I go through my work phone first, make a to-do list that'll take me a full day to get through, answer emails from colleagues and producers looking to book John, even if it's later on. They'll take him whenever they can get him. That list is long and includes everyone who is anyone not included in the original tour.

On his phone, I find calls from several of the biggest sneaker and apparel companies, a New York publisher interested in his memoir, a frozen-custard company that wants him to be their new pitch person and an agent from one of the top talent agencies on the West Coast, asking for a meeting when we're there next week.

I simply can't fathom the breadth and depth of what's coming his way. The custard thing is a no-go, but the rest of it has me intrigued. I'm glad to know he'll be able to do whatever he wants after he retires from the Navy and will have the means to live like a king. He deserves nothing less.

I'm about to power off his phone when it chimes with a text from Ava.

My heart stops when I read the words she's sent.

Hey. Are you awake?

I stare at the screen for the longest time, not sure what to say or do or think. Why is she texting him in the middle of the night? Where's Eric? I haven't clicked on the text, so she can't see that it's been read, but it may as well be lit up in neon in Times Square for the effect it has on me.

This is what it must be like to be struck by lightning, to be going along, minding your own business and then be hit with a bolt from the sky that makes every part of you feel like it's on fire.

When I have no choice but to blink, I power down the phone and stash it back in my purse. I have to tell him she texted, don't I?

I sit in the dark, reeling and trying to figure out what to do.

Does she want him back? Is that why she's texting him at three in the morning? And if she does, what will he do?

Fierce, fearless Jules isn't feeling quite as fierce or fearless after seeing that text.

CHAPTER 26

Julianne

I wake in the morning to his hand sliding from my thigh to my hip, under the shirt of his that I still have on, to cup my breast as his hard cock makes itself at home between my ass cheeks. I'm wallowing in the sensual glow of his touch when I remember the text from Ava.

"What's wrong?" he asks from behind me.

"Nothing."

"Then why did you just get all tense on me?"

"I didn't." My voice is high and squeaky, the way it gets when I lie. If any member of my family was here right now, they'd call me on it. Although, in light of who I'm in bed with, I'm deeply thankful that no member of my family is here.

"You sound funny, too."

Before I have a second to prepare, he's moved me onto my back and pushed the hair back from my face. And dear God in heaven, the man is hot in the morning with the dark whiskers on his jaw and the fierce glow of those beautiful eyes gazing down at me with care and concern.

I swallow hard. I can't lie to him, and not telling him would count as a lie. I clear my throat and lick my lips.

"What is that in your mouth?" He moves my lip and busts up laughing. "Are you wearing a *retainer*?"

"Yes! What's the big deal?"

"How old are you, Poppy?"

I offer him my best mulish expression. "None of your business."

"You are out of high school, right? Don't tell me I've been breaking the law here. That won't be good for my reputation."

"Very funny. If you must know, I'll be thirty next month."

"And still wearing your retainer." Those eyes I love so much dance with glee as he totally makes fun of me, and I don't even care. "Such a good girl." He kisses his way down my body and has me spread out before I can tell him he can't have that if he's going to make fun of me.

Who am I kidding? He can have whatever he wants, and what he wants at the moment is to lick and suck and finger me to a screaming orgasm. Before I can process that, he's on top of me, inside me, and taking me back up on the most thrilling ride of my life. I'm coming down from my second orgasm in ten minutes when I remember Ava's text.

I have to tell him.

I die at the thought of telling him, especially when he's still inside me, throbbing and filling me the way no one else ever has or ever could.

"Sweet Poppy," he whispers against my neck. "You're so damned perfect. Thank you for being there for me last night. I'm sorry I was such a mess."

I touch him everywhere I can reach, hair, shoulders, back and ass. "Please don't be sorry. You never have to be sorry with me."

"You have to take that thing out of your mouth. You sound like Elmer Fudd."

Exasperated and amused, I pop out the retainer and put it on the bedside table, trying not to think about the possible germs it might be coming into contact with. This is the Presidential Suite at the Four Seasons. There're no germs here, right? "Happy?"

"Yeah, I am," he says, smiling. "Incredibly happy when I expected to be the exact opposite during this media tour from hell."

He's happy. He's smiling. He's at peace.

And so am I.

I can't tell him about that text now. I just can't.

*

Today, we have an appearance on *CBS This Morning*, where I get to meet Oprah's best friend, the amazing Gayle King! I die when she asks if I want to take a selfie together. After that, we're at *The View*, where the ladies go wild over John, and I beat back the ugly green beast that wants to beat up all of them for daring to flirt with him.

He's mine, the beast cries out, even if that's so not true. They love him, and I should be thrilled, but I'm pissed for reasons that make no sense, even to me.

I receive a text from one of my high school friends, who's going through a hideous divorce. In our group chat, she says, *If you're single, ladies, stay that way. Men suck. They're all horrible. Every single one of them.*

Mine isn't. I'm smug as I watch him banter with Whoopi, Joy, Sunny and Meghan. He makes me so proud with the way he presents himself in the interviews. He is calm, cool, confident and composed. No one would ever know that he was sobbing in my arms less than twelve hours ago. No one will *ever* know that.

On the way back to the hotel, Muncie tells us that Amy is taking him to Chelsea Piers and asks if we want to go.

John gives me a look that melts my panties. "My head is hurting."

Apparently, he's not talking about the head at the top of his body.

"I'd love to, but I have to work," I tell Muncie. "You guys will have fun. The Piers are great." Earlier, he told me they visited the 9/11 memorial yesterday, which he found haunting and incredibly moving.

Today, I resolve, I *will* go home. I will do laundry and pick up more clothes. And by two o'clock, as if I had nothing else planned, we're back in John's bed acting as if the world will end unless we have all the sex.

I've never been happier in my life.

However, the secret I'm keeping from him nags at me like a fingernail over an open wound. It's wrong that I haven't told him, and now, too much time has gone by. If I bring it up, he's going to want to know why I didn't tell him sooner. I won't have a good answer for that. I can't very well say I kept it from him because I don't want him to talk to her or go back to her or do anything but what he's doing right now.

"You with me, Poppy?" he asks gruffly.

You'd never know the man lost a leg a few months ago or spent a month in a coma or gave himself a concussion yesterday. His stamina is admirable, as is his mastery of me. I've never come so much in my life as I do with him.

"I'm most definitely with you."

He likes that answer.

I throw myself into showing him how much I want him, how much I love this, how much I love… him. Oh God, that wasn't supposed to happen, but how could it not?

Afterward, we sleep like the dead and wake much later.

He runs his fingers through my hair. "I want to take you somewhere."

"Where?"

"I don't know. This is your city. Where should we go? I want some of that New York pizza you raved about."

I can't take him anywhere near Tribeca, where I live close to my brothers. I think of Roma's on the Upper East Side, which is one of my favorites. "I know just the place, but you can't go out looking like… well, like you."

"We'll get the security guys to take us. It'll be fine."

I'm such a girl, because the idea of going out on an actual date with him has me giddy. "Do you think we can swing by my place while we're out so I can get some more clothes?"

"Fine by me. I'd love to see where you live."

It's a risk. My place is right between Eric's and Rob's, but what're the chances I'll run into them? Slim to none. We don't show up at each other's homes without texting to make sure it won't be a wasted trip, and besides, they know I'm not there.

We shower together and get ready for a night out.

The security detail that Marcie hired is efficient and discreet. If they think it's odd that I spent the afternoon in John's suite, they would never say so. Besides, we told them we had work to do, and because I have zero fucks to give, I don't care if they know we spent the afternoon fucking like rabbits.

They get us out of the hotel and into a silver SUV. I don't see any sign of the reporters who were staking out the hotel, which is a relief.

John is wearing jeans, a wrinkled light blue dress shirt with the sleeves rolled up, aviators and a San Diego Padres ball cap. He looks nothing at all like the polished naval officer who's been on TV the last few days. Since we're getting door-to-door service, he decided to leave the crutches at the hotel.

That makes me nervous, but I'd never say so.

He holds my hand in the car, and I want to pinch myself. This is *happening*. My phone chimes with a text that I glance at, my stomach free-falling at the words from Rob to me and Amy.

This is bad, you guys. Eric won't talk to her, he won't talk to me. He's being really weird. I'm afraid they're done, and Camille is worried, too. I don't know what to do.

No. I want to scream. *No, no, no.* They are *not* done. They *can't* be done. I can't picture either of them without the other, for one thing, but if she's single again… John would drop me in a hot second for her. I have absolutely no illusions about that.

No. I just can't go there, or I'll lose my mind.

We scoot into Roma's and secure a table by one of the windows that looks out over Third Avenue. We order beer, pizza and salad, and while we wait, he regales me with funny stories about guys he's served with and things that happened on deployments, including the time he had to rescue one of his guys who was "held hostage" in a whorehouse in the Philippines.

I'm laughing so hard at his recitation of events that I have tears in my eyes. "How did you know he was being held hostage?"

"They sent a ransom note."

"No way."

"I swear! This actually happened. I had exactly four hours to get him back before the ship was due to leave without both of us. If we weren't on that ship when it pulled out of port, we could've kissed both our careers goodbye."

We devour the salad and a large fresh mozzarella pizza.

"You were right," he says over a mouthful of pizza. "It doesn't need anything on it."

"Duh, I told you."

He winks, and I melt. I am a puddle of love and desire and desperation, because I know this can't possibly last. We're living on borrowed time. As soon as the tour ends, he'll go back to his life in San Diego, and I'll return to mine in New York. Sure, I'll help him out with the offers he's receiving and continue to manage him from afar, but it won't be like this.

"Why do you suddenly look so sad, Pop?"

The nickname within the nickname kills me. "I'm not."

"You suck at lying."

"I know! Everyone can tell. Why is that?"

"Because your voice gets high like this," he says, imitating me. "And your eyes go wide, and your lips, they do this pucker thing."

I'm astounded. "I said two words. How'd you get all that?"

Shrugging, he says, "I pay attention."

Yes, he does, and that's one of the many reasons I've fallen flat on my face in love with him.

"So why are you sad?"

"I was just thinking about what'll happen when the tour is over." I may as well be truthful since he can see right through any lies I might tell him.

"I'm hoping I can convince you to move to San Diego and run my life."

I stare at him, my mouth hanging open like a fish that's been pulled from the water and left to flop on land.

With his finger to my chin, he closes my mouth, which is full of pizza. God, I'm sexy, but he only laughs. "Have I shocked the living shit out of my Poppy?"

His Poppy. I am his. If only he knew how totally I'm his. I take a sip of my beer, hoping the liquid will push the pizza past the lump in my throat. "Maybe a little."

He takes a sip of beer. "Do you think I'm going to want this to end when the tour is over?"

"I, um, I don't know."

"I don't want this to be over, Jules."

I reach down deep inside and find the courage to do what must be done. "I have to tell you something."

CHAPTER 27

John

Ava texted me. Ava texted me last night. Jules said she saw it when she checked my phone before we left the hotel.

Okay, so Ava texted me. It's no big deal. Or is it? I try not to be distracted by this news, but I can't help it. I am.

"Could I see my phone?"

Jules hands it over.

I turn it on and go right to my texts. "Do you care if I respond?"

"Of course not."

"You really are an awful liar, Pop." I caress her face and lean in to kiss her. "It doesn't mean anything. She's married, remember?"

Her brows furrow. "They're having issues."

"Still?"

"Ah, yeah. I guess it's pretty bad."

Is that why she reached out to me? I have no idea how I'm supposed to feel about any of this. A couple of weeks ago, I'd be dancing in the street at this news—or as much as a guy with one good leg can dance in the street. The thought of having another chance with Ava would've been cause for celebration.

Now? I look at Jules, pushing pizza crust around on her plate, shoulders slouched into a defeated pose, and I can't do this to her. I put the phone in my pocket. "How about some dessert?"

"Aren't you going to text her back?"

"Nah."

"Why not?"

"Because I'm on a date with you, and it would be rude to text my ex when I'm with you."

"It's okay if you want to."

I take her hand and link our fingers. "I don't want to. I'd much rather tell you about how I busted that wayward petty officer out of a Filipino whorehouse."

She forces a smile, but the easy rapport we had earlier was lost the minute Ava joined the party.

I pay the check, and when we're ready to go, we scoot out the door and into the SUV. I thank the beefy security dudes who made it possible for me to take Jules out to dinner without it turning into a circus. They deliver us back to the hotel with a minimum of fuss.

When we get up to the top floor, I realize we never went by Jules's place. I totally forgot about it. "We forgot to stop at your place."

"It's no problem. I'll grab a cab and go get what I need."

"I'm sorry."

"Don't be. I'll see you later?"

I don't want her to go. "Text me when you're back?"

"Sure."

She ducks inside her room, and when the door clicks shut, I experience a moment of panic. Have I screwed this up somehow? How? I didn't do anything. I received a text from the woman who still has possession of most of my stuff. Jules knows Ava and I agreed to stay in touch, to try to be friends, to try to be something to each other now that we aren't together anymore.

That's all this is. I'm sure of it. Except for the part about her texting me in the middle of the night less than a month after she got married.

To Jules's brother.

Complicated.

Inside my suite, I grab a beer from the fridge, pop it open and take a seat on the sofa, exhausted from the walk into the hotel and down the long hallway to my room. I raise my bottle in a toast to a successful, crutch-free outing. I'll take the progress where I can find it.

I reach for my phone and open the message app. The message from Ava is almost lost in the sea of texts from unknown numbers. Thank God Jules is handling all that.

I reread Ava's text. *Hey. Are you awake?*

Sorry, I tell her. *Just saw this. What's up?*

I can see that she's responding, so I wait, and I hate that I'm breathless with anticipation. Try to see this from my point of view. I yearned for this woman for six long years only to find out it was too late for us by the time I was finally able to contact her. Of course I want to hear what she has to say, even if I know I still can't have her. And if I could?

I can't go there.

The phone chimes when her reply arrives. *Nothing. I was just awake and figured I'd take a chance that you were too. Saw you on Fallon. You were great.*

Thanks. Not sure how I feel about all the attention.

Enjoy it. You deserve every bit of it.

Are you okay, Ava?

I'm not sure exactly. Eric and I are having some issues.

Sorry to hear that.

Why is she telling me this? What does she want me to do about it? Is she telling me because she wants me to know for some reason other than the fact that we decided to stay friends?

It'll be fine. Just some growing pains. Anyway, I wanted to see how you were doing with all the media stuff. I hope Jules has worked out well for you.

I nearly choke on a sip of beer. Jules has worked out very well for me, in more ways than one. But I can't tell Ava that.

She's great. Thank you. She saved my life.

Again, in more ways than one. Why do I feel guilty talking to Ava about Jules? They're sisters-in-law and friends. Ava is my past. Jules is my present and maybe my future. I like her a lot. I like how I feel when she's around. She's like a balm on the open wound I carry on my soul, and I've begun to depend on her in ways I never expected to depend on anyone again.

It's not just the sex, as great as that is. It's *her*.

She's the best, Ava replies. *Glad it's working out.*

Would she be glad to know how well it's working out between me and Jules? I have no idea what Ava would think of that, and I hope it's not something we have to contend with for a very long time. Although, I meant what I said to Jules last night when I asked her to move to San Diego to run my life. And even though it's still new, I'm hoping she'll want to continue our personal relationship as well as the professional one.

It's weird to me that Ava is texting me and I'm thinking about Jules. The conversation with Ava has left me feeling confused and unsettled. Why did she text me in the middle of the night? What was she hoping for? That I would tell her to come to me, since I'm in New York and so is she?

I'm so out of practice with being able to read her or this situation. Other than the guys in my unit, I haven't had much contact with people in years. I haven't had to deal with expectations or anything other than the mission, so I'm way out of my league with trying to get a handle on what's happening with Ava or how it affects me.

And then I remind myself that whatever is happening with her doesn't affect me. It's none of my business. She is married to *him*, even if they're having issues. That reminder is like a hard, cold dose of badly needed reality. No matter what she was hoping to achieve by texting me, it's irrelevant to me. It has to be irrelevant to me. That's the way she wanted it, and it would do me good to remember that.

I finish my beer and get up to grab another one. I watch a full hour of *SportsCenter*, even though I don't care about teams I completely lost track of while I was gone. I watch two episodes of *Seinfeld*, which is as good as it ever was. The show is freaking timeless.

I decide to text Jules. *Are you back yet?*

On the way.

Want me to order some dessert?

Sure, that sounds good.

I'm excited to know I'll see her again soon. I want to latch on to that feeling and ride the wave for as long as I possibly can. *What do you feel like?*

Surprise me. I'll eat anything.

Will do.

I drag myself up again and go to find the room service menu. The cut on the back of my head is hurting, but otherwise, I feel much better today than I did yesterday after the fall on the treadmill. By tomorrow, I should be good to get back in the gym, although I'll need to be more careful going forward. The last freaking thing I need is any more injuries.

It takes me a minute to figure out the menu is on an iPad. I fumble my way through the process of calling it up. Technology leaves me feeling somewhat baffled, as if I've been dropped onto an alien planet where I don't speak the language. I'm sure I'll catch up eventually, but like everything else I'm dealing with, it's going to take time.

I order a bottle of champagne along with chocolate cake and cheesecake. I'm not sure which she'd prefer, and I look forward to finding out.

I look forward.

The words resonate with me. I'm actually *looking forward* to something, which is such a huge improvement over the awful low while I was mourning the loss of Ava and the life I hoped to come home to. Even something as small as finding out whether Jules prefers chocolate or cheesecake gives me reason to hope that I just might survive the losses I've sustained.

I'm looking forward to seeing her, talking to her, having dessert with her and hopefully spending another night with her. It's such a fucking *relief* to look forward to anything after the dreadful few months I've had. I venture outside to the terrace and look down at the world going by below. Tiny yellow taxis dart in and out of lanes and between other vehicles like they're driven by NASCAR drivers trying to win a big race.

I have no idea how long I'm out there when I hear the door to the suite open and close. I turn to see Jules coming toward me wearing a dress and heels. She looks so fucking fresh and pretty and nothing at all like Mary Poppins.

Her gaze collides with mine, and she smiles as she walks across the living room to the terrace.

I hold out my arms to her, and she comes to me like she belongs in my arms, tucked under my chin in a perfect fit. I'm overcome by the alluring scent that belongs only to her.

"You look beautiful."

"Thanks. I changed while I was home."

"I see that. Did you get dressed up for me?"

"Maybe a little."

I hold her closer, wanting her as close as I can get her. "Missed you while you were gone."

"I was only gone a couple of hours!"

"I missed you."

She looks up at me. "I missed you, too."

Holding her gaze, I kiss her, and only because I'm watching her so closely do I see a hint of something resembling apprehension cross her expressive face. "What's wrong?"

"Nothing."

"You suck at lying, remember?"

She sighs. "Why do I even try?"

"Exactly. What's on your mind, Poppy?"

"Did you talk to Ava?"

"We texted a little. She just wanted to tell me she saw me on TV."

"She texted you in the middle of the night to tell you that?"

"Yeah, I guess." I place my hands on her shoulders. "What do you really want to know, Jules?"

"Did she tell you things are weird between her and Eric?"

"She did. She said they're having growing pains."

"From what Rob tells me, it might be more than that." She's madly vulnerable telling me this, and all I want is to reassure her.

"I'm sorry to hear that."

"Are you?"

"Yeah, I really am. No one wants Ava to be happy more than I do. After what I put her through, she deserves the best of everything."

"What if…"

"Jules." She seems to force herself to look up at me. "Say what's on your mind."

After taking a deep breath, she releases it slowly. "What if she wants you back?"

"She doesn't."

"How do you know that?"

"She married your brother. He's the one she wants. I've had to make my peace with that."

"If she texted you right now and told you she changed her mind and she wants you after all, what would you do?"

"That's not going to happen."

"Humor me. What if it did?"

"I just don't know, Jules. I haven't considered that possibility. She's married to him. She's not going to suddenly change her mind."

Jules drops her hands from my chest and takes a step back, forcing me to release her. She crosses her arms. "I'm way out on a limb with you. I've risked everything—my relationship with my brother and sister-in-law, my job, my reputation. I've been telling myself that it's worth the risk because I've never felt this way about anyone. We've already established that I suck at lying, so I'm telling you the truth. I'm not sure I can do this if there's any chance that you'll go running back to her if you have the chance."

I step toward her to close the distance between us and put my arms around her again. "I'm not going anywhere, Poppy."

"The entire time I was home, I couldn't wait to get back to you. I couldn't wait to see you and talk to you and be with you. I'm almost thirty years old. I've been around the block a few times. I know what I can handle and what I can't. I can't be your rebound, John. I just can't do that to myself."

"I swear to God you're not my rebound. You're so much more than that. You're my light at the end of a very long, dark tunnel. You've become the voice in my head. Your opinion is the one I most want and need. Your calm, cool, steady presence is like a lifeboat in the whirlwind that my life has become. You are *not* a rebound, Julianne. I swear to you. You're so much more than that to me."

She sags into my embrace. "I realize it's way too soon for a conversation like this, but I hope you understand—"

"I do understand. These aren't normal circumstances."

"Hardly," she says with a little laugh.

I tip her chin up so I can see her gorgeous face. "You feel better?"

"I do. Thank you for listening."

"I'd never hurt you, Poppy."

"You wouldn't hurt me on purpose, but you need to know that you have the capability to hurt me badly."

"I won't. I swear I won't. I'd like to think I've learned my lesson about hurting people."

"It wasn't your fault with Ava."

"Yes, it really was. I owed her much better than what she got from me, and I'm determined to do better this time around."

"There's one more thing I want to say."

"You can say whatever you want to me. I'll always want to hear it."

"This is a very strange time for you. The offers are rolling in. You can do whatever you want after you retire from the Navy. I don't want you to feel obligated to me because of this conversation—"

I kiss her. "I don't feel obligated. If you'd asked me a couple of weeks ago if I could picture anything remotely like this happening to me again, I would've said no way. But then my Poppy showed up, rocking the sexiest legs I've ever seen, whipped my ass into shape and gave me a reason to keep going." I frame her face with my hands and kiss the lips I can't resist. "I'm thirty-seven. I've certainly been around the block a few times, and I know something special when I'm holding it in my arms. Whatever my plans turn out to be after the Navy, I want you to be part of them. I want you to help me decide what I should do, and I want you right there with me, if that's where you want to be."

"You're making me weak in the knees," she says with a cute smile.

I'm not sure where I get the courage, but I scoop her up into my arms.

"John! Put me down! Are you *crazy?*"

"Yes, I'm crazy about you, and I can't have your weak knees causing a fall."

"Put me down. Right now, before *you* fall."

I feel stronger than Superman as I walk us inside and take the first available seat, landing in an upholstered chair with her on my lap.

"You're officially insane. You have a concussion, and you shouldn't—"

I kiss the words right off her lips, even if I love being chastised by her. I love the way she melts into my arms as we kiss. I love being with her. I love her honesty and her forthright approach to life. I love that she still wears her retainer and that she's such a good girl. I love that she's gone way out on a limb to be with me.

"Poppy," I whisper against her lips. "I'm absolutely and completely falling for you. Please don't worry about anything, okay?"

Her lovely eyes sparkle with emotion. "I'm absolutely falling for you, too."

For the longest time, we only stare at each other. She seems as stunned as I feel. The moment is interrupted by a knock on the door.

"That'll be dessert."

"I'll get it." She gets up off my lap and crosses the room to let in the room service waiter.

As I watch her go, I feel like the luckiest guy in the world to have a woman like her care about me. I'm determined to keep the promises I just made to her, no matter what happens.

And when she exclaims over the chocolate cake I ordered, I have my answer about something else I wanted to know.

CHAPTER 28

Julianne

Everything is different after our conversation on the terrace. We took a major step forward tonight, and I feel more settled after he assured me that I'm the one he wants, that this isn't a rebound but the start of something much more significant. Hours later, we're in his bed, on our sides, facing each other after making love. To call it anything else wouldn't do justice to the most intimate encounter of my life.

"Tell me something no one else knows about you."

He runs his hand up and down my arm as he thinks about that. "I don't know my real name."

"John West isn't your name?" I'm shocked by his confession.

"Nope. I was left at a fire station in West Hollywood. That's where the West came from. I think one of the nurses at the hospital they took me to decided my first name would be John. I have no clue who my parents were or the circumstances of my birth or how I came to be at a West Hollywood fire station."

"I can't begin to know what it must feel like to have no idea where you came from."

"It's weird. For the first eighteen years of my life, I felt very disconnected from the world around me. I started getting into trouble, and then I encountered the judge who gave me a choice that changed my life. I always give him credit for saving my life. After I enlisted, I found the connection I'd been missing. I immediately loved it. I worked really hard, got my degree at night and on weekends, went through an officer program, became a SEAL. I loved everything about it until this last deployment. Now I just want to be done with it."

"Your story is so inspiring."

"I don't know about that."

"It is."

He continues to stroke my arm and back, as if he can't help but touch me. "I made a lot of mistakes along the way. What I did to Ava was the worst of them."

"You said you couldn't tell her anything, right?"

"I wasn't supposed to have a girlfriend. I didn't tell her what she needed to know, and I should have. I was tortured by what would become of her after I left. She was all I thought about the entire time I was gone. I was a selfish asshole where she was concerned, and I hate that I put her through such a hideous ordeal. I'll always feel bad about that."

"You didn't want to lose her. You'd never had anyone else to call your own." I understand him and their relationship better after what he shared.

"No, I hadn't, and I didn't handle it the way I should have."

"What would you do differently if you had it to do over?"

"As soon as I realized it was serious with her, which was basically almost as soon as I met her, I should've gone to my command and come clean, asked to be reassigned. I would've taken a big hit career-wise, but with hindsight, that's what I should've done."

He doesn't say it, but the implication is clear. If he'd done that, they'd be married today.

I swallow hard, trying to manage the lump in my throat. The only reason I'm here with him, the only reason I met him, was because of her and the pain she endured for years. The thought is humbling, to say the least.

My phone rings in the other room, startling me. Why is she calling me after midnight? "I gotta get that. It's Marcie."

"Is it okay for me to say that she's a pain in the ass?"

Laughing, I get out of bed. "It's more than okay. She's a total pain." I grab the phone right before the call would've gone to voicemail. "Hey. What's up?"

"I'd like to ask you the same thing."

Why does she sound pissed? "Not sure what you mean."

"Why does TMZ have a picture of you *kissing* your client?"

My stomach drops, and my heart nearly stops. "*What?*"

"Did you or did you not dine with him at Roma on the East Side and *kiss him* in plain view of the whole freaking world?"

"Uh, I've got to go."

"Julianne! Don't you dare hang up on me."

"I'll call you back." I end the call before she can reply. My hands are shaking as I call up the TMZ website, where the picture of us is at the top of the page. "Captain Hunky and the Governor's Daughter." *Oh God. Oh no.*

My personal phone starts ringing and chiming with texts.

"Jules? What's wrong?"

John's voice sounds like it's coming from a million miles away rather than the next room. I can barely hear him over the roar in my own ears. He comes out of the bedroom, gloriously naked, beautiful and concerned. "What's wrong?"

"Someone got a picture of us at the pizza place. It's on TMZ." I hand the phone to him.

"Fuck," he mutters as he sits next to me.

"Marcie is pissed. I have to call her back. I don't know what to say."

"Quit and come to work with me. I'm going to need you far beyond the next few weeks. Whatever you're making with them, I'll raise you twenty percent and pay for health benefits and anything you want."

I stare at him as my brain struggles to catch up with what he's saying. "I can't just *quit* my job."

He tips his head. "Why not?"

"Because! I'm in line to be a junior partner and…" And I can't quit the best job I've ever had for a man I've known for three weeks. I can't do that, because it would be *insane.*

"Poppy." He takes my hand and looks at me with those blue eyes that see me in a way I've never been seen before. "*Quit.* I swear to God, you won't regret it."

The Marcie ringtone jolts me out of the stupor he's put me into by being naked, gorgeous and so very convincing.

He takes the phone off my lap and hands it to me. "Do it."

This can't be happening. I'm someone I don't recognize anymore. It's one thing to have no fucks to give, but this new version of me is brave and daring and crazy. She's nothing like the Julianne I've known for thirty years. I have to say I kind of like this new version of myself. I press the green button.

Marcie starts screaming the second I take the call.

He never blinks as he stares at me. "Do it."

"Marcie."

"Do you have any idea what a mess you've made of this, Julianne? The partners are meeting in the morning, and I might not be able to protect you from the consequences of this."

"Do it," John whispers.

"Marcie, listen to me."

"What do you have to say for yourself?"

I swallow before I leap, never blinking as I hold his intense gaze. "I quit."

"*What? You are not quitting!*"

John takes the phone from me and powers it down.

The silence is deafening.

"Breathe. Jules. *Breathe.*"

My personal phone rings with yet another call and chimes with new texts. No need to wonder if my siblings, friends and colleagues have seen the TMZ report. I suck in a trembling deep breath. Holy shit. I just quit my job for a man I've known three weeks.

"Keep breathing." He gathers me into his embrace. "Everything is fine. You're going to be fine. *We're* going to be fine. We're a team now, you and me. We've got this."

I cling to him and his assurances while my personal phone continues to blow up.

CHAPTER 29

Ava

Jules and John. Got to admit, I didn't see that coming. I stare at the photos of them taken at Roma. At first I couldn't believe what I was seeing when Skylar texted me the link with a note that said she wasn't sure she should share this with me but figured I'd see it sooner rather than later.

One thing stands out to me in the photos. They both look really happy. I tell myself I'm glad they're happy. I'm glad *he's* happy. After everything that's happened, he deserves it.

At some point in the last few chaotic months, I forgave him for the ordeal he put me through. He did what he had to do, and as hard as it's been for me to understand that at times, I've found peace with it. I have no doubt he loved me as much as it's possible for a man to love a woman. He never would've hurt me the way he did if he'd had a choice in the matter.

I get a text from Camille, who was the first person I told about the TMZ report. *Eric is enraged. He, Rob and Amy have all tried to call her, but she's not picking up or replying to texts.*

I'm sure she will when she can.

How are you feeling about it?

Not sure how to feel. They both look happy tho.

I thought that too. I've never seen her smile like that. Are you ok?

Sure, I'm great. My ex is dating my sister-in-law, and my husband isn't talking to me. Never been better.

Ugh. You want me to come over?

Nah, I'm ok.

In other news, Amy went out with that Muncie guy again. They went to see Wicked.

Good for her. He seems like a nice guy. Going to bed. TTYT.

Hope you can get some rest. I'm here if you need me.

Thx. Xoxo

I turn off my phone because I've had enough of staring at it, hoping to hear something from my husband. I'm past the point of being shocked by what's happened, and I'm cruising straight toward anger. Why is he punishing me for something I have no control over? That's what I'd like to know.

I take one of the sleeping pills Jessica prescribed for me when I was first seeing her and fall into dreamless oblivion, waking late in the morning but feeling more rested than I have in days. I power up my phone to see what I've missed while I was asleep.

There's a text from Jessica to me and Eric. *I'd like to see you both today at 3 if that works for you.*

I can be there, I tell her.

Eric doesn't reply.

I spend an hour in the rabbit hole of speculation and gossip about John's romance with his publicist, the daughter of New York Governor Robert Tilden. Naturally, there's no comment from John, Julianne or the governor about the reports. I feel strangely hollow knowing that he's moved on, which makes me angry at myself. What did I think he was going to do? Mourn the loss of me forever?

I leave for Jessica's at two thirty with no idea if Eric is going to show or not, and when I get there, there's no sign of him.

"Have you heard from him at all?" Jessica asks when we're settled in our usual chairs.

"Not a word."

"I'm sorry." She seems as dejected as I feel. "I honestly thought he'd reach out to you after I saw him the other day."

"Well, he didn't."

"And of course you've seen the news about his sister and John."

"Yep. According to Camille, Eric is enraged over it."

"How do you feel about that?"

"I'm glad he's enraged about John and Jules, but he seems to have no feeling whatsoever about his own situation."

"You sound pissed."

"Do I? Could it be because my husband has left me over something I have no control over?"

"I can't say I blame you for being upset."

"You know what makes me the maddest in all this?"

"What's that?"

"I gave up any chance I had to resurrect my relationship with John because I had faith in Eric's love for me. I had faith in *us*. I believed in us and the future we planned together. And now he's checked out, and I'm finding that my faith was misplaced. He didn't deserve it."

"You're disappointed with him."

"Yes! Wouldn't you be?"

"Probably." She leans forward in that thoughtful way of hers that's become so familiar in the months I've been seeing her. "I have a question about something you just said."

"What?"

"You gave up any chance you had to resurrect your relationship with John. Does that mean you considered that possibility?"

"No, I didn't, because I was engaged to Eric. I made a commitment to him, and I kept it, which is more than he can say. He can't even show up to do the work necessary to put things back on track between us."

"I think he will. Eventually."

"Maybe I won't be here waiting for him by the time he gets his head out of his ass."

The words are no sooner out of my mouth than the door opens, and my husband comes in. He's winded, and there's sweat on his brow, as if he ran in the heat.

"So sorry I'm late. There was an accident on the FDR, and I had to jog the last half mile."

He sits in the chair next to mine. From a quick glance, I can see that he looks like shit. He has dark circles under his eyes and hasn't shaved in days, which isn't like him. I'm glad to know I'm not the only one who's been through hell.

"We're glad to see you, Eric." Jess hands him a bottle of water from the little fridge under her desk. "As you both know, I've met with each of you individually, and I honestly believe that what we're dealing with here is a bump. I believe it's something you can get past if you both want to. Ava has indicated to me repeatedly that she wants to. I'd like to know your thoughts, Eric."

He drinks half the bottle of water, screws the top on and bounces the bottle between his hands.

I want to scream at him to say something. I recall what Jessica said about how it might be my turn to do the heavy lifting in our relationship, so I stay silent and give him room to breathe and think.

A long moment passes before he speaks. "My thoughts are kind of all over the place."

What does that mean?

"How so?" Jessica asks.

"I can't make sense of anything that's happened."

"Because it doesn't make sense that you left me." The words pop out of my mouth before I have time to think about whether I should say them.

"It doesn't make sense to you, but it did to me."

"I'm glad one of us has a clue what the hell is going on here, because I don't."

"You don't?" He raises his brows, incredulous. "Really?"

"Yes, really! Do you honestly think I wanted to be dreaming about someone else when we were on our honeymoon?"

"I honestly don't know what to think when it comes to you and him, and that's the problem."

"How many times do I have to say the same thing? I am *married* to you, not him. Doesn't that count for anything?"

"Only if that's what you really want."

"Jessica, please. Can you help me here?"

"Ava has told you that's what she wants, Eric. What can she do to convince you it's true?"

"I don't know. But here's what I do know. I don't want to be married to someone who's in love with another guy. Even if she goes through all the motions, says and does all the right things, that's not the marriage I want. I want someone who wants me and only me, and if that's not you, Ava, then all you have to do is say so. I love you. I really do. In fact, I love you so much that if you look me in the eye and tell me that he's the one you really want, I'll step aside so you can be happy, and I promise you I'll be all right."

I blink back tears because I know what it had to cost him to say those words to me. "What if I look you in the eye and tell you that *you* are the one I love, the one I want, the one I want to be married to? Would that matter at all?"

"Only if you truly mean it, and not just because he seems to have moved on with my freaking sister, of all people."

"That makes you mad, does it?" I ask, even though I already know.

"Yes, it makes me mad! She could have any guy in the world. What the hell is she doing with *him*?"

"I don't know, but what has that got to do with us?"

He balks. "You have to ask? I'm not doing holidays and family gatherings with *him* there. No fucking way. If that's what she thinks is going to happen, she's *out of her mind*."

"I doubt she's thinking of family gatherings and holidays at the moment."

"She's not thinking *at all* if she's taken up with him."

"Can I say something?"

He shrugs, as if he doesn't care when he just told me he does. I can work with that. "He will always be in my life, whether he's with Jules or someone else. He's important to me, and I've committed to staying in touch with him and remaining his friend. He's lost so much. I refuse to be one more thing that he loses forever. I made that very clear to you before we got married. You knew my intention to remain in his life. That said, I do *not* want to get back together with him. The only person I want to get back together with is you. But I have to say, the way you've behaved the last few days has given me pause."

"Why? Because for once you weren't the one in control of our relationship?"

I've never seen this side of him, but I suppose I shouldn't be surprised it's in there after what Brittany did to him and after everything that's happened with me. "No, because I put all my faith in you, and you left. You walked away the first time things got really hard."

"This isn't the first time things got really hard for me, Ava. It's about the sixth or seventh time. It's been hard for me all along, in case you haven't noticed."

"You're right. It has. And I'd apologize for that except I told you about John and what I was dealing with."

"Yes, you told me about him, but you waited until I was in too deep to turn back before you shared with me the full details of exactly what you were dealing with. I thought I could handle it, and for a long time, I did. But what happened in Spain was too much for me, Ava. I'm sorry if that makes me a dick."

"It doesn't make you a dick. It was too much for me, too. What makes you a dick is turning your back on me rather than working with me to get through it."

"I'm sorry."

"Are you really, or are you just saying what you think I want to hear?"

"I'm truly sorry for leaving, for being a dick, for all of it. I just needed some time to think, and I couldn't do that when I was with you."

"You can't think when you're with me? What does that mean?"

"I have no perspective when you're near." He sighs helplessly. "All I want to do is hold you and kiss you and be with you. I can't look out for myself when I'm looking out for you."

"Eric... You have to believe me when I tell you I married the man I love."

"I'm trying to believe you."

"What else can Ava do to convince you?" Jessica asks.

"I'm not sure."

"Will you please come home and give me the opportunity to show you that I'm exactly where I want to be and married to the man I love?"

He looks at me, really looks at me for the first time since he arrived, and I see the exact moment when he decides. "Yes, I will."

"Excellent." Jessica smiles widely. "You've made fantastic progress today, but the work is just beginning. I want to see you back again next week to check in on where we are. And if anything comes up in the meantime, I want you to call me. Any time, day or night."

We make an appointment for next week and leave together, walking down the stairs and out into the bright sunlight, where the deli smells assail my senses.

He groans. "I'm freaking *starving*. You want to get something to eat?"

"Yeah, I really do." I'm so relieved to be back with him that I'd do anything he wants if it means we get to be together. And for the first time in days, I'm actually a little bit hungry.

We go into the deli and order sandwiches—turkey for him and chicken salad for me. They're massive, which makes us laugh.

"I didn't realize we were ordering a week's worth of lunches," he says when we're seated at the table with our huge sandwiches, a bag of chips to share, dill pickles and iced tea.

We both eat like we haven't eaten in days, which I hardly have. From the look of things, he hasn't either.

He comes up for air after devouring the first half of his sandwich. "The smell of this place drives me crazy every time I come here."

"Me, too." I'm glad we're here together, but the feeling of walking on eggshells, of the fragility of our situation, remains with me.

Our phones buzz with a text from Jules.

Hi everyone. I'm sorry you heard what you did online and not from me. I would very much like to see you all before I leave for LA so I can have the chance to talk to you about what's going on. I would also like Eric, Rob and Camille to meet John. Please come to the Four Seasons, Presidential Suite, at 8 tonight if you can. I know this is asking a lot of you, Eric and Ava, but it would mean so much to me if you could be there.

Eric scowls as he reads the text. "Can you even believe this? Does she honestly expect us to hang out with him?"

"I think maybe she does."

"Well, I'm not going."

"Why not?"

"You really have to ask?"

"Yeah, I guess I do."

"It doesn't bother you that she's with him?"

"Why would it?"

"He's your ex, Ava."

I can't help but laugh at the way he says that, which he doesn't appreciate. "Thank you for reminding me of that."

"How can you laugh about this?"

"Because I'm actually happy that he's found someone amazing like Jules. I want him to be happy again. Doesn't he deserve that after what he sacrificed for all of us?"

"Sure, he can have all the happiness he deserves. As long as it's not with my sister."

"Doesn't it matter to you if she's happy?"

"Of course it does, but why does she have to be happy with *him*?"

"You're being sort of ridiculous."

"So you honestly want to go to this thing tonight and see my sister with your ex? You don't think that's in any way weird or bizarre?"

"It's *life*, Eric. Everything about life is weird and bizarre. Look at what's happened to the two of us. Did we ever picture ourselves on the journey we've each been on? Do you think Jules flew to San Diego thinking, 'Gee, I hope I fall for this guy and make everything super awkward for myself and my brother'? Shit happens. Life happens. Jules is awesome. I don't think for one second she'd ever do anything to intentionally hurt either of us."

He sighs and slumps in his chair. "When did you get so Zen-like about everything?"

"Around the time my husband left me and gave me a couple of days to think about what it would be like to live without him."

"I didn't leave you."

Raising a brow, I eye him skeptically. "What would you call it, then?"

"I took a break to get my head together."

"You *left* me, Eric. I need to know that's not going to happen again."

"It won't."

"Did you really tell Rob that you think the only reason I married you is because of what Brittany did to you?"

He glances at me, startled. "Your sister has a big mouth."

"Is it true?"

"I don't want it to be true."

"It's not."

"Okay."

"That's it? Just 'okay'? That's kind of a big bomb to drop in the middle of a brand-new marriage."

"I'm sorry you heard about that. I didn't mean for that to happen."

"Do you really think we can make our marriage work with something like that standing in the middle of it? What else do you not want me to know?"

"Nothing. That was the only thing."

"I heard what you said back there, about loving me enough to let me go if that's what I really want. You should know that I love you that much, too. If you've changed your mind about me, or if it's all too much for you to handle, you only have to say so. It would break my heart to lose you and to lose us, but I don't want to keep you prisoner in a marriage you no longer want."

He covers my hand with his. "I'm not a prisoner, and I do want this. I lost my mind a little bit when you started having dreams about him. I know that wasn't your fault, just like it wasn't my fault that it took me over the edge."

"I wouldn't have liked it if you started dreaming about Brittany."

He grimaces dramatically. "*That* is never going to happen."

"Never say never." I laugh at the disgusted face he makes. "I didn't think I'd have dreams about John either, and funny enough, I haven't had one since I told you about them."

"Well, that's good news, I guess."

"If we're going to be in this together, we have to *stay* together. No matter what happens."

"I hear you, and I'm sorry I left. I was afraid of making it worse somehow by staying. I won't do that again. I promise."

"You want to go home?"

"Yeah, I really do."

We get the rest of our food wrapped to go and head out.

"It's so nice out. Let's walk." He reaches for my hand the way he always does, and that simple gesture goes a long way toward convincing me that we're going to be able to put things back together. We take off toward home, walking east to west, through the mob scene that's Times Square on the way to Tribeca. "You're really going to make me go to this thing with Jules tonight?"

"Yeah, I am."

He groans. "It's cruel and unusual punishment to make me meet this guy."

"You'll survive it. I'll be right there with you. And remember, it's not going to be the best day John ever had having to meet you."

"I suppose that's true. Before we go, maybe we can talk about how we're going to resume our honeymoon, already in progress."

"We can do more than talk about that if you'd like."

"I'd like. I'd really, *really* like."

My heart feels lighter than it has in days, even if I'm well aware that we're a long way from back to normal. "Can I tell you something?"

"Anything."

"I'm going to see John tonight for the second time in six years, and the only thing that truly matters to me in this moment is that you're coming home. I thought you might like to know that."

Dropping my hand, he puts his arm around me and kisses the top of my head. "Thank you for telling me. Means a lot to me to know where I stand with you."

I stop walking and turn to him. "I love you, Eric, and I can't imagine life without you by my side. That's the only reason I married you."

Right there on the sidewalk, in front of a hot dog vendor, he kisses me. "I love you, too."

CHAPTER 30

Julianne

I'm so nervous about tonight that I'm afraid I might throw up. We've ordered bottles of wine and a cheese board from room service that should be here at any moment. Earlier this afternoon, we filmed *The Late Show with Stephen Colbert*, where John was asked about his relationship with Governor Tilden's daughter.

He deflected the question, but it galls me that his tour is being taken over by gossip, so I sent a note to everyone who's booked him, letting them know he won't talk about our relationship publicly, so please don't ask him about it.

I can make the request. I can't make them adhere to it, and that only adds to the boiling cauldron of stress in my belly.

John comes up behind me, puts his hands on my shoulders and kisses the side of my neck. "You're wound so tight, you're about to snap."

I love that he notices, that he pays attention, that he *sees* me so clearly. I love everything about him, even when he gets grumpy about his physical limitations, which seem to be getting fewer by the day. I love him when he has nightmares and other obvious signs of the trauma he's endured. I love him enough to invite my siblings and their significant others into this suite that's begun to feel like home to us, even knowing they may not approve of the things I want to tell them.

I hope if they see us together, they may begin to understand.

But my stomach is still not happy.

"What can I do for you?" he asks.

"Fast-forward the clock to midnight when they've been and gone and we're alone again?"

His low chuckle rumbles from his chest. "I'd do it if I could."

I turn to face him. "Are you nervous about seeing Ava?"

He shakes his head. "I'm far more nervous about meeting Eric."

"You'll like him. Everyone does."

"He probably hates me."

"No, he doesn't. He knows nothing that happened was intentional on your part."

"Some of it was. The stuff I kept from Ava was definitely my doing."

"You've apologized to her for that. It's time for everyone to build a bridge and get over it."

I love making him smile. I love the way his eyes crinkle at the corners and the right side of his face creases with a deep groove. "You look nice, and you smell fantastic."

"This is okay?" he asks of the well-worn jeans and untucked plaid dress shirt he's wearing.

"It's perfect. The Tildens are a casual sort of family when we're not being trotted out on some political stage."

"Ah, yes, your father the governor. When can I meet him?"

"Soon." I flatten my hands on his chest. "Thank you for doing this tonight. I know it's a lot to ask of you to see Ava and Eric and to meet my other brother."

"They're important to you, Poppy. I'm happy to do it."

"Even if it's hella awkward?"

He kisses me. "Even if."

I'm glad he's so chill about what feels like a huge deal to me.

"Let's get some air before they arrive." Taking my hand, he leads me to the terrace, where we make ourselves comfortable on one of the lounges. He wraps his arms around me while I use his chest as a pillow. The strong beat of his heart under my ear is incredibly reassuring for some reason. "How're you feeling about everything that happened earlier?"

"You mean the part where I quit my job?"

"And got a new one. Don't forget that."

"I'm feeling a little shell-shocked, to be honest."

"How so?"

"Well, if one of my friends was doing what I am, I'd be organizing an intervention."

"Why?"

"Um, because I've chucked my whole life for a guy I met three weeks ago, who until very recently was mourning the loss of the woman who is now married to my brother."

He doesn't say anything for several minutes while he rubs my back in small, soothing circles. "You know what I've come to realize?"

"What's that?"

"I'm always going to mourn what I lost with Ava. We had a beautiful thing that was taken from us by the same terrorist who killed all those innocent people on the cruise ship. It didn't end because we stopped loving each other, so I suppose it's only natural to grieve the loss of something so special. But I've also realized that even as I mourn the loss of what I had with her, I can still be happy with you. The two things don't have to be mutually exclusive."

"That's very profound."

"I've had a lot of time to think about these things when I could barely do anything more than sit on my ass day after day."

"You're getting stronger all the time."

"I feel better in every way since you showed up and called me on my bullshit and snapped me out of the funk that was threatening to consume me. You were like a badly needed breath of fresh air with the sexiest legs I've ever seen."

I sputter with laughter even as my heart swoons from the things he said. *This is why I'm chucking my whole life for a guy I just met. If I could bottle the feeling*

I have when I'm close to him this way, I could sell it for millions. "My legs are sexy?" I hitch one of them over his lap.

He reaches down to slide a hand from my thigh to my calf. "Oh yeah. Sexiest fucking legs I've ever seen, hands down."

I squirm as his hand travels up. "Stop." I catch it as he reaches the top of my leg. "We don't have time."

"I could be so quick."

"No!"

"You're no fun."

"I've proven otherwise on numerous occasions, and I will again later if you behave in front of my family."

"You strike a hard bargain, Poppy." He presses his erection against my side. "But I'll do my best to behave."

I crack up laughing and burrow deeper into his warm embrace. This, right here, is why I'm going all in with this guy. I've never experienced anything more perfect than this. If I'm wrong about him and this, then I never want to be right about anything again.

The doorbell ringing drags me back to reality. "That'll be room service with the stuff we ordered."

"You'd better get it. I'm a little… worked up here."

I glance down at the prominent bulge in his pants.

He scowls fiercely. "That's not helping anything."

Covering my mouth, I suppress a giggle as I leave the terrace to answer the door.

"It's not funny!"

"Yes, it is."

I open the door to the uniformed room service waiter. He wheels in a cart with the bottles of wine, beer and refreshments that I ordered. He sets everything up for us on the bar, and I sign the check. "Have a nice evening."

"Thank you."

The security personnel have been provided with a list of the guests we invited, so there's nothing left to do now but wait another half hour until they hopefully arrive. What'll I do if they don't come? None of them replied to the text, so I'm left to wonder if they'll blow me off. They wouldn't do that, would they?

In this case, I honestly don't know, and the not knowing is making me nuts. John is on with Victor Carlin at eight in the morning. Part of me wants to cancel now that I no longer work for Marcie, but it's too late to back out now. And besides, John doesn't want to back out. He's a fan of Carlin's show and is eager to meet him. Ugh. So he's not completely perfect.

"Why are you stressed again?" He takes a seat at the bar and leans in to grab one of the beers.

I hand him the bottle opener. "I'm thinking about you being on Victor Carlin in the morning."

"I can't wait."

I cringe. "I liked you better when I didn't know you're into him."

His smile is devastating. I can't get enough of it, even if it's because of that man-child Carlin. "Sorry to disappoint you, but I *love* his show."

"So you've mentioned. I don't need to know that under your sophisticated naval officer veneer, you're actually an eighth-grade boy."

"Sweetheart, *all* men are eighth-grade boys on the inside. We never grow out of poop or dick jokes, and that's why we love Carlin so much."

"You might've mentioned this before I quit my job for you."

"And miss that face you're making? Not on your life."

"I'm happy to entertain you."

"You do. Endlessly."

I pour myself a glass of wine and join him at the bar, trying to relax before our guests arrive.

"No matter what happens tonight, just remember, we've got this. You and me against the world. Don't let them talk you out of anything."

"They couldn't if they tried."

"Yeah, I think they could, but you have to stay strong and keep your eyes on the prize."

"And what's the prize?"

"Duh." He sticks out his chin dramatically. "*Me.*"

I love to see this playful side of him emerging. When I think about who he was when we first met, I never would've guessed this version of him was lurking in there waiting for someone to bring him out. I'm glad to be the one who found him. I place my hand on his sinfully handsome face and kiss him. "Thanks for the reminder."

"Any time you start to waver, just look at me. I'll remind you all over again of what we're fighting for."

I lean my forehead against his, taking strength from the connection we've found in each other. "I'll do that. Thanks."

The doorbell rings.

I'm frozen in place.

"Jules." John kisses my forehead. "Get the door."

CHAPTER 31

John

I want this to go well for her, because I know how much her family means to Jules. But I want it to go well for me, too. These people are Ava's new family, and I've been hoping to get the chance to meet them, especially the man she married, even if I'm nervous about what kind of reception I might receive from him.

Jules is stiff as she walks to the door, opening it to Muncie and Amy, who've been spending all kinds of time together since we got to New York.

Amy hugs her sister. "I told you to drop him as a client."

She did?

"You're not the boss of me."

"No, but Marcie is, and she's going to kill you for this."

"About that…" Jules leads them toward the bar. "I quit my job."

Amy stops short, and Muncie nearly crashes into her. "You did *what*?"

"I'll tell you about it when the others get here."

"No way, Jules. Tell me now."

It's hard to miss the censuring look that Amy directs my way. "Amy. Nice to see you again."

"Yeah, you, too." But she doesn't mean it. She's probably planning the intervention she's going to host for her sister, who's gone off the rails over a man. "You really quit your job?"

"I really did."

"What're you going to do?"

"She's going to work for me."

Amy's mouth falls open and then snaps shut, her disapproval apparent in every breath she takes.

There's only one way we're going to win over her and Jules's brothers, and that's to show them we intend to make this work. That won't happen tonight or tomorrow or in a week or a month. We're going to have to show them that we have what it takes to be partners in life and work by making it happen.

Rob and his wife, Camille, arrive next. I've seen pictures of Ava's younger sister, but I've never met her.

She comes right over to me. "I'm Camille."

I shake the hand she offers. "John."

"Yes, I know. The whole world knows who you are."

I wince. "Yeah, well, that's not my choice."

"You hurt my sister."

"I know. I'll always be sorry about that."

"If you hurt my sister-in-law, I'll find you and kill you."

Oddly enough, I believe her. "Understood."

"Murder will get you disbarred, babe." Rob is tall, dark and handsome, his coloring and looks closer to Amy than Jules. "I've told you that before." He shakes my hand. "She threatens to kill me on a daily basis. So far, she hasn't followed through."

"It's early days yet, my friend." Camille keeps her gaze fixed on me. "You're very handsome. The pictures and TV don't do you justice."

"Honestly, Camille." Rob huffs with amusement. "I'm standing right here."

"I'm not allowed to tell another man that he's handsome? Where is that written in the marriage laws?"

Rob rolls his eyes. "Is there beer? I need beer."

Amused by them, I point him toward the bucket of beer behind the bar. "Help yourself." When I return my attention to Camille, I find her still looking at me. "Did I cut myself shaving or something?"

"Nope. Just satisfying my curiosity about the man my sister waited five years for."

"Is she always like this?" I ask Jules when she joins us.

"Pretty much. If Camille thinks it, she says it."

"She thinks I'm handsome."

"*Duh.* Every woman in America thinks you're handsome. Don't let it go to your head."

I put my arm around her and bring her in close to me. "Too late."

"Are Ava and Eric coming?"

The trepidation in Jules's voice making me ache for the stress she's trying so hard to keep hidden from the others. But I can see it as plainly as the button nose on her gorgeous face.

"I don't know." Camille shrugs. "She didn't reply to my text earlier."

Jules sags at that news. I know how much it means to her that they come. I'm not sure how she'll cope if they don't. Although, I wouldn't blame Eric for not wanting to subject himself to Ava's ex, especially under these circumstances.

Muncie comes over to me. "How's your head?"

"Fine. Hurts where the staples are, but other than that, no ill effects."

"That's good."

"You've really taken New York by storm this week."

He's instantly flustered. "Sorry I haven't been around as much."

"I'm joking. Are you and Amy…" I roll my hand, hoping he'll fill in the blanks.

"Maybe. I don't know."

"Should I ask her?"

"No!"

I lose it laughing. He's so fun to mess with. I'll miss having him around when I retire and he moves on to his next assignment. Hopefully, he'll get something easier than dealing with me has been.

With a beer in hand, Rob returns to where I'm sitting. "I didn't get to say it before, when my wife was talking about murdering you, but thank you for your service. What you and the others did to get that bastard… Well, it means a lot to everyone."

"Thank you. I understand you're running for Congress."

"I am, although I'm not sure what I was thinking. Did you know you have to campaign *every* weekend?"

"I didn't, but I bet that's a drag."

"You have no idea."

"If I can do anything to help the cause, I'd be happy to."

He stares at me, agog. "Seriously?"

"Sure."

"I'll definitely take you up on that."

"You're one of the good guys, right?"

"Most definitely."

"Then I'm happy to do whatever I can to give your campaign a boost. You'll have to talk to my manager, though. She makes all the final decisions."

Jules grins at her brother. "We'll take it under advisement."

Jules and the others wander over to check out the cheese board, so Rob and I have a second to ourselves.

"You're being straight up with my sister, right?"

"I care about her very much. She's…" I look over at her and catch her laughing at something Camille says. I hope it doesn't involve my imminent murder. "She's amazing, fearless, beautiful, smart, competent, and she still wears her retainer. I feel very lucky to have her in my life."

"You *are* lucky, and I believe you when you say your intentions toward her are on the up-and-up. But if you hurt her, I won't stop Camille from murdering you."

"So noted." I try hard not to laugh, because I can see that he's dead serious. "I've never had sisters, but I imagine if I did, I'd feel the same way you do about yours."

"I'm glad we understand each other, and thank you for offering to help with the campaign."

"No problem."

He starts to walk away but turns back. "One more thing. I was prepared to hate you on sight because of everything with Ava. But I don't hate you."

"Thanks for letting me know. I don't hate you either."

Rob smiles and raises his beer bottle in silent toast to me. Despite the talk of hatred and murder, I feel like maybe I just made a friend. That'd be nice. I do a double take when Ava comes through the door to the suite that we've left propped open. I've seen her only one other time in six years, and damn if I don't react to her the same way I always have, with my heart skipping a beat before kicking into a faster rhythm. She's holding hands with a handsome blond man, and I experience a tiny bit of relief at seeing them together and holding hands.

I truly want her to be happy. If he makes her happy, and he's the one she wants, so be it. I stand to greet her with a hug and a kiss to the cheek. "It's good to see you. You look great as always."

"Good to see, too. You look a thousand times better than you did the last time I saw you. This is my husband, Eric Tilden. Eric, John West."

I shake his hand. "Nice to finally meet you."

"You, too." He says the socially expected words, but I get the feeling I'm the last person in the world he wants to meet or spend time with.

"Beer? Wine? What can I get you?"

"A beer would be good for me," Eric says. "Ava wants—"

"White wine." I immediately realize my mistake. He doesn't want to know how well I know her.

"Yes," he says tightly.

"Now that we're all here," Amy says, "maybe Jules can fill us in on why she quit her job."

Oh damn. Amy isn't pulling any punches. Watching the sibling dynamics is fascinating to me, as someone who's never had any.

Jules glares at her sister, then blinks and recovers. "I'd be happy to tell you about that."

"You seriously quit your job?" Rob asks. "Aren't you up for partner this year?"

"Junior partner," Jules says.

"Still. It's a promotion."

Jules glances at me. "I was offered a better opportunity."

I deliver drinks to Ava and Eric and offer a smile to Jules, hoping to reassure her and remind her of why we're taking this huge leap together.

"I'm going to work for John. He's receiving a hundred offers a day and will need someone to represent him long after this initial tour is completed."

Her news is greeted with stony silence from her siblings.

"I'm not asking for your approval."

I'm so damned proud of her.

"But I would like your support as I pursue this new direction."

Amy glances at me. "Are we going to talk about the elephant in the room?"

I clear my throat. "I take it I'm the elephant?"

"Yes, and I'm sorry that we're being forced to discuss this in front of you, but are you *out of your fucking mind*, Jules? Are you really chucking your very promising career for a guy you met a few weeks ago?"

"I don't see it the way you do, Amy. In the time I've been working with John, I've gotten to do things and meet people that would've taken me ten more years to have access to on the path I was on. Every media person who's anyone wants my number. I'm saying no to people who would've been dream contacts a month ago. This is hardly a step down for me. It's a huge step forward."

"And when the personal relationship doesn't work out?" Rob asks.

I decide it's time to speak up. "I spoke to an attorney earlier today. He's drafting a five-year contract that ensures Jules will get paid no matter what becomes of us. She's taking a huge gamble by coming to work for me. I want her protected."

Jules is stunned by this news, but that's okay. I was going to tell her about the contract later.

"I get that you all want to protect your sister. But so do I. It would be impossible for me to properly articulate the difference she's made in my life in a few short weeks. Suffice to say it's been significant. Not only has she corralled the voracious media, but she's tracking the numerous other opportunities I'm being offered and helping me figure out what's next."

They don't need to know that she's also given me a reason to get out of bed in the morning—not to mention giving me the best possible reason to *stay* in bed at other times during the day. That's our business and no one else's.

"I need her." I say this directly to her, so she can have no doubt about how I feel. Later, when we're alone, I'll tell her how much I need her in ways that have nothing to do with work.

"What about what she needs?" Amy asks.

"I need him, too." Jules holds my gaze. "This is what I want. *He's* what I want. I'm going into it with my eyes wide open to all the many ways it may turn out to be a bad idea. But it's a risk I'm willing to take."

As she looks at me and says those words, it becomes very obvious to me that I love her. I have fallen in love with her. And it's not lost on me that I'm having this rather momentous revelation while Ava is sitting six feet from me. She's my past, and I loved every minute I spent with her. But my adorable Poppy is my future. I see us moving forward together, making a life for ourselves, working and traveling together. "It's a risk I'm willing to take, too. In case anyone is wondering."

"We're not," Eric says. "But thanks for letting us know."

Touché. It'll take some time for him to come around, or maybe he never will. Either way, I can live with that if I get to live with Jules. I just hope she can handle her brother's disapproval.

"You don't need to be that way, Eric." Jules's assertiveness is a huge turn-on. "He's no threat to you. We're telling you that he's moved on.

Maybe you wish it was with someone other than me, but either way, you got what you wanted. He's not pining after your wife anymore. Sorry to be so blunt, Ava."

"No apology needed." She glances my way. "I couldn't be happier to see you moving forward with someone as wonderful as Jules. I'm truly happy for you both. If anyone deserves to be happy, it's you."

"Thank you." I'm moved by her words and the affection behind them. Having her blessing will go a long way toward convincing the others that I'm sincere in my intentions toward Jules.

Ava still means the world to me, but in a different way than she once did. I know it seems hard to believe that a torch I carried for six long years could go out in a few short weeks, but that's exactly what happened. I don't know when or how or why it happened, but I'm thankful to once again feel optimistic and hopeful about what's ahead, rather than dreading every waking moment. That mind-set was unsustainable long-term. Jules showed me that. She opened my eyes to how much life I still have to live, and that it can be a good life, full of love and affection and incredible pleasure.

I'll always regret how things went down with Ava. I'll always be sorry that I didn't take better care of her and prepare her for the possibility of a long deployment. I've learned my lesson and will do better with Jules. That's all we can do, right? Live, learn and do better.

Ava's words of support take the steam out of the objections the others might've had to our news. The conversation shifts to Rob's campaign, their father's plans for after he leaves office and whether anyone has heard from their mother.

"I have," Jules says. "She texted the other day to let me know she was proud of the job I'm doing with John."

"How does she know about that?" Eric asks.

"I told her." Rob seems sheepish. "I talked to her last week."

Eric glares at him. "Why?"

"Because she's my mother, and she called me."

"She made a mistake." Amy shrugs. "She wants to make amends."

Eric isn't buying it. "And you guys are just willing to forgive and forget like it's no big deal?"

"I'm willing to forgive because it takes a lot of energy to be pissed with her." My Poppy is amazing. "She screwed up. She knows it. She's sorry. What more do I need to hear?"

Eric doesn't like that answer, but he keeps his mouth shut when he realizes he's outnumbered.

They stick around for another hour that's passed in mostly pleasant conversation. No one asks Ava or Eric about cutting their honeymoon short, so I assume they know what's going on. They sit together on the sofa, their hands intertwined, looking very much like a newly married couple. I hope that whatever happened, they've worked it out. Just like she wants me to be happy, I want the same for her. She deserves it, too.

As they're getting ready to leave, I hear Muncie ask Amy if she wants to get a nightcap downstairs.

She agrees, and they take off together. I love the idea of them finding each other because of me and Jules. I hope something will come of it, if that's what they want. Amy has been tough on me, but only because she loves her sister. I can respect that. I know she has nothing to worry about where Jules and I are concerned, but she has no way to know that. It'll take time for me to prove myself to her, but that's time I'm willing to commit if it means I get to be with Jules.

Ava hugs me goodbye. "Let me know when you decide where you want me to send your stuff."

"I will. That's on the short list of decisions I need to make after this tour."

"I'm really happy for you and Jules."

"That means everything to me—and I know it does to her, too."

"Take care, John."

"You, too."

I offer a handshake to Eric. "Good to meet you."

"You, too." He drops my hand and starts to walk away before turning back to me. "What you did, capturing that monster who ruined so many lives… Everything else aside, thank you for that."

"You're welcome."

He nods and follows Ava, Rob and Camille out of the suite. When the door clicks shut behind them, Jules leans back against it and smiles. She's radiant. "All things considered, that went pretty well, wouldn't you say?"

I sit on the barstool and crook my finger.

She comes to me and steps between my legs, wrapping her arms around my neck.

I'm so happy to have her back in my arms where she belongs. "It went spectacularly well because of you. You were magnificent. You told them what you wanted and left no room for negotiation. I'm so proud of you."

"Thank you." She kisses me and then leans her forehead against mine. "I guess we're really going for it, huh?"

"I guess we are. Any second thoughts?"

"Not one."

"Something occurred to me tonight that I probably should've told you before you took this gigantic leap of faith and quit your job for me."

"What's that?"

"I love you."

She gasps. "You… you *do*?"

"I really do. I'm not sure how you managed to get this broken, bitter, miserable old man to feel hopeful again, but you did. You brought me back to life, Poppy." I cup her sweet face and caress her soft skin with my thumb. "You held nothing back from me, not even your retainer."

She laughs as her eyes sparkle with tears. "You're never going to let me hear the end of that, are you?"

"Never." I draw her into a soft, achingly sweet kiss. "I love you too much to ever let you hear the end of anything."

"I love you, too."

I inhale sharply. I've only ever heard those words from one other person in my life, and the impact the second time is no less profound than it was the first time. Love is not something that's been bountiful for me. I'm honored to have earned the love of this extraordinary woman. "Thank you."

"You don't have to thank me for loving you. It's the easiest thing I've ever done."

"I really do have to thank you. For everything you've already done, for taking this huge chance on me, for loving me, which is the best part. I promise you'll never regret any of it."

"I already know I won't regret it. People wait their whole lives to find what we have. I've waited my whole life for it."

"I'm so glad I found you and that Ava was the one who made it happen. There's something kind of cool about that."

"It was kismet."

"Yes, it was." I slide off the chair, and once I'm sure my legs are steady, I put my arms around her and lift her.

"John! Put me down!"

"Shhhh. I've got you." I move carefully toward the bedroom, where I put her down next to the bed.

"You shouldn't be doing that stuff."

I waggle my brows at her. "Wait till you see what I'm capable of at full strength."

She reaches for me, bringing me down on top of her. "I can't wait to see everything you're capable of."

With her by my side, in my arms and firmly entrenched in my heart, anything seems possible.

EPILOGUE

John

One year later…

I've just run three whole miles without stopping. As the doctors predicted, right around the one-year mark after the coma, I started to feel almost back to normal. Hitting the three-mile mark is a huge accomplishment. I run at the water's edge, where the sand is packed more firmly. I figure if I fall, it won't hurt as badly as it would on pavement. I still fall once in a while. I lose my balance and topple over, often without any warning that it's going to happen. The best was the time I took out an entire display of paper products in the grocery store. Since the whole world knows who I am, that was rather embarrassing.

But Jules was right there to give me a hand up, to brush me off and to continue on our day like nothing unusual had happened. She rolls with whatever comes our way and makes life easy for me just by being there.

She moved to San Diego right after we ended the LA leg of the initial media tour. She had one stipulation—that we live at the beach. We bought a beachfront condo with two fireplaces, in a brand-new complex in La Jolla that has the other thing we need—top-notch security. I still get approached everywhere we go, but things have died down a bit in recent months, or maybe I've just gotten used to the attention.

Our condo isn't far from the bench on the boardwalk where our relationship took an important turn that led us to where we are today. Every time we're in that area, we stop for a rest on our bench, where we reminisce about how far we've come from that day. We kept her place in New York for when we visit her family and have work commitments. I encourage her to go home any time she wants to, but she never wants to go unless I'm with her. Fine by me.

The initial media tour seems like a lifetime ago. I've done hundreds of interviews in the year since I officially retired from the Navy. We keep waiting for the interest in my story to wane, but it only seems to get crazier with every passing month. I agreed to an endorsement deal with Adidas. They shot me wearing only running shorts and their shoes. At first, I was hesitant to be photographed with the prosthetic showing, but Jules said, "Who cares if people see it? It's not like anyone doesn't know you lost a leg."

I love how she cuts to the chase and simplifies things for me when my inclination is to overthink everything. After years of leading my team and supervising people in the Navy, I'm more than happy to take my lead from her as I adjust to civilian life. She's never once been wrong. I joke about how I trust her gut more than my own.

The ad has gotten a tremendous amount of attention, including one of those massive billboards in Times Square, and the company is very pleased with the response. I'm very pleased with the huge amount of money they paid me to do it. Between that and my pension, we're set up rather well.

I've also agreed to write my memoir, which is turning out to be much more challenging than I anticipated. I hope that by discussing my difficult childhood and successful naval career I'll give hope to some other kid out there who may have no one pulling for them. We've heard talk of a possible movie deal if the book turns out not to be shit. That'd be something.

And I've founded the Captain John West Foundation for kids aging out of the foster system who need mentoring, direction and help figuring out what's next. If something like that had existed when I turned eighteen, I might not have ended up in front of a judge. I got lucky with someone who gave me a choice that changed my life. A lot of kids don't get those kinds of breaks, and I want to reach them before they get into trouble. We've started a pilot program in San Diego that I hope to take nationwide over the next couple of years.

Life is good—and not just for me and Jules. Rob won his election and is now representing New York in Congress. He and Camille split their time between New York and DC, and he's considered a rising star in the Democratic Party. Her firm has offices in both cities, so it works out well for them. I enjoyed campaigning for him, and he likes to say my support made all the difference. I don't know if that's true, but I was happy to lend a hand. He's become a good friend, and I really like spending time with him and Camille.

Muncie requested to be stationed in New York and is now working as a recruiter in the city. He doesn't love the job, but he *loves* living with Amy. I expect to hear any time now that they're getting married. He's remained one of my closest friends after the months we spent working together. I give him almost as much credit as I give Jules for helping me put my life back together.

Ava and Eric recently had a baby girl named Josie. She's absolutely beautiful, and they're thrilled with her, as they should be. He and I will never be the best of friends, but we're able to be cordial for Jules's sake and Ava's when we occasionally see each other. We've even gotten to the point where we can joke around a little and have a reasonable conversation about anything other than Ava. Against all odds, Ava and I have become good friends, regularly exchanging texts and keeping in close touch. I'm so glad that I get to have everything I do with Jules but get to keep Ava in my life, too.

As I jog back toward home, I think about my Poppy and the next phase of our journey together. I've had an engagement ring for weeks and have agonized about how I want to ask her the most important question I'll ever ask anyone. I'm not worried about what her answer will be, but I want it to be perfect for her, the way she's been for me.

Sometimes I wonder what might've become of me if she hadn't shown up when she did. I was in a bad place when I got out of the hospital. When I think about how far I've come since then, I owe so much of that progress to her, my light at the end of a dark tunnel. I still have occasional nightmares and wake up sobbing, mourning the losses of Tito and Jonesy as well as Ava and the life that was ripped from us by a terrorist. Jules is always right there for me, holding me through the best moments and the worst, my calm in the storm.

A few months ago, Popovicci, the master chief on my SEAL team, tried to take his own life. The shock of that incident had me spiraling for a few days as we rallied around him, got him into a PTSD treatment facility and did all the things you do when you're family to someone who's hurting. If that'd happened before I had Jules, I don't know if I could've handled it as well as I did with her by my side to help with details that would've overwhelmed me on my own.

She's a rock. She's my rock, and I want her to know how much she means to me with the perfect proposal. I've had and dismissed a thousand ideas. None of them has felt right to me. I keep hoping I'll come up with something, because I'm running out of patience. I want that ring on her finger and a plan to make her my wife as soon as possible. I want kids with her. I want everything with her. It's funny to think that when Jules and I are married, Ava's daughter will become my niece. I like that.

I arrive at our place, use the outdoor shower to clean up and navigate the stairs to our deck. Stairs are still a bit of a challenge, but like the doctors and therapists promised, everything has gotten easier with time. I step into the condo, where Jules is tending to the stove while talking on the phone. My girl is nothing if not a master multitasker.

She welcomes me home with a big smile that touches my heart. She's always so damned glad to see me. "No, he's not doing that, Victor. I don't care how much fun he has on your show, he's not dropping rubber penises from a helicopter." She rolls her eyes at me.

Laughing, I give her two thumbs-up.

She shakes her head, her expression stern.

I *love* when she's stern with me.

"No, it doesn't make a difference if it's fake poop. Both those things are beneath him." She pauses to listen. "I won't take it to him. The answer is no. Call me back when you find some dignity." Pulling the earbuds out, she tosses them aside. "He's insane if he thinks I'm letting you do any of that crazy crap he does on his show. He's lucky I let you *appear* on his stupid show once a month."

She's *magnificent*. That's the only word I can think of to describe the way she cares for me on and off the job. Sometimes I worry that she'll get tired of having only one client, but she seems to love representing me and being the "firewall" between me and the requests that continue to roll in every day. I move toward her, walking carefully on tired legs, around the counter to where she stands at the stove stirring something that smells delicious.

"What's wrong?" She gives me a quick inspection to make sure all is well. "You didn't fall, did you?" She's got her hair up in a messy bun and is wearing a formfitting tank with sexy denim cutoffs that barely cover her cheeks, not that I'm complaining.

"Not this time. And nothing is wrong." I lean in to kiss her. "I'm just checking out my warrior woman barefoot in the kitchen, fighting my battles for me the way only she can do."

"I know you love Victor, but I have to say—"

I kiss the words right off her lips. "I love *you*. *You* and *only* you." I realize there will never be a better time for what I want to do than any of the simple yet extraordinary moments we experience together on any given day.

She curls a hand around my neck. "I love you, too. How was the run?"

"Finally made it to three miles."

"Really?" Her smile lights up my world. "That's so awesome."

I used to be able to run fifteen miles while barely breaking a sweat. I may never be able to do that again, but whatever. I've learned I don't have to get back to where I was to be perfectly fine with where I am. Last weekend, I took her hiking at Torrey Pines, which had been impossible for me to navigate until I got stronger. It was nice to be back in one of my favorite places and to share it with her. "Felt good to notch that third mile."

"I'm so proud of you."

She treats each victory in my recovery as if I've just summited Everest or some equally momentous thing, which is just another on a long list of reasons why I love her desperately. "Can you hold that thought for one minute?"

"Sure." Her brows furrow adorably with confusion. "I'm not going anywhere."

That's all I need to know. "Be right back." I go into the master bedroom that's on the main floor. Jules insisted on that so I wouldn't have to deal with stairs in my own home. She's always looking out for me in big ways and small. I retrieve the ring I stashed in a dresser drawer, take it out of the box and return to the living room sofa, keeping the ring hidden inside the fist I make with my right hand. "Come here."

She stirs what's in the pan as she checks her phone. "I'm here."

"Julianne." I never, ever, *ever* call her that, and it gets her attention.

She looks up from her phone. "What?"

"Come. *Here.*"

Sighing with dramatic exasperation, she comes over to me. "You beckoned."

"Have a seat."

She sits.

It's not easy for me, but I slide off the couch onto my knees in front of her.

"What're you doing? You're going to hurt yourself!"

"No, I'm not. And what I'm doing, my sweet, difficult, gorgeous, utterly perfect Poppy, is asking if you will please marry me and make me happier than I already am, which is pretty damned happy."

Her eyes go wide, and her mouth falls open. I *love* that she didn't see this coming. Sure, we've talked about getting married, but she had no idea today would be the day.

"You, my beautiful, endlessly competent firewall, are the absolute love of my life. Spend the rest of yours with me?" I open my hand to show her the ring, and she gasps.

I went with a stunner, and judging by her reaction, it has the desired effect.

Tears run down her cheeks as she covers her mouth with her left hand. "John." The word is muted by her hand, but I hear it anyway.

I reach up to remove the hand from her face and slide the ring onto her finger. It's a perfect fit, but I knew it would be. "Remember when you couldn't find your grandmother's ring that day?"

She nods.

"I borrowed it to make sure the size was right. I felt so bad that you got upset about the missing ring and made sure you found it the next morning."

She sniffles as she looks at the ring and then at me. "I forgive you."

"I also talked to your dad about a month ago and asked for his permission to marry you. He said I had his approval, but you were the only one who could give permission."

"You really asked him?"

"I really did, and I thought you'd approve of his answer."

"I love what he said and that you did that. Thank you. I'm sure it meant a lot to him."

I kiss the back of her hand. "Do you like the ring?"

She laughs as if that's the silliest question she's ever heard. "I *love* it. It's incredible."

It's a three-carat solitaire surrounded by another two carats in smaller stones.

I kiss her again because there's almost nothing I love more than kissing her. "As the one who's usually in charge of the details around here, you're missing a rather important one."

"What am I missing?"

"You haven't answered my question. Are you going to marry me and spend forever with me? Are you going to run my life and have babies and everything else with me?"

"Yes." She caresses my face as she gazes into my eyes. "Yes to everything."

I gather her into my arms, relieved to have made it official and to have pleased her with the ring I agonized over. "You saved my life in every possible way, Poppy."

"You like to say that, but in saving yours, I found mine."

***

Thank you for reading John's story! After *Five Years Gone* was released last year, I knew I'd be overwhelmed with requests for John's book, which is why I included that opening chapter of *One Year Home* in the back of *Five Years Gone*. Everyone wanted to see him get his happy ending, too, and I hope you enjoyed seeing him get that with Jules. Writing these two books has been so much fun, and I've been delighted to hear from so many readers who loved *Five Years Gone* and have been counting down to *One Year Home*. Thank you for that enthusiasm for my books. It's much appreciated!

Join the *Five Years Gone* www.facebook.com/groups/FiveYearsGone/ and *One Year Home* www.facebook.com/groups/OneYearHome/ reader groups to discuss both books with spoilers allowed.

If you're not on my newsletter mailing list, make sure you join at marieforce. com to be notified when new books are available and to receive news of sales and events in your area.

A lot of people make it possible for me to write books all day, including my husband, Dan, and the HTJB team: Julie Cupp, Lisa Cafferty, Holly Sullivan, Isabel Sullivan and Nikki Colquhoun. Thanks go to my awesome editors, Linda Ingmanson and Joyce Lamb, as well as my stellar publicist Jessica Estep and my primo beta readers Anne Woodall and Kara Conrad. Special thanks to my final beta readers Kelly, Juliane, Gwendolyn, Betty, Nancy, Laurie, Irene, Marti, Isabel, Amy and Jennifer for their contributions. Finally, I'm super excited to have Erin Mallon and Jason Clarke playing the roles of Julianne and John for the audio edition of this book as well as Andi Arndt and Joe Arden from the *Five Years Gone* audio reprising their roles as Ava and Eric in *One Year*

Home. Thank you to this rock-star audio lineup for bringing these characters to life.

Many thanks to my author friend and San Diego resident Lauren Rowe, who made sure I got the local details correct and helped me to plan the day that John takes Jules and Amy sightseeing. A special thanks to my friend Tracey Suppo for reading *One Year Home* as I wrote and proofing one last time. I so appreciate your friendship and support, Tracey!

And thank you to my amazing readers who continue to make this the best job I've ever had.

Much love,

Marie

OTHER BOOKS BY MARIE FORCE

Book 18: Kevin & Chelsea (Episode 2)

A Gansett Island Christmas Novella

Book 19: Mine After Dark *(Riley & Nikki)*

Book 20: Yours After Dark *(Finn & Chloe)*

Book 21: Trouble After Dark *(Deacon & Julia)*

The Green Mountain Series

Book 1: All You Need Is Love *(Will & Cameron)*

Book 2: I Want to Hold Your Hand *(Nolan & Hannah)*

Book 3: I Saw Her Standing There *(Colton & Lucy)*

Book 4: And I Love Her *(Hunter & Megan)*

Novella: You'll Be Mine *(Will & Cam's Wedding)*

Book 5: It's Only Love *(Gavin & Ella)*

Book 6: Ain't She Sweet *(Tyler & Charlotte)*

The Butler Vermont Series
(Continuation of the Green Mountain Series)

Book 1: Every Little Thing *(Grayson & Emma)*

Book 2: Can't Buy Me Love *(Mary & Patrick)*

Book 3: Here Comes the Sun *(Wade & Mia)*

Book 4: Till There Was You *(Lucas & Dani)*

The Treading Water Series

Book 1: Treading Water *(Jack & Andi)*

Book 2: Marking Time *(Clare & Aidan)*

Book 3: Starting Over *(Brandon & Daphne)*

Book 4: Coming Home *(Reid & Kate)*

Single Titles

Five Years Gone

One Year Home

Sex Machine

Sex God

Georgia on My Mind

True North

The Fall

Everyone Loves a Hero

Love at First Flight

Line of Scrimmage

Historical Romances
The Gilded Series
Book 1: Duchess by Deception

Book 2: Deceived by Desire

Erotic Romance
The Quantum Series
Book 1: Virtuous *(Flynn & Natalie)*

Book 2: Valorous *(Flynn & Natalie)*

Book 3: Victorious *(Flynn & Natalie)*

Book 4: Rapturous *(Addie & Hayden)*

Book 5: Ravenous *(Jasper & Ellie)*

Book 6: Delirious *(Kristian & Aileen)*

Book 7: Outrageous *(Emmett & Leah)*

Book 8: Famous *(Marlowe)*

Romantic Suspense
The Fatal Series
One Night With You, *A Fatal Series Prequel Novella*

Book 1: Fatal Affair

Book 2: Fatal Justice

Book 3: Fatal Consequences

Book 3.5: Fatal Destiny, *the Wedding Novella*

Book 4: Fatal Flaw

Book 5: Fatal Deception

Book 6: Fatal Mistake

Book 7: Fatal Jeopardy

Book 8: Fatal Scandal

Book 9: Fatal Frenzy

Book 10: Fatal Identity

Book 11: Fatal Threat

Book 12: Fatal Chaos

Book 13: Fatal Invasion

Book 14: Fatal Reckoning

Book 15: Fatal Accusation

Single Title

The Wreck

ABOUT THE AUTHOR

Marie Force is the *New York Times* bestselling author of contemporary romance, including the indie-published Gansett Island Series and the Fatal Series from Harlequin Books. In addition, she is the author of the Butler, Vermont Series, the Green Mountain Series and the erotic romance Quantum Series. *Duchess By Deception* is the first in her new historical romance Gilded Series, that will continue with *Deceived By Desire* in September 2019.

Her books have sold 8.5 million copies worldwide, have been translated into more than a dozen languages and have appeared on the *New York Times* bestseller list many times. She is also a *USA Today* and *Wall Street Journal* bestseller, a Speigel bestseller in Germany, a frequent speaker and publishing workshop presenter as well as a publisher through her Jack's House Publishing romance imprint. She is a three-time nominee for the Romance Writers of America's RITA® award for romance fiction.

Her goals in life are simple—to finish raising two happy, healthy, productive young adults, to keep writing books for as long as she possibly can and to never be on a flight that makes the news.

Join Marie's mailing list for news about new books and upcoming appearances in your area. Follow her on Facebook at *www.facebook.com/MarieForceAuthor*, Twitter *@marieforce* and on Instagram at *https://instagram.com/marieforceauthor/*. Join one of Marie's many reader groups. Contact Marie at *marie@marieforce.com*.

9 781950 654383